FUGITIVES

A Kaley Presley Thriller

TERRY TOLER

Fugitives
Published by: BeHoldings, LLC

Copyright ©2024, **BeHoldings, LLC**
Terry Toler
All Rights Reserved

Book Cover: BeHoldings Publishing
Contributing Editor: Donna Toler

For information email: terry@terrytoler.com.

Our books can be purchased in bulk for promotional, educational, and business use. Please contact your bookseller or the BeHoldings Publishing Sales department at:sales@terrytoler.com

For booking information email: booking@terrytoler.com.

First U.S. Edition: September, 2024
Printed in the United States of America
ISBN 978-1-954710-26-9

OTHER BOOKS BY TERRY TOLER

Fiction

Save The Girls

The Ingenue

Saving Sara

Save The Queen

No Girl Left Behind

The Launch

Body Count

Save Me Twice

Powerful Enemies

Deadly Games

Don't Be Careful

Wintervention

Saving Alex

Forsaken

Cliff Hangers: Anna

Cliff Hangers: Mr. & Mrs. Platt

Cliff Hangers: The Quarterback

Cliff Hangers: Macy

Cliff Hangers: Not, Not Guilty

The Blue Rose

Triggers

Seven Year Rich

Noel

The Book Club

The Book Club Murder

The Book Club Rescue

The Longest Day

The Reformation of Mars

The Late, Great Planet Jupiter

The Great Wall of Ven-Us
Saturn: The Eden Experiment
The Mercury Protocols
The Heart of Pluto

Non-Fiction

How to Make More Than a Million Dollars
The Heart Attacked
Seven Years of Promise
Mission Possible
Marriage Made in Heaven
21 Days to Physical Healing
21 Days to Spiritual Fitness
21 Days to Divine Health
21 Days to a Great Marriage
21 Days to Financial Freedom
21 Days to Sharing Your Faith
21 Days to Mission Possible
7 Days to Emotional Freedom
Uncommon Finances
Uncommon Health
Uncommon Marriage
The Jesus Diet
Suddenly Free
Feeling Free

For more information on these books and other resources visit
terrytoler.com.

Thank you for purchasing this novel from best-selling author, Terry Toler. As an additional thank you, Terry wants to give you a free gift.

Sign up for:

Updates

New Releases

Announcements

At terrytoler.com

We'll send you an eBook, *The Book Club*, a Cliff Hangers novella, free of charge.

To the brave CIA operatives who have sacrificed everything to keep us safe.

Your courage and commitment inspire this story.

1

"The president is dead," Brad, the CIA director, said to Jamie Austen, his most famous—though now retired—operative.

"Dead!" Jamie exclaimed in shock and disbelief. "When did this happen?"

"He was assassinated about thirty minutes ago. Did you know it was going to happen?" His tone was almost accusing.

"No! I've been busy taking care of my twins. I haven't had the television on in days."

Jamie had retired a little over two years ago when she became a mother. Her husband, Alex, still ran covert computer hacking operations for the CIA through their cover company, AJAX—a combination of their names, Alex and Jamie.

Since having children, neither wanted to put themselves in harm's way again, although Alex occasionally took calculated risks. So far, he had been skilled enough to survive them without any close calls.

"You had no involvement at all?" Brad asked, sounding skeptical.

"Of course not. Why would you even ask me that question? What's going on, Brad?" Jamie asked with growing concern.

She wasn't sure she wanted to know the answer. When he used the word "assassinated," her thoughts immediately went to A-Rad and Kaley.

Surely not.

"The president was shot and killed by two gunmen," Brad said. "I believe we both know who those gunmen are."

Jamie tried to speak but couldn't find any words. Was Brad really accusing A-Rad and Kaley of assassinating the President of the United States? It seemed unfathomable.

"It could've been any number of people," Jamie finally managed to say.

The question, "Why do you think it was them?" was on the tip of her tongue, but she choked it back. She wasn't sure she wanted to hear the answer to that question.

She hadn't talked to A-Rad and Kaley in weeks and couldn't really vouch for their whereabouts or actions. The thing that gave her pause was that she couldn't deny that they were two of the few people on earth capable of pulling off such a massive feat.

Really, how could they even do it? The security surrounding the president was meant to be impenetrable.

"I know it was them," Brad stated with conviction. "Please tell me you aren't involved."

She assured him, "I'm not involved, and neither is Alex or any member of AJAX."

Brad assumed Jamie had a hand in it because he knew that she and Alex had planned and financed the assassinations of more than a dozen world leaders, using A-Rad and Kaley to carry out the missions. He had indirect knowledge and even silently endorsed them, but never spoke about them, so he could maintain plausible deniability.

For obvious reasons. Brad was the acting director of the CIA, and such activities were against US and international law. Killing the leaders of foreign countries could get them all thrown in jail for the rest of their lives.

Neither of them ever wanted to be on a call talking about the pair or the operations. Brad looked the other way because those missions had been a tremendous benefit to America and the world. But the political fallout would be unmanageable if it got out that the United States, the director of the CIA, was somehow involved or knew about the assassinations of our enemies. So he kept his distance.

Every intelligence agency in the world knew it was A-Rad and Kaley behind the killings, and everyone assumed they were Americans. But that's all they knew. The standard line was that they were rogue and had never worked for the CIA.

Which wasn't entirely true.

Jamie had recruited A-Rad to the CIA and trained Kaley herself. She loved them like they were her own family and would give her life for them. At least back in time before the twins were born.

The covert missions had been her idea, and AJAX funded them. The success of the efforts was beyond her wildest dreams. The brazen pair had taken out some of the most ruthless dictators on the planet without getting caught.

But why would they kill the President of the United States? He wasn't on the list of leaders they were tasked to kill. It didn't make sense.

"I don't think it's them," Jamie blurted after a long moment of silence.

"It is," Brad said, maintaining his confidence.

"What percentage?"

"A hundred percent."

Brad wouldn't say that unless he had undeniable proof.

Could he be wrong? If he was, it might be the first time since she had started working for him years ago. The Director of the CIA had more intelligence available to him than anyone else on the planet. If anyone knew, it'd be him.

Jamie needed to convince him she wasn't involved.

"I know nothing about it. I swear," she said.

"Were you aware that they changed their appearances?"

She lied. "No."

She had paid for the surgeries—at least AJAX had.

After A-Rad and Kaley assassinated the prince of Norway, they were caught and put on trial. Alex and Jamie helped them escape, but their covers as CIA operatives were blown and their faces plastered all over the media.

A world-wide manhunt had been going on for more than two years making running missions in foreign countries virtually impossible. With advanced facial recognition software becoming more prevalent, the pair couldn't step foot in any major city or take a plane or train without being detected.

The last time Jamie checked, the reward for their capture had reached twenty million dollars. Dead or alive. Preferably dead.

Desperate for a solution, Jamie found a surgeon in India who completely restructured their faces. They didn't even look like the same people. The ploy had worked, and it allowed them to move around the world freely on passports Alex and Jamie provided for them.

She wondered how Brad knew about their new look.

"They were spotted in Russia a few days ago," Brad said, interrupting her thoughts. "I've been tracking their movements. As far as I know, I'm the only one who knows about the new look, and I used facial recognition software to find them."

"What are they doing in Russia?"

"That's where the president was assassinated."

Instantly, Jamie felt a wave of relief and disbelief at the same time. She had been worried that the president was killed inside the United States. She couldn't imagine A-Rad or Kaley being stupid enough to come into the US and try such a brazen operation. The southern borders were porous enough for them to get in, but operating inside the United States was a risk they'd never take.

"I didn't realize our president was in Russia," she said, truthfully.

"It's his first foreign trip. He made Russia a priority. As you know, relations have been strained since they sort of blame us for the deaths of their previous two presidents."

A-Rad and Kaley had assassinated the president of Russia eighteen months ago. He was a despot who deserved it. He was replaced by someone even worse. A-Rad and Kaley returned to Russia and took him out as well.

In response, the Russians surprisingly installed a more moderate leader, someone friendly with the West. Both men were highly popular in their countries. The President of the United States campaigned on improving relations with Russia. He had won his election in America by a landslide and had only been in office less than two months.

Brad was named CIA director shortly thereafter and easily confirmed by the Senate since he had already been the assistant director for a number of years.

"Why would they kill the president?" Jamie asked.

"You tell me."

"How would I know?"

"I have a theory. The president made it a priority to capture them. One purpose of the Russian trip was to assure the Russian president of that fact."

"They wouldn't kill him over something so trivial as him vowing to capture them."

"Well, they did. The reason doesn't matter. And there's going to be fallout. People are going to blame Russia for this. I'm trying to keep World War III from breaking out."

"I won't believe it until I see it or hear it from their own mouths."

"Watch the video I sent you."

Jamie walked to her office, her heart pounding as she fired up her computer. She opened her email, and her breath caught in her throat as she watched the shocking video. The president was gunned down while standing at a podium giving a speech at an airport welcoming him to Russia.

The satellite image clearly showed the two assassins. It captured their forms as they fled the scene. One shot briefly captured Kaley's face. No doubt about it. It was them.

"There must be some explanation," Jamie said, her voice trembling, though she couldn't think of one.

"The explanation is that they let their powers go to their heads. Having the ability to end someone's life comes with a great deal of responsibility. They began to think of themselves as gods, deciding when killing was justified. This time, they took it too far."

Jamie didn't answer. She had no way to defend their actions without it looking like she might've been complicit.

"It doesn't matter now," Brad said, with a bitter tone. "It'll be over for them soon."

"What do you mean?" she asked, dread creeping into her voice.

"Turn on your television. The Russian army has them trapped in a warehouse about a mile from the scene. I watched them on satellite run into the building, and I didn't see them come out."

"Are you sure it's them?"

"Positive. I saw their faces there as well. Clear as day. It's them. The Russians know it too."

Jamie turned on her television and was met with footage from Russia playing on all the major networks. The warehouse was surrounded by a small army, including tanks and hundreds of soldiers with machine guns.

The press was even showing pictures of A-Rad and Kaley as the suspects. Accusing them of the killing of the President of the United States and the two Russian presidents. Brad obviously wasn't the only one who had images of their new look.

If they were inside that warehouse, their lives were in grave danger.

"I can send you the pictures of them running into the warehouse if you want," Brad said. "You can see for yourself."

"No, that's okay. I believe you."

"I can only hope A-Rad and Kaley are killed quickly. Otherwise, the torture will be unimaginable."

This was the first time Brad had used A-Rad and Kaley's names since the Norway incident. He had avoided being associated with them in any way. It must truly be over if he was willing to speak their names so freely.

Jamie decided to end the call.

After she hung up the phone, she turned off the television. She couldn't bear to watch two of her closest friends being killed by the Russian army or dragged out of the warehouse like animals.

The pain in her heart was unbearable.

She collapsed into a chair, buried her head in her hands, and sobbed uncontrollably.

2

Somewhere in the Indian Ocean
Two Years Earlier

Our new normal was anything but normal.

After A-Rad and I escaped Norway with the help of the AJAX team, we were taken to Alex and Jamie's small island north of Aruba. Within two weeks, it became clear we couldn't stay there—too risky for them. If caught, it'd link the entire team directly to the assassination of the Crown Prince of Norway.

As a solution, Jamie had the yacht brought to the island, and A-Rad and I set sail for international waters, away from any patrolled areas. That led us to the Indian Ocean, as far away from land as possible, safe from any threats.

The downside was that we had been battling rough seas for more than two months. It wasn't ideal, but our best option considering the alternatives.

We were now considered the most wanted terrorists on the planet. Every Western intelligence agency, including the CIA, was hunting us. They considered us more dangerous than some of the worst terrorists in the world.

Which wasn't fair.

The prince was the one who trafficked college-aged girls and murdered them right before our very eyes. He deserved to die and I hadn't lost a second of sleep over it. Our actions weren't just to seek revenge for the girls. A man like that couldn't be allowed to ascend to power in a NATO country.

But few people knew our motives. Jan Sealy, the Norwegian prosecutor who helped us escape knew the truth but couldn't reveal it without risking his life and exposing his involvement.

The Norwegian monarchy had effectively covered it all up. Consequently, the truth remained buried, and our fate was sealed. The only consolation was that the prince was dead and would never harm another girl again.

The consequences were that A-Rad and I would be forced to live on the run indefinitely. Since we'd never have a normal life again, Jamie had the idea to use our skills to kill as many evil world leaders as possible.

The worst of the worst. The despots who oppressed their people, funded terrorism, and wreaked havoc around the world. Our lives would have some purpose then, although it was only a matter of time before we met our inevitable demise.

Death.

Not even the normally optimistic A-Rad could deny what the end would be for us. The unspoken truth we shared. The only question that remained was how many tyrants we could eliminate before that happened.

We waited for our first assignment. I thought it'd only take two to three weeks, but it had been more than two months. Jamie said she'd contact us when she had a plan. All she could tell us was that Colonel was working on it and that the task was complicated for obvious reasons.

A-Rad and I were growing impatient. We weren't the types to sit around and do nothing. If we were in a tropical location, it might've been easier to wait, but we were near Antarctica, where the weather was relentless and bitterly cold.

"I'm so tired of this, Kaley," A-Rad said with frustration one morning, a rarity. He was normally the tolerant one who never complained about anything.

"I couldn't agree more," I replied. "I prefer to have my feet firmly planted on the ground."

Thankfully, seasickness didn't bother either of us, but being trapped on that yacht was weighing on our emotions and mental well-being. We'd been in worse conditions for sure but being in a confined space with no freedom to leave was a challenge.

"Where do you think they'll send us first?" he asked.

"Maybe Somalia or some other smaller country with fewer resources to stop us. By resources I mean a full military complex. Nuclear weapons and all. I can't imagine they'd throw us into the fire by sending us to Russia, Iran, or even Pakistan. I'm guessing they'll start with the easiest target first."

"Easiest is a pejorative term," A-Rad said, flashing a pained smile.

I felt my eyes widen in surprise. "You never cease to amaze me, A-Rad. Where did you learn the word 'pejorative'?"

He pointed at his chin. "This isn't just a pretty face you're looking at."

"I'm not sure pejorative really applies in that sentence, but nice try."

"I think it applies perfectly."

"Do you even know what pejorative means?" I asked, pointedly.

"Not really. But I'm sure you'll tell me."

I thought I knew but wasn't completely sure either. Not enough to explain why he was wrong.

"Let's look it up," I said.

One good thing about being on the yacht was having access to some modern amenities. We had an entertainment library full of movies and music, as well as internet access. As long as we didn't search for anything that might alert those monitoring the web to our location, we could use it.

We walked over to the computer in the main living area and I typed the word 'pejorative' in the search. I read the definition aloud for both of our benefits.

"Pejorative means expressing contempt or disapproval."

"See, it does fit in the sentence."

"No, it doesn't," I said a little more strongly.

"What was the sentence again? I forgot now."

Our laughter filled the air as the conversation was more playful banter than disagreement. Even though we were living in close quarters, both of us had handled it well, and hadn't resorted to taking the frustrations out on each other.

We hadn't had a single fight. I would've thought we would annoy each other more than we had. Things could be a lot worse than cruising on a yacht. Something we had reminded ourselves on more than one occasion.

Once we did start our dangerous missions, the thought occurred to me that we could very well wish we were back on the yacht. I struggled to remember the conversation that prompted us to look up the word.

"I said that Alex and Jamie would send us on the easiest mission," I said, after I remembered.

"Right."

I continued. "You didn't like the term 'easy' and said it was a pejorative term. That doesn't fit based on the definition."

"How does it not fit, Kaley?" A-Rad said, his tone rising slightly. "Pejorative means disapproval. I disapprove of the term easy. I was expressing my disapproval of the characterization."

"The word *easy* is not pejorative, it's your disapproval that is."

He contorted his face in confusion and annoyance. "I find your whole attitude pejorative."

"Now, that's a correct use of the term!"

"I know. So is the other."

I decided to change the subject before things got heated and turned into our first fight as a married couple.

"What about going to China?" I suggested.

"What about it?"

"That might be a good place to hide. Don't they still wear masks?"

One of our biggest concerns about traveling on land was encountering face recognition software. Not every country and city had it, but all the major airports, train stations, and borders in the bigger countries did. We were certainly on every watchlist around the world and wouldn't get past even lax security.

"I don't want to wear a mask," A-Rad stated firmly.

"Me neither, but it might be worth it to get us off this boat."

He vehemently shook his head no.

"China would be the worst place to go. You can't even sneeze there without the government knowing."

"You're right. The regime is one of the worst at controlling its people. I wonder why the President of China isn't on the kill list."

"The devil you know," A-Rad said. "That's probably why this is taking so long. Colonel has to think through all the political ramifications. We don't want to take out a dictator and have someone worse take his place. You break it, you have to fix it."

"That's true," I said. "What about Alaska? We could go there. At least it's in America. And close to Russia. We could hop on over there and take out the Russian President and be home in time for dinner."

"Too cold."

"Africa then. We could go on a safari and hunt big game. Keep our skills sharp."

"Too hot."

"I'm out of suggestions then. You think of something."

"I think we should hang tight until we hear from Alex and Jamie."

I drummed my fingers on the desk in a show of boredom.

"What do you want to do now?" I asked.

"I don't know. What do you want to do?" he answered.

"Want to fool around?" I suggested with a mischievous grin.

We'd done a lot of that to pass the time. There weren't any shortages of opportunities for intimacy since we were alone and technically still on our honeymoon.

Alex had married us when we got to the island. If we were going to be on the run together for the rest of our lives, I had insisted we get married. While it lacked the formality of a real wedding and wasn't the wedding of my dreams, the ceremony on the beach was special.

Jamie was there by video link and acted as my maid of honor. Bond stood in as A-Rad's best man, although he would've chosen Alex had he not been officiating.

We wrote our own vows and the whole thing was moving. The only downside was that we had to use makeshift rings made from soda cans.

When the yacht arrived at the island, Jamie rectified that. She had included a velvet box in our supplies. When we opened it, I was shocked to see real wedding rings. My heart swelled with emotion as I slipped the ring on my finger.

A-Rad made me take it off, so he could formally put it on. He had actually picked it out without me knowing about it. I held out my hand and looked at it now, like I still did a dozen times a day.

"You want to have sex now?" he asked. "I thought you liked later in the day rather than in the morning."

His eyes glistened with excitement. Every time I mentioned hooking up, he got a silly boyish grin on his face that sent waves of desire through me as well.

Out of the blue, a strange thought popped into my head.

"I could wear that outfit," I blurted.

"What outfit?" A-Rad's forehead burrowed in confusion.

"The one Jamie made for me in Norway."

As a disguise, Jamie sent me a sexy outfit complete with a specially made bra that gave me huge, pointed boobs. We had left the outfit behind when we fled Norway, but Jamie put another one on the yacht. Partly as a joke but mostly because, admittedly, it was a good disguise.

To my humiliation, Jamie made me try it on and model it for them. It had become a running joke for several days.

Since we were never around other people, I hadn't had a chance to wear it, but when I wore it in Norway, A-Rad seemed to like it. At first, I was offended. Now I thought it might be a way to spice things up between us.

Not that we needed any more heat.

A-Rad's eyes widened, and a wide grin came on his face, apparently figuring out what costume I was talking about.

"You mean the outfit with the—," he said, making a gesture with his hands in front of his chest.

"Yes! That one. It might be fun," I said, eagerly.

"Eww. That would be cheating!" he exclaimed.

"You're not cheating on me if it's me in the costume, silly."

"That's disgusting. I'm attracted to you, not some random blonde lady in a costume."

"You said you liked it. I thought she was your type."

"I was just playing with you. You're my type. That's who I want to make love with. Not some bimbo."

My heart was warmed by his words.

"You could dress up, too," I said, with a lustful grin.

"Kaley!" A-Rad's tone had turned from disapproval to disgust.

I hadn't expected such a strong reaction.

"I thought guys liked this kind of role playing."

"Not this guy."

I was surprised. I figured he'd be into it. Even though I'd always known A-Rad was a bigger prude than me and he was certainly proving it now.

The whole thing was cracking me up, so I decided to continue teasing him.

"You could dress up as the pool boy on a cruise ship! No. You could be the captain and wear one of those captain hats."

"I am extremely pejorative about that idea," he retorted with a grin that took up half his face.

I couldn't hold back my laughter. Both in the words he used incorrectly in the sentence and his tone of voice.

"That's *not* how you use the word pejorative in a sentence."

"Whatever," he huffed, his jaw clenched to keep from bursting out laughing. "Let's go."

He walked over to me and picked me up like a rag doll and carried me into the bedroom.

Even though A-Rad didn't like my idea to dress up in costumes, I made sure to show him a good time regardless.

Twice.

3

Six weeks later

Jamie still hadn't called.

I was starting to worry that the satellite phone wasn't working. If she had tried to call and couldn't get through for some reason, how would we know?

Alex had devised and installed an encryption program on the satellite phone so we could talk freely when they did call. It had worked when we left the island, but it could be affected by all kinds of things, including the weather. We couldn't call them or test it in any way. All we could do was wait.

A-Rad was taking a nap on the couch, while I read a book at his feet. Without warning, the buzzer sounded, so loud it shook the room. Alex had wanted to make sure we could hear it even if we were outside on the deck.

We both jumped to our feet instantly.

I rushed to answer the phone connected to a speaker. A familiar voice filled the room replacing the shrill of the buzzer. My ears were still ringing.

"Hello. Do you remember me?" Jamie asked.

"I thought you forgot about us," I replied, not completely joking.

"Sorry about that. It took some time to get the mission plan together, but I think we're finally there."

"That's good to hear," A-Rad chimed in.

"Hey, buddy," Alex said.

"Hi Alex," A-Rad responded. "Have you been busy pillaging terrorist bank accounts?"

"Not exactly. I've actually been focused on domestic stuff."

"Really."

That surprised me. Alex and Jamie never ran domestic operations. The CIA wasn't allowed to operate on US soil, which meant it had to be an AJAX initiative. Even though AJAX wasn't technically part of the CIA, it had a close alliance and there were many constitutional issues to consider. Due process and the like. Banking regulations. Hacking into computers and bank accounts were crimes even if the motives were pure.

Alex explained. "There's a group targeting elderly women and scamming them out of their money. One of the women in our church lost thirty grand to them. She got a call from someone claiming her granddaughter was in jail and needed bail money. The woman withdrew the cash, met the man, and handed it over, only to find out her granddaughter was safe and away at college."

"That's pure evil," A-Rad said. "I hope you make them pay."

"I already have. As soon as I heard about what they did, I got to work and found out who was behind it. I emptied their bank accounts which had more than five million dollars in them. Some of the elderly women lost hundreds of thousands of dollars."

"That's incredible."

"Some lost their entire life savings," Alex said. "One of the things they did was send out spam emails that looked legitimate. When the women clicked on the emails, it corrupted their computers and allowed the bad guys access. Once they knew their banking passwords, they took the money directly out of their accounts without them knowing about it until it was too late."

"I can imagine they were devastated. And embarrassed."

"One woman committed suicide. I was able to identify most of the victims and I put the money back into their bank accounts. If their accounts were closed, I sent them a cashier's check. Anonymously, of course. There wasn't enough to pay everybody, but AJAX made up the difference."

"You're a good man, Alex."

"It's dirty money we stole from the bad guys. At least some good can come out of it."

"Keep up the good work."

"I will. I've got my sights on more companies that need to be taken down."

"I hope you bring them all to justice."

"I intend to. How's married life?"

"You won't hear me complaining," A-Rad said.

"He'd better not," I said.

A-Rad was sitting next to me and put his hand on mine. "You know what it's like, Alex, being married to someone who can kill you a hundred different ways with her bare hands. You avoid fighting with them like you avoid a great white shark."

"I hear that. I'd rather tangle with a pool full of sharks than pick a fight with Jamie."

"Me too. Pick a fight with Kaley, I mean."

"I hope you two lovebirds enjoyed your honeymoon," Jamie said, "because it's about to come to an end."

Before I could respond, Alex said, "That reminds me. Speaking of marriage, I got my license."

"What license?" I asked.

"My ordination papers," he clarified.

"I don't understand."

"Your marriage is legal now."

"Wait a minute, I thought it was legal before."

"It was ... kind of ... sort of. When I said I'd marry you on the island, I didn't actually have my papers. When I got home, I went online and made an application for ordination papers. They came in the mail a few days ago so now I can officially marry people."

"But you married us three months ago! Are you telling me we aren't officially married?"

"You are now," Alex said, matter-of-factly.

"That means we've been living in sin for three months!" I exclaimed.

"Don't worry. I had it backdated to the day I married you."

"You can do that?" A-Rad asked.

"They'll do anything for an extra hundred bucks. Anyway, the important thing is that my ordination is effective as of the day of your wedding."

"Is that legal?" I asked, hesitantly.

A-Rad squeezed my hand. "Does it matter?" he said. "We're married in God's eyes. That's all that matters to me."

I nodded. Still unsure.

We hadn't actually filled out a marriage license and filed it anywhere anyway, so technically we weren't married as far as any legal jurisdiction was concerned. The upsetting part was that I didn't know Alex wasn't authorized to marry us. I don't know if I would've agreed to it.

"Who's going to challenge it?" Jamie said. "You guys are together. That's all that matters."

"Enough about that," I said. "Are you calling with a mission?" I was anxious to get to the business at hand. A wave of nervousness had come over me as I desperately wanted to know where our first assignment would take us.

"Yes," Jamie confirmed. "Colonel is here with us."

"Hi guys," Colonel said.

"It's good to hear your voice," A-Rad greeted him warmly.

I saw a pain flash in his eyes. Hearing his best friend's voice had probably sent a dart through his heart. I felt it too. It reminded me that we'd probably never see any of them again.

"Likewise," Colonel said, in his friendliest voice, while not being able to avoid his military aloofness that was as much ingrained in him as the stripes on a tiger.

"Sorry it took me so long," Colonel said sincerely. "I created a plan for everyone on the kill list, before deciding which target to pursue first. I figured we'd start with either the most dangerous person on the list or the easiest mission to pull off. As it turns out, they were one and the same."

A-Rad grinned at me when Colonel said the word 'easiest'. I gave him a "Don't say it" look. He said it anyway.

"Easiest is pejorative," A-Rad said, to my stiff frown.

"What?" Colonel asked, in a confused voice.

"Never mind," I said. "Where are we going?" The anticipation was bursting inside of me.

Jamie answered, "In a global game of hide and seek, where is the best place to hide?"

"I have no idea," I admitted. "It could be anywhere."

"North Korea," Jamie declared emphatically.

I was shocked. That's probably the last place I thought they'd send us. I had no clue why Colonel might think it'd be the easiest.

"I would think North Korea would be the hardest place to hide," I said, expressing my concerns aloud. "And an even harder place to kill the leader."

"On the contrary," Jamie said confidently. "Actually, it's the perfect place to start."

"It's a closed country."

"Exactly. Very few people are allowed into the country and none of the citizens are allowed out. What better place to hide? That's the last place anyone would look for you. And Alex has contacts there."

A few years ago, before I joined the CIA, I remembered that Alex had gone to North Korea in an attempt to shut down a computer hacking organization run by a man named Pok. Alex and Pok had a running, and often dangerous, feud for years. I think Pok was dead now, although that's not a subject anyone talked about in AJAX circles.

"I already have a place for you to stay," Alex said. "You can stay at Momma's place."

"Your mom lives in North Korea?" I asked.

Alex chuckled. "No, Momma-son. She runs a diner in North Korea. She took me in and saved my life."

I was still skeptical. "Neither of us speaks Korean. How will we communicate with her?"

"Momma speaks English," Alex said. "And she makes the best pancakes on the planet."

Pancakes sounded good. We had been eating the same thing for more than three months.

"Tell us about the mission, Colonel," I said. "How do we pull it off? And why will the leader be so easy to kill?"

"Min Yang is the Divine Leader," he answered.

I knew his name, but that's about it.

"He's anything but divine," Jamie added, with bitterness behind the words. And he's the most dangerous threat on the list. Which is saying something."

"Right. He's been making a lot of noise in the region," Colonel said. "Threatening the West and test-firing missiles into the Pacific. As you know, he has nukes and would use them if he thought he could get away with it. He's contained for now, but who knows for how long."

"I've been wanting to get rid of him for ages," Alex interjected. "The man is ruthless. Not only is he a threat to the world, he's a tyrant when it comes to his own people. The government owns everything. Everyone is separated into classes and told where to live and where to work. No one owns anything. If you even think about dissenting in any way, you and your entire family are thrown in jail. It's the most oppressive regime on the planet, by far."

"That actually works in your favor," Jamie said. "Yang is arrogant and thinks he has things so under control that he's let his guard down."

"That's why I said it's an easy kill," Colonel said.

"How is it easy?" I asked.

"Every Friday, Yang likes to go on a long motorcycle ride. He leaves the palace on his bike and rides for hours in the countryside. All you have to do is follow him and put a bullet in his body."

"What about security?"

"They don't go with him," Colonel said. "Like Jamie said, he thinks he's invincible."

"That does sound easy enough," A-Rad said.

"Where are we going to get motorcycles?" I asked.

"All that will be provided," Colonel said. "You'll take the yacht to South Korea and moor there. You'll make your way to the DMZ and cross the border through the secret CIA route."

"The DMZ is heavily guarded on both sides, isn't it?" A-Rad asked.

"I'll show you how to do it," Alex said. "I've crossed many times with no problems."

Colonel continued. "Once you're across, there'll be two motorcycles waiting for you at a hidden location along with weapons and everything else you'll need. You'll ride them to Momma-son's diner. She'll be expecting you. You can hide there. When you're ready, you kill Yang."

"Sounds simple enough," I said.

"Just one more problem," Jamie said.

It did sound too good to be true.

"Yang has a sister. A twin. A few hours younger. He was put into power by his father because he was the first born. You're going to have to kill her, too. She's more dangerous than her brother."

"Do you have a plan for that?" I asked.

Colonel answered. "We do. She loves horses and has a stable of them. Every Friday, while her brother is riding his motorcycle, she goes for a horse ride on the palace grounds. After you kill her brother, you'll have to go to the palace and kill her as well."

"Any security?" I asked.

"Only around the palace grounds," Jamie said. "None that rides with her. At least as far as we know. We have a source, but information is sketchy so you may have to play that one by ear."

"I see at least one complication," A-Rad said. "We'll have to kill her before the word gets back to her that her brother is dead. Otherwise, she'll go into a bunker and we'll never get her out."

"That's something you'll have to take into account," Colonel said. "You'll have a short window. From minutes to maybe several hours if you're lucky."

"If you're successful, and you will be, this would be huge," Jamie said. "There's no other family member to take Yang's place. It'll create a vacuum. A power struggle. We don't know who will emerge on top, but they couldn't be worse than Yang."

"You can count on us. We'll kill them both," I said.

"There's one other problem," Alex said.

I let out a groan that they could hear. "Of course there is. What is it?"

"Have you seen the weather lately?"

"Not recently," I said, anticipating what he was about to say.

"There's a tropical cyclone headed your way. Category 5."

"I saw that," A-Rad said. "I thought it was headed north."

Alex's tone was urgent now. "No. It's turned south and you're right in its path. There's no way to avoid it. It could hit you as soon as tomorrow."

My heart was beating faster now.

"Then we'd better get off the phone and get to work preparing the yacht," I said. "Hopefully, she can withstand it."

"I'll send the mission plan to your inbox," Jamie said.

"Thanks, Jamie. You can count on us," I said. "Colonel, thank you for all your hard work."

Saying goodbye prompted an emotional storm to rise up inside of me along with the worry of the physical storm bearing down on us.

"You're welcome," Colonel and Jamie said in unison.

The call ended abruptly and A-Rad and I sat there in stunned silence for too long. The weight of our mission and the potential impending disaster felt like a heavy stone, crushing any excitement we felt about finally having a mission.

"It's never a good sign when a mission starts off on the wrong foot," A-Rad finally said.

"It sounds like the next few days might be the most treacherous part of our journey."

4

The moment we hung up the phone from the much-awaited call with Alex and Jamie, A-Rad and I sprang into action. We immediately checked the radar and saw that the tropical cyclone was no longer a distant threat—it was bearing down on us with full force.

The yacht was our only hope for sanctuary, and we had to make sure it could withstand the imminent onslaught. We secured everything on the deck, double-checked all hatches, and stowed any loose items. A-Rad checked the engines and power systems, while I covered and reinforced the windows to the main cabin.

The sky turned an ominous gray, and the wind picked up significantly, howling like a wild beast.

I could feel the tension in the air as we hurried to prepare for the storm with a sense of urgency. The yacht creaked and groaned under the growing intensity of the wind, making me doubt if our preparations would be enough.

A-Rad occasionally glanced at me, his expression a mix of determination and concern. "Be careful out there," he shouted over the roaring wind as I struggled to secure a small craft attached to the yacht and had to lean over the side to do so.

The first raindrops began to hit my skin, cold and foreboding.

A sudden loud crack split the air, followed by a powerful jolt that nearly knocked me off my feet. Panic surged through me as I realized the storm was already upon us with all its fury and unpredictability only moments away.

Not sure the small boat could make it through the storm anyway, I left it as it was and made my way to help A-Rad. The deck was slick and unstable, and I stumbled forward, grabbing onto the railing to steady myself as the yacht pitched violently.

A-Rad was at the back, frantically trying to secure a loose fender that was being whipped around by the wind. I saw the panic in his eyes as he battled against the storm's increasing wrath.

"Help me tie this down!" he shouted over the raging wind.

Without hesitation, I rushed to his side and together we wrestled with the unruly rope, struggling to bring it under control.

The rain hammered down on us, drenching us as we worked frantically.

Without warning, a massive wave struck the yacht causing it to tilt dangerously to the side, knocking me off balance. I slipped on the wet deck and fell hard.

The yacht suddenly lifted into the air. I desperately tried to grab hold of something—anything—to brace myself. The only thing within my reach was the stray rope to the fender which I quickly wrapped around my right wrist.

The yacht was momentarily suspended in the air before plummeting down like a roller coaster in an amusement park. It slammed on the ocean waves below.

When we hit with a jarring impact, the momentum threw me into the air, and I screamed as I went over the side of the yacht headed for certain death in the churning and frigid ocean.

The rope around my wrist stopped my fall and slammed me against the side of the yacht. Somehow, I managed to hang on with all my might. The rough fibers burned my bare hand and wrist causing intense pain, but I couldn't let go. The violent waters below would swallow me up faster than water sucked down a drain.

The icy water sprayed up at me as I dangled precariously. The wind howled in my ears, urging me to surrender. The lurching waves slammed me against the side of the boat several more times knocking the remaining breath out of me.

A-Rad's voice pierced through the chaos. "Don't you dare let go! Pull yourself up!"

He leaned over the side of the yacht, his hand outstretched toward me, but still out of his reach. If he leaned over any further, I was afraid he might fall into the ocean. If another wave hit, we'd both be powerless to stop it from happening.

Summoning every ounce of strength and willpower, I pulled myself up hand over hand on the rope. The storm continued its relentless assault around me, but I refused to yield. Inch by agonizing inch, I hauled myself towards safety until I was within reach of his outstretched hand.

"Take my hand," A-Rad shouted. "I'll pull you up."

I hesitated. If I reached for his hand, I had to let go of the rope. If his wet grip didn't hold, I'd fall into the ocean. My chance of survival, impossible.

Is this how I'm going to die? In a watery grave?

A-Rad's words were surprisingly resolute and filled with confidence. "I've got you. Trust me."

My strength was fading fast. With one final surge of energy, I released one hand from the rope and reached up towards A-Rad's hand, immediately losing the grip with my other hand.

I felt myself falling. A second scream stuck in the back of my throat.

The next thing I knew, I was lying on the deck. It all happened so fast I couldn't describe it in detail. All I knew was that A-Rad's strong hand had wrapped around my wrist at the last moment and jerked me over the railing, and onto the deck.

He fell to his knees gasping for breath. I collapsed beside him, my heart pounding like a drum in my chest. A-Rad's face was etched with relief and gratitude.

"Are you okay?" he asked.

I did a quick assessment of my body which was shaking from the cold and the adrenaline rush. It felt battered and bruised, but nothing seemed broken.

"You're a madman," I said, scooting closer to him so we could embrace tightly. "You could've been killed trying to save me."

"That's better than the alternative. If you had gone in the water, I was going in after you."

"Then we would both be dead."

"Like I said, this was a better alternative."

I managed a weak chuckle.

It felt comforting to be in his arms surrounded by his warmth. I drew strength from it.

The rain began to pelt down harder, so we retreated inside to get out of the wet clothes and to secure what we could on the inside. Once satisfied that we'd done all we could, we collapsed onto the couch and prepared to ride out the storm in each other's arms.

The yacht's interior felt suffocatingly small with the windows boarded up, and in some ways, I wished I could see what was happening on the outside. The storm made its presence felt through the constant violent movements of the vessel, and eventually I was glad I couldn't see it.

Our life jackets sat on the table next to us, but we didn't bother to put them on. If we ended up in the freezing water, we wouldn't survive five minutes.

Why prolong the agony with a life jacket?

I braced myself for the worst. So many things could go wrong and my mind was spinning out of control with all the possibilities.

The boat could capsize. It wouldn't take long to fill up with water and sink to the bottom of the ocean, never to be found. It could break apart like a flimsy toy made of sticks and splinter under the onslaught. Perhaps some remaining pieces of the yacht might wash ashore hundreds of miles away.

Even if the yacht survived the storm, there's no guarantee we'd make it out alive. If we lost all power and couldn't fix it, we'd be at the mercy of the current that would drift us rapidly towards Antarctica, where we'd either strike an iceberg or get stuck on a desolate ice floe.

I didn't think we could survive the cold long enough for Alex and Jamie to find us. Even if they tried, which was no certainty.

The last thought sent shivers down my spine.

But I couldn't let those thoughts consume me and I chastised myself for giving them a place. Jamie had drilled in me to always remain optimistic. To never give up even in the face of overwhelming odds.

As long as we had breath, we had hope.

And yet, the sense of impending doom hovered over us like a thick fog suffocating my emotions under its weight.

Desperate for comfort and security, I sought refuge in A-Rad's arms and snuggled against his shoulder. His strong presence had already saved me once that day, and even though I knew he was no match for the storm, his grip on my shoulder reassured me he'd do it again.

Whatever confidence I mustered was short-lived as the storm hit with a fury and unlike anything I had ever experienced before. The yacht was tossed about like a toy in a bathtub by the merciless beast whose unrelenting waves slammed into us from all sides with bone-crushing force.

The wind screamed a howler monkey wail that drowned out everything else, making it impossible to communicate without shouting even though we were inches from each other.

With every violent pitch and roll, it felt like we were being tossed into the jaws of death. We'd find ourselves almost at a ninety-degree angle, then we'd slam back down the other way, repeating the excruciating roller coaster ride again and again. All we could do was hold on and pray for it to be over.

Time lost all meaning as our ark put up a courageous battle. Minutes felt like hours, and hours felt like days.

At one point, we were thrown off the couch and onto the floor. The impact sent a sharp pain through my ribs as I slammed against a chair.

We were now at the mercy of the storm that lifted us high in the air and then slammed us down causing us to fly into the air and then slam back to the floor. When the yacht tilted to the side, we would follow it and slide down to one end of the cabin. When it was met by an opposite wave, it'd throw us to the other side of the cabin.

We could not survive this. We had to find something to hold onto.

"A-Rad!" I called out, panic rising in my throat as I struggled to get up.

He was stunned as well, but his face was a mask of grim determination as he struggled to stand and make his way back to me. We managed to huddle together on the floor with our feet and arms wrapped around two chairs securely bolted to the floor, determined not to let the storm toss us around again.

The storm had no concern for our struggles and raged on outside, un-relenting in its assault. Every muscle in my arms and shoulders cried out begging for relief as we stayed that way for several hours. If I let go, I knew I wouldn't be able to find my way back to the spot that had turned out to be the best place to ride out the storm.

"Stay strong! We have to make it through this," A-Rad shouted into my ear over the deafening roar of the wind. "We have to get to North Korea."

That was the last thing on my mind. I hadn't given our mission to kill the leader of North Korea a second thought.

His words helped me though. I nodded and clenched my jaw and grip on the chair with a newfound resolve. Determined to survive so we could fulfill our mission and make the world a better place.

As if we had any choice in whether or not we survived. Living through this was mostly outside of our control. It depended on the strength of the yacht. Could it withstand the onslaught?

So far it had.

And if it hadn't given up yet, neither would I.

I said silent prayers to God. Hoping for protection and peace through the terrifying ordeal.

Exhaustion tried to weaken my faith in God, but I pushed through the pain, focusing all my energy on praying us through the chaos. The storm seemed determined to break us, but I refused to let it conquer my will.

Hours passed in a blur of adrenaline and fear, each wave feeling like a mini battle we had to fight and win. Our entire world had shrunk to the confines of the yacht, our only hope depending upon the faith in my prayers and the construction of the hull.

The power flickered and then went out completely, plunging us into darkness as if we didn't have enough problems.

"We've lost power!" A-Rad shouted, his voice filled with urgency.

"Nothing we can do about it," I said.

The emergency backup lights flickered on, casting a faint glow over our surroundings. It wasn't much, but it was better than being engulfed in darkness.

When I thought we couldn't take any more, the storm's fury began to lessen. The wind still howled, but the deafening roar had subsided. The waves were still rough, but they were no longer as violent or as high.

Everything suddenly became eerily calm.

"We're in the eye of the storm," A-Rad said, his voice weary but hopeful.

"Thank goodness," I replied, feeling a surge of relief.

"We don't have much time," he said. "We need to check for damage and make sure we're ready when the other side hits."

My legs felt wobbly as I stood to my feet. My arms felt like I had been lifting heavy weights for hours.

Once we got our bearings, we moved quickly, going outside to assess the damage. The yacht had taken a beating, but it was still seaworthy. Several of the windows were cracked, and the deck was a mess, but overall, the yacht was intact.

As we worked to shore things up again, I felt a strange sense of peace settle over me. It seemed almost impossible to believe that we were totally surrounded by such a destructive power and yet things were so calm in the eye.

Once we did all we could, we hurried back inside knowing what lay ahead. The eye of the storm was only a brief respite.

We barely had time to catch our breath before the other side of the storm hit. At first, it wasn't as fierce as the first half, but it was still brutal. We hunkered down in the same spot and rode it out, praying that the yacht would hold out a little longer.

It didn't take long for the storm to hit us with renewed ferocity, as if nature itself was determined to test our resilience. The waves grew larger and crashed against the yacht with relentless force.

"We can't take much more of this!" A-Rad shouted over the din, his voice strained with exhaustion.

I nodded grimly, my knuckles white from grasping onto the leg of the chair.

When I thought it couldn't get any worse, the storm unleashed a final ferocious attack. Like a winning fighter not satisfied, going for a knockout in the last round.

Mercifully, it finally ended.

We made our way outside after we got our bearings. We didn't find the same calmness we experienced in the eye. The sea was still rough, but the wind had died down and the rain had stopped. We walked around the yacht assessing the damage, not bothering to try and fix things, exhausted and battered, but thankful to be alive.

"We made it," A-Rad said, his voice filled with disbelief and relief.

"We did," I agreed, feeling a deep sense of gratitude. "Now let's get this yacht back in shape. We've got a mission to complete."

My own voice was surprisingly firm with determination.

A-Rad's forehead was furrowed and his eyebrows narrowed.

"What's wrong?" I asked.

He pointed to the storm in the distance that seemed to be getting closer.

I let out a disapproving yelp as the fear returned with a vengeance.

"It's sucking us back into it," he said, urgently. "I've got to get the power restored so we can steer away from it."

"Can I help?"

"No, you stay here. If we get dragged back into the storm, go inside and brace yourself again."

That's the last thing I wanted to hear.

He rushed off to the engine room while I stayed on deck, nervously watching the dark cloud drawing closer. If it took any longer, I'd have to seek safety.

My heart leapt to the top of my chest when I heard the powerful diesel engines come to life. I cheered when I saw A-Rad emerge from the engine room and climb the walkway.

I flashed him an appreciative wave then joined him as he took control of the helm. After we were safely away, I went back on the deck to repair what I could.

The sun began to peek through the clouds, casting a golden light over the ocean around us and bringing with it an overpowering optimism.

A-Rad joined me on the deck, having put the yacht on autopilot. A sense of camaraderie and mutual respect filled the air, binding us together in a shared sense of survival. The yacht looked like us, battle-scarred warriors who had emerged victorious from a great conflict.

We stood side by side on the deck, staring in the direction of the cyclone that was now out of sight. I took A-Rad's hand, and we knelt together to thank God for saving us.

The storm had tested us, but we had survived. And now, with North Korea on the horizon, our next challenge was about to begin.

5

Seoul, South Korea

For the first time in three and a half months, our feet were on dry land. Technically, we stood on a dock in Indonesia when we stopped to refuel, but that didn't count in my mind.

This did. We were walking through a park, feeling the grass under our feet.

We had docked the yacht in a secluded inlet on the northern coast of South Korea and used our small boat to reach the marina. The same boat that almost cost me my life when I tried to secure it before the cyclone was upon us. Turns out it was as resilient as the yacht and came through the violence with some scars but mostly intact.

Passing through security in South Korea was surprisingly easy. Jamie had created fake passports for us that worked perfectly. She made some slight alterations to our pictures, but they went unnoticed by the security personnel and didn't trigger an alert.

We were certain our faces were on a watch list, so going through customs was nerve-wracking, but we had chosen that checkpoint for a reason. Our backpacks were searched, but the only things we were armed with were a change of clothes, bathroom bags, and American currency. They didn't even call us into a room for questioning since our passports showed frequent visits to South Korea.

After we made it through security, we wore masks whenever we thought it necessary and avoided the limited number of cameras on the streets. Half the people were wearing masks, so we fit right in. In a bustling city of ten million people, we blended, and I doubted anyone even noticed us.

Even then, our plan was not to go straight to the DMZ and cross into North Korea. The park was too enticing, and we indulged in a few minutes of relaxation. While it felt good to be on dry land and around people and activity, we were still constantly aware of our surroundings and kept our heads on swivels.

The constant anxiety of having to watch our backs was a stark contrast to the monotonous days spent on the yacht.

A-Rad surprised me when he said, "Hey Kaley, let's do some exploring."

"What do you mean?"

"I mean that we've been cooped up on that boat for ages. It feels good to be back in the real world. We aren't under any timetable to get to North Korea. So let's enjoy ourselves while we can."

I took a quick glance around our surroundings. "Do you really think that's a good idea? What if someone spots us?"

"What are the odds of that happening? I'm not suggesting we do anything reckless. I'd just like to sit down at a restaurant, eat some good food, and feel like a normal person for a few minutes."

"But you aren't a normal person."

"And you are?"

"No," I nervously chuckled. "You know what I mean."

"You're as normal as tornadoes in Oklahoma or like cyclones in the Indian Ocean are normal."

I shuddered remembering how close we came to dying in the Indian Ocean at the hand of one of those cyclones.

"Did you know why hurricanes are usually named after females?" I asked.

"No, Kaley, tell me."

"Because when they leave, they take your house with them."

We both laughed at my joke, and I felt some tension release.

We spent the next hour wandering aimlessly through the streets. With no real purpose. We did some window shopping and watched some street performers. Eventually, we found a small restaurant that looked like an authentic Korean restaurant.

As we settled into our seats, A-Rad scanned the menu and blurted out, "I wonder if they have cheeseburgers and fries."

I groaned in disbelief. "A-Rad! We finally have a chance to eat at a real restaurant and you want a burger and fries?"

"Yes, Kaley. I haven't had one in three months. I'd love to bite into a juicy burger with cheese fries on the side. Do you think they have that here?"

"Yeah. It's right next to the kimchi and bibimbap."

A-Rad made a face. "What's kimchi?"

"I'll look it up."

Before finding the restaurant, we stopped at a store and bought two burner phones. In case we got separated, we'd have a way to communicate with each other. The phone also had internet access, so I searched for kimchi.

"Kimchi consists of salted and fermented vegetables."

A-Rad wrinkled his nose in disgust.

"Salty is okay but I don't like the sound of fermented."

"It's a traditional dish made with a variety of vegetables like cabbage, with garlic, chili peppers, fish sauce, and can include carrots, radish, cucumber, and scallions. Depending on the region."

"No to cabbage. No to fish sauce. No to scallions. No to ... No to all those ingredients. I'll stick to my burger and fries."

"Kimchi sounds good to me." My stomach was starting to growl.

"Even the name, kimchi, sounds unappealing."

"I'll have you know that in South Korea, kimchi is eaten at almost every meal, including breakfast."

"I'm afraid to ask what's in bibimbap. Did I say that right?"

He butchered the pronunciation, but I knew what he meant and typed it into the search engine on my phone.

"I'll tell you what's in it. Bibimbap is a beloved Korean bowl dish. It incorporates steamed rice with fresh vegetables and meat. It's always served with an egg on top."

"Now you're talking." He rubbed his hands together in excitement.

The eggs we had onboard the yacht were powdered. Having fresh eggs did sound good. I was also looking forward to trying Momma-son's pancakes that Alex raved about.

"They also have tofu and rice," I said, jokingly, knowing the response I'd get from A-Rad.

He grimaced.

"Rice guys finish last." He grinned like a mischievous boy and seemed proud of himself for coming up with the quip.

"Did you just make that up?"

He flexed his muscles that were bulging out of his tight t-shirt. "This boy needs some real meat. Some steak and eggs."

The waitress approached our table with our drink order, and I chose the kimchi, and A-Rad ordered the bibimbap with steak and an egg over-easy.

"Good choices," the waitress said, before leaving.

"I'd settle for anything that doesn't come from a can," he said.

"Or freeze-dried," I added, with a cringe. "I never want to see another packet of instant noodles again."

"Hey, don't knock the noodles. They saved us more than once."

"True," I admitted, "but they're not exactly gourmet cuisine."

A-Rad continued to study the menu. "I should've gotten the bulgogi. Look, it has a picture."

I looked it up on my phone. "Bulgogi is a Korean dish for meat lovers."

"Oh man. I should've ordered that."

"'Bul' means fire and 'Gogi' means meat. Fiery meat. You can get it with ribeye, tenderloin, or sirloin steak."

"Definitely tenderloin. No wait, ribeye. Definitely ribeye."

A-Rad took the next few minutes trying to pronounce the other menu items. I didn't bother looking them up but was amused watching him butcher the words.

Our food arrived with steam coming off the top of the bowls, filling the air with a tantalizing aroma. My stomach rumbled with approval.

"Can I have some ketchup?" A-Rad asked the waitress.

I stared at him in shock.

The waitress seemed confused. Her English was good, but she obviously couldn't understand why anyone would put ketchup on any dish they served. I doubted they even had ketchup in the restaurant. The only things on the table were a collection of sauces.

"He's kidding," I said to her, even though I knew he wasn't.

She walked away with a frown on her face, still perplexed.

"I wasn't kidding. I like ketchup on my eggs."

"You're going to ruin it. It already comes with a sauce on it."

He must've liked it anyway because he devoured it within a couple of minutes. I ate slower, savoring every bite.

Our conversation was limited since our mouths were full. I wondered if A-Rad would order seconds, but the portions were big, and he didn't mention it. It could be because we had a big night ahead of us, crossing the DMZ. He wouldn't want to be weighed down by too much food.

As we waited for our check, A-Rad leaned back in his chair and surveyed the bustling street outside the restaurant. He ran his hand through his hair. "I feel like I need a haircut."

"I cut your hair yesterday!"

"No offense, but I'd like to have a barber do it. And get a shave."

I laughed. "Tell me about it. My hair is a mess. I don't think anyone is going to ask me to be on the cover of a magazine anytime soon. I look like I just came off a deserted island."

"You almost did."

I laughed so hard I nearly choked on my water. Maybe A-Rad was right. Taking a moment to enjoy the simple pleasures, like a good meal and some light-hearted banter, was exactly what we needed.

The waitress sat two fortune cookies down in front of us. I handed one to A-Rad and he snapped it open.

"An alien will appear to you soon," he said.

I snatched it out of his hand and read it. "That's not what it says."

It said something about contentment came from more than riches.

"Open yours," he said.

I cracked mine open. "It says a wise man listens to his wife. A foolish man disagrees with her."

"You lie. What does it really say?"

"Nothing." I tossed it on the table. "These things are stupid."

A-Rad picked it up and read it out loud.

"Success is not final; Failure is not fatal."

A grim reminder of the task awaiting us hit me out of the blue. Where we were going, failure could very well be fatal. That's why I had tossed it aside. I'd been struggling for days to try and push the risk of our mission out of my head.

A-Rad tossed the paper on the table without comment, but I knew he was thinking the same thing. As we left the restaurant, he took my arm and squeezed it and I felt reassured.

"I guess we should head for the DMZ," he said. "It's getting dark."

"Dark is better."

Without even trying, my focus changed. I could sense it in A-Rad as well. We switched into full mission mode and implemented counter surveillance techniques to make sure we weren't being followed, just in case.

Satisfied we weren't, we approached the DMZ, and saw our first security personnel. I felt A-Rad stiffen his entire body, as did I. Armed soldiers guarded the area with machine guns, and I felt vulnerable.

We didn't have any weapons on us, not that we'd use them. The soldiers on the South Korean side of the border weren't our enemies. We also weren't doing anything wrong. Not yet anyway. As soon as we attempted to cross the DMZ, we were breaking all kinds of international laws.

Alex had warned us that the Demilitarized Zone was one of the most fortified borders in the world, but nothing could've prepared us for the reality of it. We stood in awe at the sheer magnitude of the military presence before us.

This wasn't a typical border control area. It was a fortress with a small army guarding it. The high fences and bright strobe lights that illuminated the area made me wonder why Alex had said this would be easy.

Every step we took felt like an increasing risk. Like any moment we could be caught never to see the light of day again. The thought occurred to me that if we were caught, it'd be better if it were on this side of the border.

But getting caught wasn't an option.

We followed Alex's instructions and stayed a good distance away from the massive wall that separated the two countries.

We hiked several miles to the secret passageway—an old, abandoned tunnel from the Cold War era. Finding the entrance was no easy task either. It was hidden beneath layers of an overgrown thicket, camouflaged to the point of being nearly invisible. We moved the foliage aside and found a rusted hatch, the door to the tunnel.

A-Rad worked getting the door opened while I kept watch, my heart pounding in my chest.

"Got it," he whispered, the hatch opening with a creak.

We descended into the darkness, the air cool and damp. Our phones provided the only source of light as we made our way through the cramped space.

The narrow passageway led us into the unknown. We moved quickly but cautiously, our footsteps echoing in the confined space. Every sound seemed amplified, and I couldn't shake off the feeling that we were being watched.

A number of foreboding thoughts flooded my mind.

What if the North Koreans knew about the tunnel and had guards waiting for us at the other end?

What if we weren't successful on our mission and we ended up dead or worse, in prison for the rest of our lives?

But there was no turning back now. This was what we signed up for. Our vows to each other., for better or for worse. This wasn't what most people meant when they spoke those words.

After we walked more than a mile at least, we came to the door at the other end of the tunnel, presumably in North Korea. We were in enemy territory now, and I could feel it down to my bones.

"Are you ready?" A-Rad asked, with one hand on the door.

"I'm ready," I said.

A resolve overpowered me as I spoke the words. A fire ignited inside my soul.

We were about to strike the first blow in a war that would change the world forever and our enemies had no idea what was coming for them.

Victory or defeat awaited us on the other side of that door, but one thing was for sure: nothing would ever be the same again.

6

North Korea

A-Rad reached for the latch on the door at the end of the tunnel, his face tense with determination. I grabbed his arm and stopped him.

"Wait," I whispered, urgently. "What if there's a guard on the other side? We'll be easy targets."

"Stand against that wall," he said, "and turn off your phone light."

We plunged into total darkness. I couldn't see my hand in front of my face. But I did what he said and pressed my back against the wall. I presumed that A-Rad did the same on the other side as I heard him rustle into position.

Pressed against the wall was the safest place. Safe was relative. If a guard was out there and opened fire, he'd likely aim for the center of the tunnel. If that happened, we could close the door quickly and retreat to the other end of the tunnel.

"Are you ready?" he asked.

"Go."

A-Rad pushed the door open slowly. The loud creaking sound from the rusted door reverberated through the tunnel. If someone was out there with a gun, he heard us. Couldn't be helped.

I held my breath, bracing for gunshots that never came.

At least the opened door sent a glimmer of light into the tunnel, and I could see A-Rad leaning out listening intently for any sound before deciding to exit the tunnel.

"It could be a trap," I whispered. "He might be waiting for us to come outside."

"Wait here," A-Rad said, crouching low and moving cautiously. He disappeared from view, then reappeared and motioned for me to follow, signifying he thought it was safe.

As I emerged into North Korea, the oppressive darkness and musty smell of the tunnel gave way to a moonlit landscape, with eerie and unfamiliar stillness.

A-Rad nervously scoured the area, looking for any sign of trouble, as did I. Every shadow potentially held a threat. My senses were on full alert, and I had to remind myself to breathe normally.

Once we were satisfied the coast was clear, A-Rad closed the hatch behind us and covered it, ensuring no trace of the tunnel remained visible. At some point, we'd have to escape through that same lifeline. Hopefully.

"Are you good?" he asked in a hushed voice. "I don't think anyone's around."

I nodded, my heart still pounding in my ears. "Let's move."

Following his lead, we set out to look for the small makeshift lean-to where we hoped to find the motorcycles and weapons based on Alex's directions. I'd feel better once I had a gun in my hand.

We navigated the rugged terrain as fast as possible, but quietly. A-Rad's confident steps gave me a sense of security.

The landscape was uneven and a stark contrast to the vibrant city we had just left. Here, it was barren and silent, the air heavy with an ominous presence, making me feel uneasy. Being on enemy soil even smelled different. Which was a ridiculous thought, but I'd noticed over the years that danger had its own feel and smell, even if it was only in my imagination.

A-Rad picked up the pace as he became more confident in his surroundings. I didn't know if we were going the right way, but I trusted him. He had an uncanny sense of direction. Always had.

Alex had laid out the directions clearly in the mission plan and A-Rad knew where to go and didn't hesitate once.

As we made our way through the forest, which kept us too close to the border wall for my preference, two North Korean soldiers appeared not too far off, their silhouettes outlined by the night sky. We saw them in time and ducked behind a row of trees, holding our breath as they spoke in normal voices, not trying in any way to hide their presence.

One of them lit a cigarette, its pungent odor filled the air alarmingly close to our hiding spot. The men didn't appear to have a sense of urgency about them. A-Rad signaled for us to continue moving and we crept along the tree line with every muscle tensed. One snap of a twig could reveal our presence.

The soldiers seemed bored. From what I read in the mission plan, there weren't many incidents at the border anymore and these soldiers probably had little to do. In the old days, many people tried to escape. After the crackdown and the installation of the more oppressive regime, the North Koreans became resigned to their fates, and few attempted to risk it now. Those who did try were usually caught and imprisoned or shot.

I'm sure the soldiers thought no one would be foolish enough to escape *into* North Korea.

The thought almost made me laugh.

When we were safely away from the soldiers, I felt my breathing return to normal. Still painfully aware that more soldiers could be anywhere. A-Rad kept his eyes focused ahead and I watched our backs.

Our destination was a small, nondescript building hidden in a dense forest. Alex said it'd be easy to miss. The last thing I wanted was to be lost and wandering around in enemy territory.

"There it is," A-Rad said excitedly when he spotted it a few minutes later.

We hid behind a tree and watched the dilapidated building for a few seconds, scanning the area for threats. We didn't wait long. The sooner we found the motorcycles and weapons and got on our way, the better.

A-Rad went to check inside, while I stayed outside and watched the perimeter.

After a few moments, he emerged with a huge grin on his face. "They're here, just like Alex promised."

I followed him inside and was surprised to see two sleek motorcycles sitting in the middle of the room. These were not your average bikes; they looked brand new and powerful.

I couldn't imagine how Alex managed to get them there. He obviously bought them in South Korea and brought them through the tunnel, at considerable risk. I silently thanked him.

A-Rad let out an excited whoop and ran his hand along the smooth surface of one of the bikes. "Wow. These things have some power behind them. I bet these babies can do 150-200 miles per hour."

I remembered seeing similar bikes on the freeways back home, weaving in and out of traffic effortlessly.

"That makes sense," I said. "Yang probably has one. We need them to keep up with him."

Two helmets were strapped to the bikes, along with two backpacks. Inside, we found weapons, ammo, and North Korean currency.

"This one's mine," A-Rad said, looking like a kid at an amusement park as he mounted it.

I hesitated before getting on mine.

"Don't go too fast," I warned. "At least not until I get used to it."

"You'll be fine. It's like riding a bike."

He laughed at his joke, but I wasn't laughing inside. "Seriously, don't lose me. Our phones won't work in North Korea."

"If we get separated, we'll meet at Momma-son's diner."

"If we get separated, don't even bother coming to the diner because you'll regret it." My tone was rough and threatening and meant to get the point across.

"I hear you."

We donned our helmets, which not only provided protection but also had built-in communication devices. I felt better that we could communicate with each other, but I wasn't sure of the range. They probably only worked if we were in close proximity to each other. If he left me in the dust, then the radios were useless, and he was in deep trouble.

"Let's hope these start," A-Rad said.

We rolled them outside. He turned the key and his engine roared to life. He revved it several times. I wasn't sure that was a good idea. We were probably outside earshot of the soldiers, but we couldn't be sure.

I started mine, anxious to get out of there as soon as possible. He looked at me and gave the thumbs up sign. I flashed it back.

The hum of the engine filled my ears, and I could feel the power between my legs as I touched the throttle and the bike lurched into action. I steadied it and couldn't believe how smoothly it handled even with my inexperience.

Heeding my admonition, A-Rad took it slow at first. It didn't take long until I was actually enjoying it.

"How you doing back there?" his voice reverberated clearly in my ears.

"Good. You can go faster now. I can keep up."

He let out a yelp and sped off. I struggled to keep up but managed to.

At first, the rough terrain made the ride bumpy and uncomfortable, but the adrenaline coursing through my veins dulled any discomfort. Eventually, we found smoother roads. Riding through the North Korean countryside was surreal, and I felt almost invincible on that bike. I envisioned chasing Yang through the countryside and surprising him when we pulled our guns.

The moon was bright and illuminated our route. Noticeably absent were any streetlights. All the houses we saw were dark. I'd read that electricity wasn't dependable and even the wealthy were subject to rolling blackouts.

The roads were also empty of vehicles. The only ones we saw were old and dilapidated and parked outside modest houses.

We avoided the main routes, sticking to back roads. The only official-looking vehicle we saw was parked along the side of the road and seemed like it had seen better days. No sign of who it belonged to.

Seeing the condition of the vehicles provided a sense of comfort. On the straightaway, we had our motorcycles up to over a hundred miles an hour. We clearly didn't have to worry about anyone catching us if we had to make a quick getaway.

After several hours of riding, the first hints of dawn began to break, casting a pale light over the landscape. I had hoped to get to the diner before sunrise, while still in the cover of darkness. Two people speeding through the towns in those bikes would certainly draw unwanted attention.

"We're close now," A-Rad said a few minutes later. He pointed ahead.

Off in the distance was a small, well-maintained building that looked like a diner. A nondescript structure in the middle of a small community. We parked our bikes behind the building, concealing them from the view of the street. The diner was closed, but a single light flickered inside, signaling that someone was there.

A-Rad knocked on the back door in a specific pattern, as instructed. Moments later, the door creaked open, revealing a petite, elderly woman with sharp eyes and a warm smile.

"Momma-son?" A-Rad asked.

She nodded and ushered us inside quickly, closing the door behind us. Once inside, she hugged our necks like we were relatives returning home from a trip.

The interior was simple but cozy, with a few worn tables and chairs scattered about. The smell of something delicious filled the air.

Momma-son led us to a spot in the back of the diner, a storage room filled with supplies. She stood in front of a wall, staring at it, lost in thought, as if she wasn't sure what to do next. For a moment, I wondered if she suffered from some sort of dementia.

A few seconds later, she pushed a hidden lever behind some supplies and a secret door opened, confirming that she knew exactly what she was doing. We descended steps to a fairly large room with a bed and a desk along with a computer and satellite phone.

Alex had called it a safehouse and Momma-son had gone to great risk to let him set it up there. If discovered, no telling what the authorities would do to her.

In surprisingly good English, Momma-son said, "Alex told me you would come. Sit, eat. You hungry from your journey. Momma-son make you something nice."

We took a seat at a small table as Momma-son disappeared back upstairs. She returned a few minutes later and placed two steaming bowls of rice in front of us, along with a plate of kimchi, and a pot of tea.

"Eat," she insisted. "You need your strength."

As we ate, Momma-son sat down with us, with curious eyes. "I help you as much as I can," she said. "But be careful. Many eyes watch, many ears listen."

We nodded and mostly ate in silence. She didn't ask any questions, and we didn't offer any information. The less she knew, the better. We had to protect her at all costs. Alex had a deep affection for Momma-son, and we needed to stay out of sight and not do anything that could lead the authorities back to her.

"The diner open soon," she said abruptly. "I'll be back."

She bounded up the steps. Alex had said she was over ninety now, but she looked to have the energy of someone half her age.

After we finished eating, we laid down on the bed and slept for a few hours. We'd been up all night and still had two days before we'd leave to execute our plan.

Momma-son had more food waiting for us when we woke up. I started to mention that I'd like to try her pancakes that Alex raved about, but kept my mouth shut thinking that might be rude.

"I've been thinking," I said to A-Rad after Momma-son removed the dish plates and disappeared back up the steps. "Why do we have to shoot Yang?"

A-Rad's eyes widened with surprise.

"Don't tell me you're having second thoughts? What are we even doing in North Korea then?" His voice was laden with disbelief.

"That's not what I mean. What if we made it look like an accident?"

A thoughtful expression crossed his face as he stared up at the ceiling.

"We can force him off the road," he finally said. "Is that what you mean?"

"Yes."

"But he'll be wearing a helmet."

"Then we'll force him off a cliff."

"I don't know if North Korea has any cliffs."

"Okay. Okay. I'm just spit balling here. We can crash him into a tree or blow out one of his tires. As long as he's dead, that's all that matters. If they think it's an accident, then they won't be looking for us."

"What about the sister? We have to kill her too."

"People have horseback riding accidents all the time. She could fall off and break her neck. Or we can force her off and I'll break her neck. We'll make it look like she had an accident."

A-Rad paused, deep in thought again.

"I don't know. Two accidents on the same morning? Won't they be suspicious?"

"Of course they will. But if we do it right, they'll never know for sure."

"I like the idea of getting out of here without anyone looking for us. We already have enough heat on us to cook a steak."

"Part of me wants the world to know we did it," I said. "The more rational part of me wants to live to fight another day. In this instance, live to kill another leader. If we can get out of this one without anyone knowing we're behind it, then that's better."

"I agree."

A-Rad fired up the computer and pulled up the mission plan that Colonel devised. It had maps and the route Yang normally took on his rides.

We studied the maps and satellite images, looking for the perfect spot to carry out our plan. We came upon a curve in the road that looked promising.

"We'll force him off the road here. He won't stand a chance," I said, pointing at the map.

"Alright, now let's figure out what to do with the sister," A-Rad said, scrolling through the images of the palace grounds.

"I like your idea to make it an accident, but I'm not sure how we do it," he said, after studying it for several minutes. "I don't think we can get the motorcycles onto the property. We'll have to chase her by foot. She could easily ride away from us."

"We have to figure out how to surprise her."

We studied the satellite images of the palace grounds for at least ten more minutes.

"We'll have to play it by ear," I finally said. "There are plenty of places to scale the wall. We'll find the best one when we get there."

"We could go there tomorrow and do some reconnaissance."

I shook my head. "Normally, you're right. But I don't think that's a good idea in this instance. We have to avoid being seen. Two expensive motorcycles on the roads around the palace will draw unwanted attention."

"We can do it on Friday. We'll get there early. We need to see the curve anyway. That'll give us time to check things out and get into position."

A-Rad had a hint of excitement in his voice.

I nodded, feeling optimistic for the first time since we arrived in North Korea.

7

Friday

The sun was still hours away from rising when A-Rad and I left Momma-son's diner on our high-speed motorcycles. We had spent the last two days meticulously planning and rehearsing our ambush of the leader of North Korea and going over every possible scenario.

Momma-son had been a gracious host, providing us with a safe haven and all we could eat. She even got up early and made us pancakes that morning. I could see why Alex raved about them and especially why he loved Momma-son and was so protective of her.

We said our goodbyes. I felt a range of emotions.

"Good luck," she said.

She may not have fully understood the gravity of our mission and certainly didn't know any details, but she clearly grasped the importance of it.

As we sped off, I couldn't help but wonder if we'd ever see her again.

The moon cast long shadows across the empty roads as we sped through the North Korean countryside. A-Rad led the way, his focus unwavering. He had memorized the route and didn't make a single wrong turn.

My mind raced with thoughts, with as much speed as the bikes we were on. I tried to push them aside and concentrate on the task at hand. The upcoming confrontation kept playing in my head like a B movie in a theater.

According to the mission plan, Yang's usual route took him through a series of winding roads and sharp turns, making any number of places perfect for our ambush. When we arrived at the beginning of the route, we did a dry run and followed it, paying close attention, committing every bend and bump along the way to memory.

When we reached the crucial curve where we intended to strike, we were even more convinced our plan would work. This was where we would force Yang off his bike and make it look like an accident. The spot was ideal. Isolated and dangerous, even if someone wasn't trying to kill you there.

The plan was solid—until it wasn't.

When we drove to the palace grounds, that's when things became complicated.

The sprawling palace grounds covered over five hundred acres and was surrounded by a ten-foot wall, resembling a medieval fortress. There were heavily guarded gates at both the front and back entrances.

The rest of the wall was not secure at all. No cameras, no motion detectors. Scaling it would be easy.

But then what? We'd be on foot.

"How do we chase a horse?" I asked. "I can't run that fast." The absurdity of the last statement made me chuckle despite the seriousness of our mission.

"We have to figure out how to get a motorcycle inside the gate," A-Rad replied, scratching his head as if the solution might be hiding in his hair.

"Can we lift it over the wall?" I suggested, imagining us as some sort of characters in an action movie.

"I'm guessing it weighs five hundred pounds," he said, while shaking his head with a noticeable frown of disappointment.

"What about a ramp? Could we construct something?"

I was only half-serious.

"That's a good idea. We could build something, or buy something that would work, but not today. We'd have to come back."

His voice tinged with frustration.

"Well, it's not like it has to be done today," I said. "He rides every Friday. I'd rather wait and plan than rush something and make a mistake."

"I say we go back to Momma-son's and regroup," A-Rad suggested. "Either that, or we scale the wall and take our chances. We'll take the first shot we get. It won't look like an accident, but like you said, it doesn't really matter in the end."

"I have an idea," I said, my words hanging in the air like the moment before a curtain opens at a Broadway play. They came out before I had even given it any thought.

"Let's hear it," A-Rad replied, leaning in as if I were about to say something brilliant.

Before I had the chance to tell him, the rumble of an engine caught our attention. Yang appeared at the front gate. The guards saluted him, and he gave them a wave before speeding off right past us. Alone and oblivious to the threat hiding in the woods.

Adrenaline spiked through me.

"What do we do?" A-Rad asked. "It's either now or we come back next Friday."

Convinced my plan to kill the sister and make it look like an accident would work, I replied excitedly, "Let's do it now."

A-Rad didn't hesitate. He pulled out of our hiding spot, and we began to follow Yang, keeping a safe distance behind so he wouldn't see us.

Yang rode like a maniac, making it difficult to keep pace with him. We had to take risks in order to close the gap before he got to the curve where we intended to launch our plan. A-Rad revved his engine and raced ahead, taking some risks, but catching him almost immediately.

He didn't see A-Rad until it was too late. When he saw A-Rad, he was momentarily confused and slowed down, giving me a chance to catch up to them.

Once he saw me, he sensed the danger and sped up again. A-Rad reacted immediately and passed him, cutting him off. Startled, Yang swerved to avoid a collision, but I was coming up next to him on the other side and he had veered away to avoid hitting me.

"I'm going in!" I shouted, accelerating and aiming for his back tire. I clipped it. The impact caused Yang's bike to skid, but he somehow managed to regain control. It took all my skill to stay upright on my own bike.

"He's good," A-Rad muttered in my headset, as Yang rushed ahead trying to escape. A-Rad's tires squealed as he hit the throttle and went after him.

"I got you!" I heard A-Rad shout the threat through the communicator. "You aren't getting away this time."

"I'm right behind you," I confirmed.

I pushed my bike harder, beyond what I thought were my limits. But I was getting closer to Yang. He was obviously an experienced rider and navigated the twists and turns of the road with perfection. I had to slow down on the curves.

A-Rad had thrown caution to the wind. I prayed he'd stay upright.

"Get ready!" A-Rad called out, "He's a dead man."

I tensed. All I could do was watch it unfold.

Yang sensed the threat and that he wasn't going to be able to run away from us. He began to serpentine back and forth, but A-Rad was relentless, staying right on his tail.

It allowed me to catch up and enter the fray. I moved in from the side, just as Yang swayed in my direction. Our bikes nearly touched. He yanked his away at the last second.

His bike wobbled, and for a moment, I thought we had him.

But then, everything went wrong.

Without warning, Yang slowed down and swerved sharply right into A-Rad's path, clipping A-Rad's bike and sending him sliding sideways across the road. I watched in horror as A-Rad's out-of-control bike teetered on the edge.

"Hang on!" I shouted, but A-Rad's bike slid off the road, and he tumbled out of view.

"No!" I screamed, but I couldn't stop now. Yang was getting away and I had to finish the job or we might not get another chance.

I gunned my engine, closing the distance between us. This time I was the one with no concern for my safety. If A-Rad was dead or dying, then I didn't care one way or the other about myself.

My heart ached though. Was A-Rad okay?

I had to push it out of my mind. This was my chance to get Yang and I had to take it.

Yang pushed his bike to its limits, and I followed, weaving through the narrow, winding roads. The roar of the engines echoed through the country-side, a dangerous symphony that promised a deadly outcome for one of us.

I gritted my teeth. "You are not getting away this time," I growled.

We continued our high-speed chase for several miles. Sometimes reaching speeds of a hundred and fifty miles per hour on the straightaways.

Whatever was off the road was a blur as we sped by. Yang's skill on the bike was impressive, but I matched it. Every time he tried to shake me off, I closed the gap, relentless in my pursuit.

"Should we just shoot him and call it a day?" A-Rad's familiar voice resounded in my head, sending my heart leaping inside my chest.

He was back on his bike, and I could see him rapidly approaching in my rear-view mirror.

"Let's give it one more shot." I desperately wanted to make it look like an accident rather than an assassination.

"We're approaching another curve," A-Rad said. "He'll have to slow down."

I knew exactly which curve he was talking about. We had considered it but wasn't sure if Yang would make it this far away from the palace. This was our next best chance. We'd be coming into some towns soon.

We hadn't ridden it earlier that morning, but I remembered seeing it on satellite photos and how dangerous it was. Yang would have to slow down.

When he slowed down as expected, I accelerated, and bridged the gap in seconds, positioning myself alongside him. He glanced at me, but I couldn't see his eyes because of the darkened visor of his helmet.

"This is it," I thought, preparing to make my move.

I pulled up beside him after we made it through the curve. A-Rad suddenly appeared on the other side of Yang.

How did he get there so fast?

Yang took his right hand off the handlebars and reached into the front of his pants and pulled out a gun, aiming it at A-Rad.

Panicked, I shouted a warning. "He's got a gun!"

Yang fired several shots, but they all missed. It was difficult to aim and fire at such high speeds on those bumpy roads.

But I wasn't going to give him another chance. With determination, I leaned in and swerved hard, aiming to force Yang off the road. I kept pushing him closer and closer to the shoulder as he struggled to counter my attack but didn't dare swerve into me. He'd kill both of us.

When he ran out of road, his bike hit a patch of loose gravel on the shoulder, and he lost control. The motorcycle veered sharply sending the bike into a skid.

For a moment, time seemed to slow.

Yang braked hard and tried to turn into the slide. It didn't work and he went airborne. Flying through the air like a human cannonball at a circus. His arms and legs flailed. He landed hard with a sickening thud and bounced several times before finally coming to a stop in the middle of the road.

I winced at the gruesome sight.

The sound of Yang's motorcycle screeching across the ground echoed in my ears, followed by an eerie silence.

I skidded to a stop, my heart pounding from the adrenaline. I took off my helmet and parked my bike then cautiously approached the motionless body. Yang's arms and legs were a mangled mess. Twisted into unnatural angles from multiple fractures.

If he survived, it'd take a team of skilled doctors to put him back together again. We'd never give them the chance.

A-Rad came up from behind me and checked for a pulse.

"He's dead," A-Rad confirmed, his voice flat.

I nodded, feeling a mix of relief and unease. We had accomplished our mission, but it hadn't gone as smoothly as planned. The chase had been chaotic and we nearly died several times. My heart still pounded in my ears.

I looked around to make sure no one saw us.

"Let's hide his body in those trees over there," I said, pointing towards a cluster of trees on the side of the road.

"I say we leave it here. This is perfect. It looks like an accident."

Ignoring him, I proceeded to take off my jacket, then my shirt.

"What are you doing?" A-Rad asked in disbelief.

I took off my shoes, then my pants, which left me standing on the road in my underwear.

"I don't think now's the time to fool around. Not that I'm opposed to it," he said with a hint of humor behind the words.

"Help me get Yang's clothes off."

I bent down and removed Yang's helmet and inspected it. It had a large dent on the side but was otherwise intact.

Yang was wearing a leather jacket and leather pants, and thick black combat boots.

"Take off his shoes, A-Rad," I said. "Hurry up before someone comes."

"What are you up to?" he asked.

"I'll explain in a minute."

Once I had Yang's clothes off, I began putting them on me. Putting on the shoes last after A-Rad got them off. They didn't fit perfectly, but they'd have to do.

"Check Yang's bike and make sure it's functioning properly," I said.

A-Rad walked over and picked it up and looked it over before announcing, "It's good." I was relieved. If it wasn't, my plan wouldn't work."

A-Rad walked the bike over to where I was standing.

"Let's put Yang and my bike behind those trees over there."

"I think I understand your plan now."

A-Rad picked Yang off the ground and easily carried him over to the nearby cluster of trees and laid him down unceremoniously behind the tree. I rolled my bike over there and laid it down on the ground next to him.

"Here's the plan," I said.

"I know what you're thinking. Are you sure it's a good idea?"

"I'll ride Yang's motorcycle back to the front gate. The guards will think I'm him and they'll let me through."

He nodded approvingly.

"I'll chase down the sister and take her out. I'll make it look like an accident."

"Assuming you can get past the guards. Maybe I should go instead. I could handle any trouble that comes up with the guards."

I laughed. "You're too big to pass for Yang. I am a similar height and weight. You stand at six feet tall and weigh two hundred fifty pounds."

His brow furrowed. "I'll have you know that I only weigh two hundred and fifteen pounds," he said roughly. "I've lost some weight since we got off the yacht."

During our three months at sea, we worked out daily, but it wasn't the same as real fitness training. We pushed ourselves, but the rest of the day was spent lounging around. As a result, we both gained a few pounds.

"Anyway, point taken," he said. "I wouldn't fit in his clothes anyway, and they'd know it wasn't him. You, on the other hand, might be able to pull it off."

"After I kill the sister, we'll come back here. We'll move Yang back on the road and stage it to look like an accident. Then ride off into the sunset."

"It's ten o'clock in the morning," A-Rad joked.

"You know what I mean."

He agreed with the plan, we mounted our bikes and sped away from the scene. We had successfully eliminated Yang, but our mission wasn't over yet.

We still had a target. I had to intercept his sister and make her death look like an accident as well.

As we rode towards the palace grounds, a satisfaction came over me. At the very least, we'd shaken the fabric of the world order.

That didn't change my resolve to kill the sister. We had come too far to fail now. Jamie had warned us that if we couldn't kill the sister, then we shouldn't kill Yang. The sister was even worse than Yang.

I approached the guard gate. A-Rad lagged behind and hid a distance away.

I touched the gun in my waistband for reassurance.

I had no choice. I had to succeed.

8

I approached the guard gate to the palace with trepidation. The less than intimidating structure was flanked by average sized walls and two armed sentries. Despite my helmet visor hiding my face, I still felt exposed and vulnerable. Not because I couldn't easily take out the two guards, but because if I had to, my plan would be shot to pieces before I even got a chance to execute it.

The guards stationed on either side of the entryway were in a state of high alert. As I drew closer and they saw who it was, they scurried like scared ants to open the gate, their hurried movements betraying a mixture of fear and blind obedience.

Such is the power wielded by a ruthless dictator over his loyal subjects who he could have killed or imprisoned simply at his spoken word. I had counted on that when I devised the plan.

The gate swung open with a slow, heavy groan, revealing the massive residence on the palace grounds beyond.

So far, so good.

It seemed I'd be able to enter without any issue.

A wave of relief washed over me, but it was tempered by the awareness of the dangers still ahead. With a quick rev of the engine, I rode through the gate, glancing back to make sure someone wasn't about to shoot me in the back. All I saw was the gate closing behind me with an ominous finality.

I touched the gun tucked in my waistband for a second time. My Plan B. If I had to use it, I would, but ideally, the plan was to infiltrate the palace undetected and eliminate Yang's sister without having to fire a shot. Then drive out through the same gate. If I could somehow make the sister's death look like an accident, our mission would be successful beyond my wildest imagination.

Even Jamie would be impressed.

My thoughts turned to A-Rad waiting outside the gate. He watched me from a distance disappear inside the grounds, close enough to help me with the guards if I ran into trouble. Now he'd just have to wait. Knowing him, he'd be a nervous wreck until he saw me again and we were safely away from danger.

The palace grounds sprawled before me, a maze of grandeur and luxury. Buildings shrouded in opulence and excess. The sun was further in the sky now and cast long shadows across the meticulously manicured lawns and gardens.

Time was of the essence. Hampered by the fact that I had no idea where the sister was. She could be anywhere. In the stables. On the trails. Still in bed, for all I knew.

With my eyes scanning in every direction, I navigated through the grounds, looking for any sign of the sister. Each passing second felt like I was taking too long.

She wasn't near the stables, and I let out a sigh of relief. For obvious reasons, I couldn't kill the sister in front of other people. Well, I could, but not and make it look like an accident. That's what I'd do if it came down to it, but I preferred to do it away from the buildings, out on the trails.

A couple of hired hands snapped to attention when I zoomed past them, their startled expressions reminding me that this was probably out of the ordinary. Yang should be riding his bike on the roads. I had no idea if he ever rode his bike out that way.

What if I didn't find her? That'd be my worst nightmare.

Panic surged within me as I realized how vast the palace grounds were—dozens of riding trails spread over hundreds of acres. It looked much bigger than it had on the satellite images.

Indecision struck me. Should I choose one trail and risk her emerging from a different one, or should I continue searching for her in the open?

To my left, a sprawling riding arena caught my eye. The jumps and obstacles were meticulously arranged. According to Jamie's intel, the sister was the only one who rode horses. All of that expense and maintenance was for the benefit of one person.

A rage stoked inside of me as I thought of the plight of the masses, forced to live in poverty while millions of the country's resources were wasted on Yang and his sister's lavish lifestyles. The maintenance alone on that arena could feed an untold number of families for a year.

The state's central distribution system controlled the food supply. The wealthy and the loyal soldiers and subjects received the best and the most. Whatever was left over was rationed to the masses.

Meat was a luxury for everyone but Yang and a chosen few. The only reason we had it at the diner was because Alex periodically came through the tunnel and brought Momma-son everything she needed. He even offered to give her a tidy sum of cash on more than one occasion, but she refused.

"What am I going to do with it?" she had said. "All it will do is draw attention to me."

She had relayed the conversation to us during one of our meals.

She also described the illegal grasshopper markets. They earned their names, not because they sold grasshoppers, but because of how fast they came and went. Smugglers would set up stalls. Folks would come and buy everything they could. If they didn't have money, they'd have to barter something or go without.

Most of what they sold was rice, kimchi, and bean paste. According to Momma-son, two in five North Koreans were undernourished. When she was younger, a famine killed as many as a million North Korean people. Tears welled up in her eyes as she described the horror of it.

I was glad Yang was dead and that I had executed some revenge on behalf of the North Korean people. I couldn't wait to find his sister, so she'd meet the same fate.

Seeing firsthand the extravagant way Yang and his sister lived, only stoked the anger burning inside of me.

I had to find her first.

Since the sister was clearly not at the arena, I searched frantically in the area around the entrances and exits to the trails. Time was slipping away, and with it, my chances of success.

For a good twenty minutes, I rode back and forth along the tree line, keeping myself between the trails and the stables. My heart sank further in my chest with each passing moment, fear of failure waging an inner battle with my optimism.

What if she wasn't on the trails?

What if she was and I didn't see her exit them?

What would I do then?

I'd have to comb through every inch of the palace grounds to find her, taking out anyone who stood in my way. Then figure out how to get out of there without dying. As soon as my cover was blown, things would disintegrate in a hurry.

I could get away with the ruse as long as I kept my distance. Disguising myself as Yang would be impossible at close range to the guards and staff.

What if she wasn't even on the palace grounds?

Colonel said she rode every Friday, but what if this Friday she went to town? Or was on vacation? Yang and his sister had several houses throughout North Korea. Including three beach houses.

As despair began to take hold, movement caught my eye. A figure emerged from one of the trails and galloped away from me. The opposite direction of the stables. It had to be the sister.

I didn't think she saw me.

Without a moment's hesitation, I tore after her, my tires spinning wildly in my haste.

She disappeared onto another trail, but I followed without pause, my mind focused on the chase. The trail weaved through a dense wooded area, the thick foliage lined the rough path barely wide enough for a horse or a motorcycle to pass through.

The air was thick with the scent of pine and earth.

The trail narrowed even further, forcing me to weave through the trees with precision. Branches whipped against my helmet; the sound muffled by the roar of the engine.

I was closing the distance, but not fast enough.

The trail widened again. As I rounded a corner, the sister came into view again. With grace and skill, I watched her guide her horse over a fallen tree that blocked the trail. In a seamless jump, her silhouette framed against the dappled sunlight filtering through the trees.

"Dang it!" I said under my breath, frustration boiling within me as I had to stop when I came to the obstacle.

I revved my engine and let out a shout to get her attention. It worked. She glanced back, her eyes wide with surprise. Clearly, she wasn't expecting to see her brother on the trail.

She turned around and rode back toward me. I dismounted the bike and my hand instinctively moved toward the gun in my waistband. The fallen tree was still between us. As she got closer, her eyes widened again. Panic flickered across her face as she realized I wasn't her brother.

I saw her reach for a radio, then abruptly turn the horse and gallop away.

Without hesitation, I pulled out my gun and took careful aim before firing a shot that struck her in the right shoulder. Not an easy shot from that distance. She fell from her horse and hit the ground with a sickening thud.

I jumped over the log and rushed to her. She hadn't moved since she landed on the ground. Her lifeless eyes stared up at the sky while a pool of blood slowly spread beneath her.

She was dead, but it wasn't my bullet that killed her; it was the fall.

A sickening feeling twisted in my gut as I realized the whole thing would've looked like an accident except for the bullet lodged in her back.

I retrieved her horse, calmed it down, and led it back to where she lay. I positioned her body carefully, making it look like she had been thrown. I then remounted my bike and sped back towards the gate, my heart racing with adrenaline-fueled anticipation.

Did she have time to alert the guards on the radio?

Did anyone hear the shot?

If I saw anything suspicious, I'd turn around and speed away. I could scale the fence on the other side of the grounds and find A-Rad.

The guards opened the gate without question. I gave them a curt wave of the hand. Once outside, I hit the gas and raced to the designated spot where A-Rad was waiting, hidden from view.

I didn't bother to stop. He emerged on the road as I flew by. I took one last look back for any sign of trouble. When I didn't see anything, I turned my focus to the road ahead.

We raced toward the curve where Yang's body was hidden, our bikes tearing through the winding roads with speed and precision. I didn't take any chances on the curves, but also didn't take my time either.

The sooner we got out of North Korea, the better I'd feel.

Even then, my mind kept replaying the confrontation with Yang's sister, wondering if there was anything else I could've done differently. Jamie would chastise me if she could read my thoughts. She said the time for reflection and criticism was after the mission was over.

And yet a nagging feeling tugged at my heart. In a way, I had failed A-Rad. And Jamie for that matter. Things would've been so much easier had it looked like an accident. It made all the risks we took taking down Yang unnecessary. We could've just shot him and been done with it.

But deep down, I knew they'd understand. I did what I had to do when it came to the sister. If she had gotten away, I might not have gotten another chance to kill her.

"Everything go smoothly?" A-Rad asked as we got to our destination and I dismounted Yang's bike.

"Yes and no," I responded, trying to steady my breathing and not let my tone give away any of my emotions.

"She's dead. That's all that matters."

I didn't want A-Rad to dwell on the same thoughts that threatened to consume me.

"Good," he said with cold satisfaction in his voice. "Let's move Yang's body and get out of here."

Together, we worked to stage the crash, placing Yang's body a few feet away from his bike and making it look like he had lost control and crashed. We made sure to cover our tracks, erasing any evidence of our involvement and making it look like a tragic accident.

Satisfied, we mounted our bikes and sped off, leaving the scene behind. Mission accomplished, but it felt like a hollow victory that still bugged me.

When they discovered the bullet in the sister's back, they'd know it wasn't an accident. They'd look into it further. An investigator would see that it wasn't Yang that came through the gate. It was an imposter. Yang's death would be called into question.

But what difference did it make?

Our ultimate goal was to kill Yang and his sister. We had succeeded. I needed to let go of any regret. Nothing I could do about it now.

As we rode away, the sun climbed higher in the sky, warming the cold thoughts that plagued me. This mission may be over, and we could claim victory, but the sobering reality was clear.

They wouldn't all be this easy.

9

South Korea

When we returned to the yacht, we could finally relax. We settled on the top deck, sipping cold drinks as the ocean breeze gently swayed the boat. The sunset painted bright colors across our faces warming my body and bringing a calm to my soul—a sharp contrast to the adrenaline rush from the events earlier that day in North Korea.

The loud buzzer to the phone interrupted the peace and sent my heart skipping as I leapt to my feet. A-Rad was already walking with a purpose toward the main living room.

It had to be Jamie. We sent her an email letting her know we had accomplished our mission. She didn't know the details, which was probably why she was calling.

I was surprised she was calling us so soon. Probably because she was enjoying living vicariously through us. If she couldn't kill Yang and his sister herself, this was the next best thing, and she wanted all the juicy play by play.

A-Rad pushed the button that put the call on speaker. "How did you pull it off?" Jamie asked, her voice filled with excitement.

We exchanged glances to see who was going to respond. I still hadn't told A-Rad what happened with the sister, and he didn't press me for information. I had accepted the fact that I couldn't make the sister's death look like an accident and refused to let that fact rob me of the spoils of our victory.

In our line of work, we didn't get money or accolades. The only spoils were self-satisfaction. If I couldn't find fulfillment in what was a successful mission by any measure, then something was seriously wrong with me.

"It was a stroke of brilliance," Jamie said, with pride behind the words.

"Kaley deserves all the credit," A-Rad said, sending a smile my way.

I smiled back. I still wasn't sure what Jamie meant was brilliant, and was somewhat confused, since I rarely heard her be that effusive towards me.

I humbly shrugged off the compliment, even though Jamie couldn't see my gesture.

"Making Yang's death look like an accident was pure genius," she added.

So far, Jamie hadn't mentioned the sister. Perhaps she didn't know about it.

"The sister is dead as well," A-Rad said, reading my thoughts.

"Oh yes, I heard about that," Jamie said. "What timing!"

"Yes, it was quite fortunate," I replied, trying to push away any lingering feelings of remorse.

Jamie continued on, unaware of my inner turmoil. "I can't believe Yang killed his sister on the same day you killed him."

"What?" I said, stunned by the words.

"Yang didn't kill the sister," A-Rad clarified. "Kaley did."

Jamie paused before responding. "The news reports said Yang killed her. The guards saw him ride his motorcycle onto the palace grounds, hunt her down, and shoot her while she was riding her horse."

"Kaley was the one on the motorcycle," A-Rad said. "She was pretending to be Yang."

Silence fell over the line as Jamie processed this new information.

Within a few seconds, she laughed out loud. "You were the one riding the motorcycle, Kaley?" she asked incredulously.

I nodded, even though Jamie still couldn't see me.

"Yes. After we killed Yang, I put on his clothes and took his motorcycle and went back to the palace. The guards thought it was him and let me in. That's when I shot his sister."

"Like I said, brilliant. Truly remarkable work," Jamie said. "I always knew you were good, but this is next level."

A-Rad grinned proudly while I just felt relieved that our plan had worked and that Jamie was happy with me.

"The best part is that nobody suspects you," Jamie added.

"That's what we were counting on," I said. "We wanted to make both deaths look like accidents. That wasn't possible. I had to shoot the sister."

It had never dawned on me that they might think the brother was the one who killed her. It should've been obvious, now that I was hearing it for the first time.

"This is even better," Jamie said, barely able to contain her excitement. "The whole world thinks Yang killed his sister, then karma struck, he didn't negotiate the curve, crashed his bike and died."

"I wish I'd thought of it," Colonel said, interjecting himself for the first time.

"Hey, buddy," A-Rad greeted him. "You would like to take the credit, wouldn't you?"

"It was essentially my plan. With some improvisation. Good job, soldiers."

"I appreciate it, sir, but Kaley deserves most of the credit. She did all the heavy lifting."

"I'm sure your time will come."

"I suppose sooner rather than later."

"We did it as a team," I said.

"Of course," Jamie said. "Still, a lot of people back here are really happy with what went down. It's only been a few hours, but this opens all kinds of possibilities."

I hadn't really had time to think about all the political ramifications. Those were above my pay grade.

Jamie continued. "I spoke to Brad, and he said that the CIA was moving quickly to try and find a way to fill the leadership void."

"Does Brad know we were behind it?" I asked.

"No. Not at all. And he will never know. But he's sharp. He sees an opening. As we speak, Alex is hacking into the North Korean nuclear weapons facility. He's going to disarm the nukes and fire them off into the Pacific Ocean."

"We're on the Pacific Ocean!" A-Rad said. "Tell him not to shoot them in our direction."

"I'll be sure and tell him," Jamie said while chuckling.

"What do you want us to do?" I asked. "Should we take the yacht back to the Indian Ocean?"

"No," Jamie said, her tone turning serious. "Stay put. We have another mission for you."

Both A-Rad and I immediately snapped back to attention. I had hoped for a few days to enjoy this one before our next mission.

"Where are we going?" A-Rad asked.

"Iran," she stated bluntly.

The name alone carried enough weight to make both of us sit up even straighter. I was surprised. Jamie had assured us that we weren't going to target any Middle Eastern leaders. The reason was because it was futile. Even if we killed one, another would rise to take their place the same day. We simply couldn't eliminate all the threats. The real enemy was the ideology, not any individual person.

"Iran? Going from the fire into the furnace," A-Rad remarked, echoing my thoughts.

"Yes you are," Jamie confirmed. "Do you remember what I taught you in training, Kaley?"

I laughed. "You told me more things than I can remember."

"I told you that I wanted to help you learn how to be comfortable when you're uncomfortable."

"I remember."

"That will be crucial in this mission. You're going to have to keep your wits about you, or you won't make it out alive."

"Tell us the mission," A-Rad said, soberly.

"We've received intelligence that Iran is dangerously close to securing a nuclear weapon," Jamie revealed.

"I thought the INWA was inspecting their facilities," A-Rad said.

The INWA, or International Nuclear Watchdog Agency, was in charge of curtailing nuclear proliferation around the world.

Colonel responded. "As you know, Iran has been pursuing a nuclear weapon for some time now, and Israel has threatened war over it. That's a line in the sand that they cannot cross. They simply can't be allowed to get a weapon that will annihilate Israel, particularly since they would be willing to use it."

The thought sent chills down my spine.

Colonel continued. "I spent a lot of time in the Middle East, and I know it well. Iran has always insisted that their nuclear program was for energy purposes only, not to build a bomb. We didn't think they had the capacity to take nuclear material and turn it into a weapon. At least not until recently."

"What's changed?" I asked.

"The prevailing wisdom among the CIA has been that Iran didn't have the intellectual knowledge to finish building a bomb. And as you said, Iran agreed to inspections in exchange for lifting sanctions. Israel stood down, and inspectors have been monitoring those facilities for several years now."

"I still don't understand what that has to do with us," I said. "Why are we going to Iran?"

"I'm getting to that," Colonel said.

"I certainly hope you aren't expecting us to destroy the entire nuclear facility. I wouldn't even begin to know how to do that."

"Your target is Berthold Kunkel," Jamie interjected. "That's who we want you to kill."

"Who is he?"

"Kunkel is a German nuclear physicist," Colonel explained. "He's one of the foremost in the field. If not the most highly regarded. He's in Iran helping them build a bomb."

"Why would a German help Iran?" I questioned.

"Because he hates Israel," Colonel answered. "He's old school. He's nearly sixty years old and longs for Germany to return to the glory days of Hitler and fascism. As his last hurrah, he wants to be the one who helped Iran blow Israel off the face of the earth."

"Kunkel," I repeated, the name leaving a bitter taste in my mouth.

"Your mission is to infiltrate their nuclear facilities and eliminate him," Colonel stated.

"How are we supposed to do that?" I asked.

"You'll find all the details in your inbox," Colonel said.

"I can hardly wait," I said sarcastically.

"Can you at least give us a general idea?" A-Rad asked.

"We've arranged for you to enter Iran and pose as INWA inspectors," Colonel said.

"You make it sound easy," I said. "They'll shoot us on the spot."

"It should be fairly easy to get you in," Colonel retorted.

"That's what you said about North Korea. I wish you'd quit using that word," I said. "It may be easy on paper, but it's a lot harder when your neck is on the line. Iran and easy should never be used in the same sentence."

"Point well taken," Jamie said. "But I can't stress enough how important this mission is. The most dangerous man in the world right now is Kunkel. Your job is to take him out. If you don't, then Israel will attack Iran, and it might spark World War III. Millions of people could die."

"No pressure," I muttered.

A-Rad leaned forward, fully engaged now. "How do we get into Iran? Are we going in through the CIA's secret route, like we did North Korea?"

"Nope. You're going in directly. On a private plane. Iran will know you're coming."

"Where do we get a plane?" I asked.

"Like I said, it's in the plan."

"Humor us," A-Rad said.

"It'll be on its way to South Korea in the next few days. It'll be waiting for you at a private airport. All your credentials and everything you need will be on that plane. All you have to do is fly it directly to Tehran."

"That's all." I chuckled uneasily.

"Be sure to pack a couple of doses of courage in there," I added as a joke.

"You have plenty of that already," Jamie said. "I'm not even sure I could do what you're doing, even back in my heyday."

"We both know that's not true," I said.

I had never met anyone as fearless as Jamie.

Colonel got us back on track. "Kaley will be the inspector. A-rad, you'll be her bodyguard. That way, you can take a weapon with you."

"How do we get past security?" I asked.

"That shouldn't be a problem," Jamie said. "Inspectors have access that most people don't have. You should be able to fly right in."

"Won't our faces be on a watchlist?" I asked.

"They're scrubbed," she said. "For now."

"Thank you, Alex," I said, certain his computer hacking skills was what pulled that off.

"What if someone recognizes us?" I asked.

"That's a possibility. Kaley, I'd suggest you put your hair up and wear glasses. Change your appearance in any way you can. Don't wear the Norway outfit. That won't work in a Muslim country. You know why. They wouldn't let you in dressed like that."

"Got it. I still don't think it's going to be that easy. It shouldn't be hard for them to do a little checking and see that we aren't with the INWA."

"We've taken care of all the details," Colonel said. "Alex will take care of the plane. He'll make it look like the plane is owned by the INWA. Your pictures will be on their website when they go to verify your identity."

I nodded, absorbing every word. "Okay, assuming we get in with no problem, then what?"

"Then," Jamie said firmly, "you take Kunkel out. Cleanly and quietly. Make it look like an accident if you can. I don't care. Eliminate the threat. The world is counting on you."

The responsibility was suddenly heavy on my shoulders. We'd only had a few hours to decompress from North Korea, and now we were thrown back into another high-stakes operation. North Korea was a piece of cake compared to this.

"Once you're inside," Jamie's voice was stern, "you'll assess the facilities, making sure to note security protocols and routines. See if you can get us some intel. They'll give you full access. If they don't, throw your weight around. Threaten them. They are supposed to cooperate with inspectors. You're going in under the guise of a surprise inspection."

"It's going to be a surprise all right," I quipped.

"The hardest part will be to figure out how to get close to Kunkel. That won't be easy. You'll have to convince him you really are an inspector."

"I don't know anything about nuclear power," I said. "I wouldn't even know how to speak the language."

"You're an actress, playing a part. That's what I meant about being comfortable while feeling uncomfortable."

At the moment, I felt anything but comfortable.

10

Iran

The AJAX plane touched down in Tehran as dawn was breaking. A-Rad landed it smoothly as the sun's first light cast long shadows across the tarmac, giving the place an eerie, desolate feel. As the plane's wheels contacted Iranian soil, the anxiety already coursing through my veins spiked to unsustainable levels.

Was there a more dangerous place on earth than Iran for us? If there was, I couldn't think of one.

We landed on a runway far from the main terminal at Imam Salahuddin International Airport. Under normal circumstances, we might be impressed by the beauty and the grandeur of the modern facility. Hard to be inspired by a facility named after a tyrant.

The Grand Ayatollah Tajweed Ubab Salahuddin was a ruthless dictator who rose to power pledging Death to America and the extinction of the Jewish infidels. When he died unexpectedly of natural causes a few years back, more than ten million people attended his funeral. He was so beloved the airport was renamed in his honor.

His dishonor in my humble opinion.

Landing there was a stark reminder of how many people in that country would tear us limb by limb if they knew who we were. As if we needed to remind ourselves of that fact. Tension filled the cockpit so thick it felt like I was suffocating, like being trapped in a cave surrounded by scorpions or venomous snakes. Except the vipers were real people with real weapons, with a real hatred for us simply because we were different from them.

I hope we aren't making a huge mistake.

A-Rad taxied us toward the designated spot provided by the air traffic controller. Ahead of us, we could see three armed soldiers standing next to two large black SUVs.

"Let's hope Alex didn't make any mistakes," I said.

"He didn't," A-Rad responded, less confidently than I would've liked.

Without Alex and his computer hacking skills, this trip wouldn't have been possible. He made our plane look like it was owned by the INWA. In reality, the plane was owned by AJAX, stolen from a Russian oligarch. Its entire history had been scrubbed and now it was whatever Alex wanted it to be to fit the mission.

He also filed a fake flight plan that showed us coming in from Germany rather than South Korea. I had no idea how he changed the radar to make it look like that's where we came from.

A-Rad brought the plane to a stop, shut off the engines, and we went to the back to gather our belongings. I double checked my passport and documents, praying they'd withstand the scrutiny I knew was coming.

I was Dr. Mina Volk. My business card read Senior Authorized Nuclear Inspector.

I'd seen my impressive resume on the INWA website and couldn't help but laugh out loud. I had a B.S. in Physics from Oxford and a Ph.D. in Nuclear Physics from the University of Stuttgart.

I barely finished high school.

Among the many skills on my resume, I was proficient in nuclear chemistry techniques including liquid scintillation counting, ion chromatography, and gamma-ray spectroscopy.

I couldn't spell any of those words with a gun to my head, but apparently, I had conducted extensive research and experiments on nuclear structure.

My cover was extensive, and Alex had gone to great lengths to create it. I was born in Bavaria, an only child. That way I wouldn't have to remember the names of any siblings. Currently, I resided in Vienna but happened to be in Germany when I was sent to Tehran for a snap inspection.

A-Rad's name was Wolf Bierman. I might start calling him Wolf after this. The night before we left for Tehran, we were in our bed on the yacht. In the throes of passion I cried out, "Yes, Wolf, yes!"

He didn't like it. Said it killed the mood entirely. Further confirming my increasing belief that he was the biggest prude I'd ever met.

At least he was my prude.

I found it cute and liked teasing him about it.

"Are you ready?" he asked me.

"No," I said, honestly.

He nodded with a stiff expression and lowered the steps to the plane. As we exited, the Iranian heat hit us like a wall.

I half expected the armed soldiers to immediately swarm us and force us face down or at least search us and the plane. They didn't do either. They maintained their positions with their weapons pointed down.

A-Rad had a gun in a holster strapped to his chest under the black suit he was wearing. If anything went wrong, our plan was to retreat back to the plane and fly out of there if possible.

If it came to that, the odds of success were slim to none. The Iranian Air Force would shoot us down before we reached the border. The only odds that might be considered worse was trying to fight it out on the ground with men holding automatic weapons.

A door on one of the SUVs opened and a stern-looking man in a dark suit stepped out and walked toward us. He extended a hand in greeting. I eyed him cautiously, while trying not to make it obvious.

I could feel A-Rad tense up.

Easy big fella, Wolf.

The joke inside my head caused me to snicker slightly.

"Dr. Volk, welcome to Tehran," the man said with a heavy accent, but in fluent English. "My name is Jeric Beri."

Can I call you Jerry Berry?

Stop it, Kaley!

The strangest thoughts popped into my head at the most inopportune times.

"I'll be accompanying you during your stay," Jerry added warmly.

"Thank you, Mr. Beri," I said, shaking his hand. Making a mental note not to accidentally call him Jerry or Jerry Berry.

He gave A-Rad a quick once over, then motioned for us to follow him to the vehicle. I didn't bother introducing A-Rad to him. From my experience, high level authorities like Jerry didn't acknowledge the hired help. He didn't introduce the three soldiers to me either.

I'd taken Jamie's advice and pinned my hair to the top of my head and covered it with a blue flowing scarf, following the customs of what would be expected of me in Iran. I was also modestly dressed, suitable for a Muslim country.

A-Rad and I would have to be careful not to show any signs of affection for each other. Not only were public displays of affection frowned on in Muslim countries, but we also had to maintain a degree of professionalism to pull this off.

We'd have separate hotel rooms, and we couldn't discuss anything unless we were certain no one could hear us. Our rooms were likely bugged, maybe even equipped with hidden cameras. Until we were safely out of Iran, we had to be extremely careful.

The glasses perched on the rim of my nose felt uncomfortable and I had to continually reach up and push them back. It wasn't much of a disguise, but between the scarf and glasses, it'd be hard for anyone to associate me with the woman in Norway who killed the prince.

A-Rad didn't try to disguise his features other than dark sunglasses that made him look like a Hollywood action hero. He wore a solid black suit, sleek and polished, that hugged his muscular frame.

The soldiers and A-Rad eyed each other as A-Rad retrieved our two duffel bags from inside the stowage compartment. The black bags were official looking with the INWA logo on the side. I'm not sure how Alex and Jamie were able to go to these lengths on such short notice.

Jerry opened the door for me, and I slid into the back seat, almost losing my glasses on the way. I scooted over to the far window anticipating that Jerry would get in next to me, which he did.

The point of no return.

A-Rad closed the doorway to our plane, then quickly walked over to the SUV, put our bags in the back, then got in the front seat on the passenger side. The three soldiers got in the other SUV and followed us when our driver pulled away.

Once we were moving, we were committed to whatever we faced.

A-Rad glanced back at me and nodded. His expression oozed confidence. Like, "We've got this, Kaley. Just like North Korea."

I smiled at him.

Jerry noticed the exchange, but it wasn't out of the ordinary and he maintained his friendly demeanor. Colonel had assured us that having an armed bodyguard accompany an inspector was normal, especially for a woman traveling alone.

Despite Jerry's attempt to make me feel comfortable, the air was thick with suspicion. I expected probing questions and anticipated them starting right away.

This was one of those anticipated crucial moments in the mission. One wrong move and I could blow our cover. I'd spent hours memorizing my background and resume. Jerry would no doubt commit my answers to memory and go to extensive lengths to verify them.

He'd be looking for any inconsistencies or red flags. Anything out of the ordinary that didn't check out.

Our plane was probably being searched as soon as we were out of sight.

The SUV left the airport and headed west. I glanced out the window, trying to steady my nerves.

Jerry cleared his throat and turned slightly in his seat to face me. "Dr. Volk, I hope you had a pleasant flight."

"Yes, thank you, Mr. Beri. We flew in from Germany, about a five-hour trip."

The flight from South Korea actually took more than nine hours. Under normal circumstances, I'd be glad to be off the plane.

"Everything was quite comfortable," I replied, offering a polite smile. "It certainly beats flying coach. My employer takes good care of us."

Jerry nodded, his eyes sharp and assessing. "Good to hear. Where did you do your studies?" he asked, out of the blue, even though I was anticipating that question.

"In Germany, actually. Well, my undergrad was at Oxford, but I received my Ph.D. from Stuttgart."

"So you're from Germany?"

"No, sir. I studied in Germany but was actually born in Bavaria."

"I'm having a hard time placing your accent."

"Good. I've worked extremely hard to lose it. Are you a nuclear physicist as well?" I asked the question I had to get out of the way, but also to change the subject off me to him.

If he answered yes, then this part of our mission was doomed. There's no way I could talk for two hours with someone who would see through my ruse with the simplest of questions.

We had a contingency plan for that as well. If things went south, A-Rad would take out the driver. I'd kill Jerry. We'd commandeer the vehicle. There'd probably be some kind of chase. We'd have to lose the soldiers in the second SUV and then go dark.

That'd make killing Kunkel harder, but we'd have to find a way. Knowing we'd have to avoid a massive manhunt.

Every mission from here on out was going to be like this. Fraught with danger. Dangling on the precipice of disaster was our new normal.

It'd only be by the grace of God if we survived them.

My anxiety level didn't lessen one bit when Jerry answered, "No. I'm not a physicist, I'm with the Ministry of Intelligence Services."

Good information to have, even if it was unnerving. Jerry was a highly trained killer as well.

I didn't expect them to send a low-level grunt to escort us, but I didn't think they'd send someone at the top of the food chain.

It made sense, though. The organization was mandated to protect Iran's nuclear program.

Colonel had mentioned Jerry in the mission report although he didn't actually know if we'd encounter him. One of Jerry's jobs was to prevent the assassinations of Iranian nuclear scientists, so that's obviously why he personally came to watch us.

My heart fluttered. He was already suspicious, or he would've sent a lower level person to babysit us.

"How did you find the transition from academia to the practical field of nuclear inspections?" Jerry asked, keeping the questions coming with little pause in between.

"I never saw myself in inspections," I said, sticking to the rehearsed story. "But I quickly discovered that I had a knack for it. The practical applications of my work in the field were both fascinating and crucial for global security. Ensuring that nuclear materials are accounted for and used safely is something I take very seriously."

"Of course," Jerry said, his tone still polite but with an undercurrent of curiosity. "We share the same views. Our nuclear program has always been for peaceful means."

Yeah right.

"And what brings you to Tehran specifically?" Jerry asked. "We did not have any scheduled inspections on the calendar."

"This is a surprise inspection. It was a surprise for me as well. I was in Germany when the call came to travel to Iran immediately."

"That's highly irregular. We were given no notice. They didn't even tell me who was coming."

"That's why it's called a surprise," I said, with a smile hoping he'd notice my playful tone which immediately turned more serious. "It's in the joint comprehensive plan of action agreement. I hope that's not going to be a problem and that you intend to fully cooperate with my efforts."

"What are your efforts? And what is your mandate? Which aspects of our facilities do you plan to inspect? I should at least be informed of that."

His tone turned more serious but not combative. Not yet.

I reached into my briefcase and pulled out an official looking document on INWA letterhead. It specified the purpose of my visit. I didn't understand most of what was on there.

I took a deep breath, preparing for this part of the conversation which I had rehearsed more than a dozen times.

"I'll give you a brief overview," I said. "My focus will be on verifying the integrity of your centrifuge arrays and ensuring that all isotopic measurements align with declared activities. It's a routine procedure, but vital for maintaining trust and transparency."

That's the extent of my knowledge. The delivery went smoother than I had practiced it. I could envision A-Rad smiling under his breath while listening to it.

If our lives didn't depend on me getting it right, it might've been amusing.

"Understandable," Jerry replied, though I sensed a hint of skepticism. "Is this your first trip to Iranian facilities? Are you aware of the protocols and the parameters of the inspections?"

"Yes," I said, nodding. "I have reviewed numerous reports and findings from my colleagues, so I'm quite familiar with the protocols and standards expected here."

Jerry leaned back slightly, his eyes staring off into the distance. "Well, we strive to maintain the highest standards, Dr. Volk. I'm sure you'll find everything in order."

"I have no doubt," I said.

The conversation fell into a brief lull, and I took the opportunity to steal a glance at the cityscape. The tension in the car was as thick as a dense fog, but I felt a small surge of confidence. So far, I had held my own without a single misstep. At least, none that I was aware of.

"Tell me, Dr. Volk," Jerry said, breaking the uncomfortable but welcomed silence. "Are you married?"

I paused, considering my response. "I'm not," I said. "But I'm glad you mentioned my love life. I'm looking forward to seeing Dr. Kunkel again."

And there it was. I'd just dropped a nuclear bomb into our conversation.

What in the world was I thinking?

11

Mentioning Kunkel's name out of the blue was a calculated gamble.

"I'm not familiar with that name," Jerry said, his voice smooth and controlled.

His words were a lie, easily detectable by my trained instincts. The subtle movements of his body and the slight twitch of his lips betrayed his true knowledge. A smugness seemed to radiate from him, pleased that he was able to deceive me. But I could see through his facade.

"Oh." I feigned surprise. "I thought he was helping you with your nuclear program."

"Why would you say that?" Jerry's gaze suddenly became fixed on my eyes, clearly searching for any signs of deception. Not only was I trained to spot liars, I was trained to lie while hiding my own deception.

His entire demeanor had changed as soon as I mentioned Dr. Kunkel.

"I know Dr. Kunkel," I said, meeting his gaze. "He graduated from the University of Stuttgart, as did I."

That's the reason we chose that university for my resume.

"I'm looking forward to seeing him again," I added. "Can you arrange a meeting?"

"I'm sorry, but we don't have a Dr. Kunkel working with our program." Jerry's denial only fueled my determination.

I leaned in closer and whispered, "Oh, I'm certain you do. We had a bit of a drunken moment together in Stuttgart. Not that long ago. At a bar in Stuttgart. Right before he came to Iran. He let it slip."

I put my hand over my mouth playing up the charade for added effect. "Oh my! Was he not supposed to tell me?"

This time, Jerry looked straight ahead. Avoiding eye contact. I couldn't help but feel satisfied that I had thrown him off his game.

"I'd just taken a job at the INWA," I continued. "Bertie, I mean, Dr. Kunkel, said to look him up if I ever came to Iran to do an inspection." I added that detail hoping it would add credibility to my story.

Jerry's mask of composure continued to slip as he processed my words. "What was the nature of your relationship with this ... Dr. Kunkel?"

I playfully slapped Jerry on the arm while letting a seductive smile spread across my face. He stiffened further when I touched him.

"A girl never kisses and tells," I purred.

A-Rad's jaw stiffened in the front seat. I'm sure he didn't like this conversation even though it was pure fiction.

"But I'm certain that Dr. Kunkel will want to see me as much as I want to see him. I was simply delighted when they told me I was coming to Iran. I understand that you want to maintain secrecy, but can you arrange for him to call me at my hotel?"

"I don't think that's possible since I don't know a Dr. Kunkel."

As the SUV continued its journey, Jerry clammed up. Had I made a mistake by mentioning Kunkel? It was interesting but not surprising that the standard line was denial. The fact that Jerry seemed flustered by the line of questioning told me everything I needed to know which was why I brought it up.

I'd taken a risk for sure by mentioning Kunkel in that way. At the same time, we needed intel. We were going into this mission blind, with no idea where Kunkel could be located within Iran's numerous nuclear facilities.

In a short period of time, Jerry had given me tons of information. He verified that Kunkel was indeed working in Iran. He'd also confirmed that Kunkel wouldn't be at the facility he was taking us to.

I decided to remain quiet and not push the issue further. It'd only raise suspicion. We were now deep into the mission, and every word, every action, had to be carefully calculated. There was no room for error.

Jerry's brows were knitted together in confusion. He obviously didn't know what to do with me or that information.

And neither did I. It wasn't part of the script. I had come up with it on the spur of the moment. It didn't get us any closer to Kunkel, but it confirmed what I had to know. Kunkel was in Iran. If he wasn't, then I wanted to know now. No reason to risk our lives chasing a ghost. While I trusted Jamie's intel, it could be wrong.

Now I knew it was accurate, although it created a different problem. If Iran denied that Dr. Kunkel was involved in their program, we'd have no way to insist on a meeting. But if I hinted at a romantic connection between us, then it might get back to Kunkel and pique his curiosity.

Of course, instead of being curious, Kunkel might be immediately suspicious. If he was certain he'd never met me, then Jerry would know that I wasn't who I said I was. Then we'd be in immediate and grave danger.

We drove the rest of the way in relative silence. After two hours and forty-five minutes, we finally arrived at the nuclear facility.

It's showtime.

* * *

Nuclear Facility
Arka, Iran

We pulled up to a massive gate, guarded by armed soldiers. It felt like we were entering a military base. The facility was surrounded by a chain link fence that had to be twenty feet high with barbed wire at the top.

Once A-Rad and I were inside, the only way out would be to shoot our way out.

The SUV came to a halt, and Jerry motioned for the driver to lower the window. He exchanged a few words with the guard, who signaled for the gate to open.

As we passed through, I couldn't help but feel a growing sense of unease. This was it. We were about to step into the heart of Iran's nuclear facilities. Every move, every word would be scrutinized.

I was about to meet people who had expertise in nuclear energy. Who would immediately be able to see through my ruse if I made one misstep. The vehicle came to a stop in front of the reactor itself.

We exited the vehicle and were greeted by a man in a lab coat, his head covered with a white turban, flanked by several associates and a couple of armed guards.

"Dr. Volk, let me introduce you to Dr. Mahmoud," Jerry said.

"Welcome, inspector," he said to me, his eyes narrowing as he studied us. "We were told to expect you."

I held out my hand. He didn't shake it but bowed his head instead.

"It's my pleasure to meet you, Dr. Mahmoud," I said, trying to keep my voice steady. "I look forward to working with you."

"Of course," he replied, a hint of skepticism in his voice. "Please, follow me."

It took nearly half an hour to clear the security protocols. Each second seemed like an hour. This would be where our credentials would be more closely scrutinized. If things fell apart, it'd be now.

"Don't you have any equipment with you?" Dr. Mahmoud asked, with suspicion.

My heart skipped and did a lap around my chest. I pushed the negative thoughts aside, since I had anticipated that question and had prepared an answer.

"No. We have a specific mandate. I'm only here to inspect entrance logs and security camera footage. We'll only be here for a few hours."

The entrance logs would confirm that Kunkel didn't work out of that facility. I was convinced he wasn't there, based on what Jerry had said. Even the entrance logs wouldn't tell me anything. Kunkel could enter under an assumed name.

The security cameras, on the other hand, would tell me if he entered the facility. Assuming they hadn't been tampered with.

I didn't expect to see him on any of the footage. If Jerry was going to deny knowing Kunkel, they wouldn't be stupid enough to let him show his face on a camera monitored by the INWA.

Jamie had wanted me to do a deeper inspection of the facility, but I nixed that idea. She wanted pictures inside the nuclear reactor. It would've required carrying in equipment that we didn't know how to operate.

That wasn't happening.

We'd have to put on protective suits to enter the heart of the facility. She wanted me to stand on the bridge that extended across the spent fuel pond. Then record it with a camera to verify the presence of spent fuel. They'd try to match it with the amount disclosed.

That seemed too risky. It wouldn't be hard for the workers to realize my inexperience if we entered restricted areas or handled specialized equipment. They might even know I was a fraud as soon as they saw me try to put on one of their protective suits.

"Let's stick to the mission. Killing Kunkel," I had insisted. "That'll be hard enough as it is."

I bit my lip to keep relief from washing over my face when we were waved through security. Inside, the building was a maze of corridors and more security entry points. Each one manned by vigilant guards.

Jerry suddenly disappeared which added to my angst. I could see him trying to verify our story. Or worse, he could already know we were fakes and was preparing to arrest us.

Nothing I could do about it now.

Finally, we arrived at a conference room where a few men in lab coats were waiting.

"Dr. Volk, this is Dr. Reza Pahlavi and Dr. Amir Hosseini," Dr. Mahmoud said. "They will be assisting you during your inspection."

I studied their faces. Neither were Kunkel, even though I didn't think they'd be.

"Pleasure to meet you," I said, shaking their hands.

Dr. Pahlavi, an older man with graying hair, smiled warmly. "Welcome, Dr. Volk. We've been informed of your visit and are ready to provide any assistance you require."

Dr. Hosseini, younger and more intense, nodded in agreement. "Yes, we have prepared everything for your inspection. Please let us know how we can facilitate your work."

"Thank you," I said, trying to appear as confident and professional as possible. "All I need are the entrance logs to this facility and all other facilities. Along with access to security camera footage."

"Of course," Dr. Pahlavi said. "Please have a seat and make yourself comfortable. There are drinks in the refrigerator."

I glanced at A-Rad, who gave a subtle nod. We were still in the game.

The secure room was small but well-equipped, with a large table covered in documents and a computer terminal. Dr. Pahlavi and Dr. Hosseini excused themselves. I downed two bottles of water to sate my parched throat and mouth.

A few minutes later, they returned with the visitor logs. I began going through the documents, knowing full well that we were under surveillance.

I didn't see Kunkel's name on any of the entrance logs for any of the facilities.

"Everything seems to be in order," I said aloud for the benefit of those watching us.

A-Rad didn't respond, but I could see the tension in his posture. He was on high alert, ready for anything.

A couple of hours later, they led us into a room that had all the security footage. I went through three randomly chosen days and didn't see Kunkel on any of them. The footage could be easily doctored, but I doubted Iran would go to that trouble.

Kunkel wasn't there and hadn't been. That meant he was working at one the inspectors didn't know about. More confirmation that Iran had a secret facility. That's where they'd be building the nukes.

Find Kunkel and we'd find where Iran was building the bomb.

That was the burning question. How do I find Kunkel?

* * *

Tehran

Later that night

When we finished at the nuclear facility, Jerry drove us back to Tehran and we checked into our hotel. After dinner in the lobby, I said to A-Rad, "Let's go for a walk."

Outside of the hotel we'd be away from watchful eyes and prying ears.

Jerry had assigned someone to guard us, or so he claimed. In reality, the guard was there to monitor our every move. He kept his distance during dinner, but I still didn't feel comfortable talking freely.

As we exited the hotel and onto a street, the guard followed. We didn't try to lose him but kept him far enough away that he was out of earshot.

"Kunkel isn't at any of the facilities that we checked," I said.

"I didn't think he would be," A-Rad said.

He was as tense as a puma on a hunt. Constantly looking in each direction. Watching for any threat.

"Me either," I said. "He is in Iran though."

"How do you know?"

"Jerry confirmed it."

"Who's Jerry?"

"Oh right. Jeric Beri. The one in the backseat with me. I call him Jerry."

"Speaking of that, what were you thinking? Implying that you had an affair with Kunkel."

"It's the only thing I could think of. When Jerry lied and said that Kunkel wasn't part of their program and that he'd never heard of him, I knew we were wasting our time going to the nuclear plant. Kunkel is working in a secret facility."

"Or maybe he really isn't working with them."

I shook my head. "Jamie confirmed he was, and Jerry did too when I mentioned Kunkel's name. I could tell he was lying when he said he didn't know him."

"A girl doesn't kiss and tell?" A-Rad said, sarcastically for emphasis. I knew as soon as I said it, that he'd be bothered.

"There's a method to my madness," I said. "Rather than finding Kunkel, I'm hoping he finds us."

"And you think that's the way to go about it?"

"He's a man. He'll be curious."

"Don't you think if he had an affair with you that he'd remember it? He'll know you're lying and then our cover is blown?"

"It's possible. But I said we were a little drunk. What man hasn't had a little fling and doesn't remember all the details?"

"I haven't."

"I'm not talking about you. You're weird. I'm talking about the average man. You're anything but average. A lot of men couldn't tell you how many women they've slept with, much less their names or the circumstances behind it."

"One. Kaley. On a yacht. Actually, on the island first. Then the yacht."

I waved my hand dismissively. "Like I said. You're different. Kunkel is a lifelong bachelor. I'm sure he's had his fair share of one-night stands, especially after a few drinks."

"You don't even know if he drinks."

"He's from Germany. Drinking beer is a national pastime there."

"I'm not convinced."

"I'm not either. It's a shot in the dark. But what else do we have to go on? Do you have a better idea? Jerry expects us to return to the nuclear facility tomorrow, then leave the next day. I don't think we should go back to the facility. It's a waste of time. We aren't going to find anything there and it's not worth the risk. Someone is going to ask a question I can't answer and figure out that I'm not a nuclear physicist."

"I agree."

"We can buy ourselves one more day by telling Jerry that we're going to review our paperwork at the hotel tomorrow."

"Then what?"

"Our next move is to sneak out of the hotel and hunt down Kunkel."

"Then our cover is blown, and we'll be on the run. They'll seize our plane. We'll have to find another way out of Iran."

"We're not leaving Iran until Kunkel is dead."

"And how are we going to find him?" A-Rad asked. "I wouldn't even know where to start looking and neither do you."

"That's the mission."

"Once our cover is blown, Kunkel will know that we're looking for him. He'll have more guards around him than a queen bee in a hive."

"I didn't say it's going to be easy."

"I say we leave tonight then."

"Let's give it one more day. I'm certain Jerry will call Kunkel. Maybe you're right and Kunkel will know I'm lying. Or maybe we'll get lucky and Kunkel will call me at the hotel. That's why I want to hang around there one more day, just in case."

"It's worth a shot."

"We maintain our cover for as long as we can. In the meantime, I'll try and come up with another way to smoke him out."

"We could tell Jerry we want to visit a different facility. On the way, we kill Jerry and the driver and dump their bodies in the desert. Then we'll have a vehicle. We'll also have Jerry's phone. You said Kunkel will call Jerry. That means his phone number will be in that phone."

"That's a good idea. We'll make that plan b."

"You mean make it plan c."

"What's plan a?"

"Don't die."

"I'm on board with that," I said with a nervous laugh.

"I'll be sleeping with one eye open tonight," A-Rad said, his voice filled with deep concern.

"I wish I could sleep with you," I said, playfully. "You wouldn't get much sleep though. I'd have so much fun ravishing you that you wouldn't be able to close either eye."

His cheeks turned red. "Is that all you think about?"

"Jamie and Alex said their best sex was when they were on a mission. The danger increased the intensity. I want some Iranian danger sex."

"You're the one who's weird."

I laughed. "I can't help it that you're so sexy, Wolf."

"Stop calling me that!" he said, though the smile on his face betrayed his amusement.

We walked back to the hotel in silence and said a professional goodbye before going into our separate rooms. As much as I wanted to kiss him goodnight and go back to his room and do what I said I'd do to him, it wasn't possible. The guard was a few steps from us. He'd be stationed outside of our rooms all night.

As I entered my room, the phone was ringing. I rushed to answer it.

"Hello," I said.

"Dr. Volk," the voice on the other end said.

"This is Dr. Volk."

"I'm Berthold. Berthold Kunkel."

My hand was trembling so hard, I almost dropped the phone.

12

The next day

The restaurant in the Majesque Palace Hotel in Tehran was elegant, bathed in soft lighting with plush furnishings that exuded a sense of refined luxury. I sat at a corner table with my back against the wall, a glass of water in hand, waiting for Dr. Kunkel's arrival.

He had called my room the night before, inquisitive, borderline suspicious. He had looked up my picture on the INWA website and said I looked familiar. I played it up and convinced him we had met in Stuttgart Germany and that I was eager to see him again.

We agreed to meet at eight o'clock. It could very well be a trap, and my senses were heightened, fueled by the anxiety raging inside.

A-Rad was nearby, strategically positioned to act if I got into trouble. Jerry's guard, who had been tied to us for the last two days, was in close proximity as well, although across the room from A-Rad.

Best to keep those two separated. They'd been eyeing each other warily since the moment we stepped off the plane.

A critical moment in our mission was upon us, a do-or-die moment, and I needed everything to go perfectly. If Kunkel showed, he was essentially a dead man. As soon as he was in our sights, he wouldn't get out of them without us killing him.

The plan was for me to lure him back to my hotel room and kill him there. Then we'd sneak out of the hotel in the middle of the night and figure out how to get across the border of Iran into Turkey. From there, we'd have to find a way back to South Korea.

We'd worry about the details of our escape later. For now, my only concern was convincing Kunkel that we had a moment in Stuttgart and that we should continue it now.

A-Rad and I didn't fight over the plan, but I could feel the tension. I could see it in his rigid posture and clenched jaw. He didn't like the idea of me trying to seduce Kunkel. He particularly didn't like my choice of outfit.

I opted for a sleek, black dress that clung to my body like a second skin, exuding allure. Its plunging neckline hinted at my intentions. The fabric hugged my curves in all the right places and shimmered subtly under the restaurant's soft lighting.

"Why does it have to be so short?" A-Rad had argued.

"I want my legs free. In case I need them as a weapon, or I have to run away in a hurry. If my dress is too long and form-fitting, I won't be able to move like I might have to."

The dress was paired with simple yet striking accessories—a pair of diamond stud earrings and a delicate silver bracelet. My dark red hair was styled in loose waves that cascaded over my shoulders, and my makeup was understated but accentuated my features, with a bold red lip gloss adding a touch of drama.

At precisely eight o'clock, Dr. Berthold Kunkel walked into the restaurant. He scanned the room, his gaze finally landing on me. I waved subtly, and he made his way over, looking slightly puzzled but intrigued.

To my relief, he was the one who showed up instead of a bunch of armed soldiers coming to drag us away.

Kunkel was in his mid to late fifties and smartly dressed in a classic navy-blue suit that spoke of quiet confidence and professionalism. Impeccably tailored, it fit his medium-sized frame perfectly. Open collar, he wore a crisp white shirt underneath paired with polished shoes that completed the outfit.

He had a classic German look, with neatly trimmed hair and mustache, thick bushy eyebrows slightly above a pair of stylish glasses that gave him an intellectual edge. The overall effect was one of a man comfortable and confident, but not overly flashy.

I stood to my feet and surprised him by hugging his neck, then kissing him on each cheek. His cologne had a subtle mix of cedarwood, amber, and a hint of musk. Not too strong but enough to pleasantly tickle my nose.

"Dr. Volk?" he said, helping me with my chair as I sat down.

"Please, call me Mina," I insisted.

"Mina it is," he replied with a warm smile. He studied me closely, his brow furrowing slightly. "I must apologize, but I don't seem to recall our fling in Stuttgart."

I stuck out my lower lip, pretending to be hurt. "I guess I wasn't very memorable."

"That's not what I meant."

"I wouldn't call it a fling. We had a few drinks, maybe more than a few. But nothing else happened."

"Ah, I see."

Hopefully, that made more sense to him. I saw some confusion leave his face and his shoulders relax slightly. He'd likely remember a woman he slept with which was why he was so skeptical, but he couldn't possibly remember every woman he'd shared a drink with.

I had a prepared answer if he asked which bar, but that's where things could go south quickly. If he said he never went to that bar, then I'd have to adlib. Pretend I got it wrong. If that didn't work and he saw through the ruse, then I had to kill him and run out of the hotel as fast as possible.

"You're quite beautiful," he said. "You'd think I'd remember such a pretty face."

I chuckled softly, dismissing his comment with a wave of my hand. "Oh, don't worry about it. It was one of those wild nights. A group of us from the university were celebrating a little too much. Things got a bit … shall we say, rowdy. I can be an impetuous flirt when I drink."

"Then we need to get you a drink," he said laughing, signaling the waiter who was standing off to the side patiently waiting for a command.

Kunkel ordered a bottle of wine without looking at the menu. He was settling into the role of lady's man which gave me some hope that my plan might work.

"Those nights can be rather memorable," he said, "yet so easy to forget the details."

"Exactly," I said, leaning forward slightly. "But I do remember you. You were quite the charmer, as I recall. I liked it."

He smiled, clearly pleased. "Well, I'm flattered you remember me. I'm so glad you reached out to me. I hear that you're working with the INWA now."

"That's right." I leaned in, lowering my voice slightly. "To be honest, I was hoping to run into you. I've been thinking about that night in Stuttgart, wondering what became of you. If you were still in Iran. I hoped maybe we could pick up where we left off. Unfinished business, as they say."

Kunkel's eyes sparkled with interest.

"Or should I say, unfinished pleasure," I flashed him a seductive smile, while making sure I avoided looking at A-Rad, who was probably itching to kill Kunkel.

If for no other reason than that the man was hitting on his wife right in front of his face.

I realized I might be overdoing it, so I decided to dial it back some. Not so much for A-Rad's benefit, but so Kunkel didn't get suspicious. Men preferred to chase their prey.

The waiter arrived with our bottle of wine and Kunkel loosened up even more after consuming a couple of glasses. It looked like my plan was working. Whatever suspicions and inhibitions he had were fleeing by the moment.

Our conversation became more intimate and flirtatious. I complimented his intellect, and he reciprocated, noting my charm and wit.

The chemistry was undeniable, and I could see that he was enjoying the attention.

Every once in a while, I caught a glimpse of A-Rad out of the corner of my eye, with steam coming out his ears. If looks could kill, Kunkel would already be dead.

Kunkel downed a third glass of wine like he was gulping water. I had only taken a couple of sips. I wanted my wits about me. He moved his chair closer to mine and proposed a toast. We clicked glasses.

Without warning, he leaned in and kissed me on the lips. I immediately pulled back.

What I really wanted to do was throw up in my mouth.

I was surprised that A-Rad didn't kill him on the spot.

Kunkel looked angry. Like he was offended that I had rejected his advances. I had to act quickly, or my plan could be ruined.

"I'm sorry," I said. "I was told that public displays of affection were against the law in Iran and that I could be arrested. That's why I pulled away. Not because I'm not interested."

He nodded, the anger in his face faded away.

"It is against the law, but I have connections. They won't do anything to me. Forgive me. I was being somewhat presumptuous. Did I come on too strong?"

"Not at all," I said, trying to regain my composure and take back the initiative. "I just wasn't expecting it. But it's kind of awkward here. With the guards watching us."

He didn't know the half of it.

"Why don't we continue this up in my room?" I asked. "How does that sound?"

"What about our dinner?"

"We'll order room service. Afterwards. I don't want to wait."

He hesitated for a moment, making me think he was going to decline. Instead, he nodded and said, "I'd like that very much. Good idea."

Was this too easy?

Kunkel left some money on the table for the wine. I offered to put the charge on my room, but he insisted. He helped me with my chair again and we left the restaurant and walked in a straight line to the elevator.

Kunkel seemed in a big hurry to get back to the room.

A-Rad and Jerry's guard entered the elevator with us, making things extremely awkward.

I couldn't shake the feeling that something was off.

I'm standing in an elevator with my husband and a strange man I'm taking back to my hotel room who thinks we're about to have sex. Of course, something was off!

But was Kunkel wanting to get me alone in my room so he could kill me?

I wasn't too worried about that, but what if Jerry and his goons were waiting in my room to ambush me? If so, the first priority was killing Kunkel followed closely by making it out of there unscathed.

It didn't seem like Kunkel was planning anything nefarious. His intentions were clear. His hands were all over me in the elevator. A-Rad stood so rigid, his face so racked with tension, that he looked like a statue in a wax museum.

The elevator finally reached my floor. We exited and the other two followed us. I couldn't wait to get into my room. It seemed like Kunkel felt the same way as we walked quickly down the hallway, the anticipation building.

My heart fluttered in relief when I found the room empty.

Inside, I poured each of us a glass of brandy and handed him one. We clinked glasses, and I took a sip, watching him cautiously over the rim. Prepared to strike at the first sign of a threat. I didn't intend to wait long to kill him.

"To old memories and new beginnings," I said softly.

"To both," he replied, downing his with one gulp.

It seemed like he was about to kiss me again, so I took his hand, and we sat on the couch facing each other. I edged closer, placing a hand on his thigh. His hand was immediately on my upper thigh, practically groping me.

My instincts were to knock it off, but I resisted the urge.

Our faces were inches apart now. He looked deep into my eyes, desire and curiosity exuding from every feature on his face.

I remembered how much I hated the man. How he was plotting to kill millions of people. That stoked the rage inside and made me feel powerful.

"You know, Bertie," I asked, seductively in a low voice, "May I call you Bertie?"

He nodded eagerly.

"I have a feeling that you're not going to forget me after tonight."

"I have that same feeling."

He made his move, coming in for a passionate and aggressive kiss.

I leaned away.

His eyes widened. Then was replaced with fear, when he saw the rage on my face.

With a swift, precise movement, I struck him on the side of his neck with an open hand, targeting the vagus nerve. The blow found its mark.

His eyes rolled back in his head, his body tensed for a brief second before he collapsed back on the couch, unconscious within seconds.

The maneuver was tricky, but Jamie taught me how to execute it with precision. The heart nerve, when struck at the exact right spot, caused a sudden drop in blood pressure. If hit too sharply, it can cause immediate death.

I struck him with the exact force I had intended. Hard enough to kill him, but not hard enough to leave a bruise. The red mark would fade by morning.

My heart raced with adrenaline as I made sure he was dead. Filled with satisfaction that the plan had worked.

The room was eerily silent, and I focused on calming myself down. I took a deep breath to collect myself.

Even though I didn't have to be in a hurry, I wasted no time. I removed Kunkel's clothes and arranged his body on the bed, to make it seem like he died in his sleep.

I carefully ruffled the bedclothes and climbed into bed for a few moments, to create the illusion that I had been sleeping there too.

His clothes were a pile on the floor, and I went through them, looking for anything that might give me a clue as to the location of the secret nuclear facility.

He didn't have any kind of badge on him, but he did have a phone in his pocket.

It was locked and I didn't know the password. I walked over to the bed, turned him over and held it to his face, hoping that the face recognition software was activated. It opened and I let out a slight squeal of delight.

I thoroughly searched his text messages and emails, memorizing every detail that seemed important. What I saw in one text message sent shivers down my spine. Addressed to Jerry.

Good news. We're about a month away from having the bomb weaponized and ready for launch.

My heart, which was starting to calm, was racing again.

One month!

13

A hurricane of conflicting thoughts assaulted my mind as I stood in the hotel room, Kunkel's phone in hand. My initial shock had turned into a jumble of fear, anger, and uncertainty.

The text message I had read revealed a deadly plan. Kunkel was helping Iran acquire a nuclear bomb. Was it too late to stop them or were we in time?

The gravity of this knowledge pressed down on me like a boulder on my chest, but I needed more answers before I could act.

Did they need Kunkel to complete the bomb?

Would his death be enough to thwart their plans?

But the most crucial question burned within me like a wildfire: Where is the secret facility?

If I didn't know its location, all my efforts would be futile.

My original plan to leave on our flight tomorrow morning after successfully killing Kunkel felt like a distant memory now. The urgency to find the facility grew with each passing second.

A-Rad and I needed to sneak out tonight and start searching. But where do we even begin to look? Panic set in as I realized I didn't know. Even if we did find the nuclear facility that housed the bomb or bombs that could potentially wipe out millions of lives, it'd almost certainly be heavily guarded by a small army.

What were A-Rad and I going to do? Attack it with a single handgun.

The only option was to locate the facility and alert Jamie. She could contact Mossad and then it'd be their problem. Unlike us, they had the resources to take out a nuclear facility.

Was one month enough time to activate all those moving parts?

The clock was ticking, the countdown to disaster rapidly approaching faster than any of us had even realized. With every day starting tomorrow, Iran's bomb grew closer to completion and the threat of nuclear war loomed over Israel.

Regret crept in alongside my other emotions. My idea to make Kunkel's death look like an accident was no longer viable. Once I vanished, Jerry would surely come looking for me with the tenacity of a bulldog.

Kunkel's death was a small victory, but it wouldn't buy us much time. Would the one-month time frame be affected by his death? Did we have two months, six months, a year if he wasn't there to manage it or was it far enough along that they didn't need him?

Since we didn't know, we had to assume the one-month time frame was still in play.

I was getting ahead of myself. I needed to tackle one problem at a time. I had to figure out how to get out of the hotel tonight without anyone knowing.

My mind raced with possible escape plans, each one riskier than the last. A-Rad could create a distraction, allowing me to slip away. He could then meet me outside the hotel ... but then what?

We didn't have a vehicle. Even if we did, we wouldn't know which direction to drive.

I scolded myself for thinking so far ahead. *One problem at a time*, I reminded myself sternly. Right now, my priority was finding a way out of this hotel alive.

Regret clawed at my insides for a second time as I realized it may have been a mistake to kill Kunkel so quickly. My grip tightened on his phone as I thought of what I could have gained by keeping him alive and forcing him to divulge the location of the facility.

But then a new plan formed in my mind, sparked by A-Rad's earlier suggestion. Jerry knew where the facility was, and he could lead us there. I could use my charm and manipulation to convince Jerry to give us one more day of inspections under the guise of wanting to see another plant.

On the way, A-Rad could overtake the driver while I overpowered Jerry. We would threaten him, and if necessary, torture him until he revealed the location of the secret nuclear plant.

That's not necessary.

My hand trembled and the phone shook as I thought of a better plan. I powered up the phone and frantically searched for the location services.

"Please be on," I begged under my breath, my heart pounding in my chest. The fate of our mission might rest on this one small detail.

A shriek escaped my lips, echoing through the room. The guard was almost certainly still outside the door, and he might've heard it, but I didn't care. He'd think Kunkel and I were having a wild time.

I frantically scanned the locations on Kunkel's phone screen. I almost let out a bigger shout when I found only two places he had been going to everyday for months. One had to be where he stayed and the other, without a doubt, was the location of the secret facility since that's where he was all day, every day.

I memorized the coordinates to what I was certain was the location of the secret facility. As confident as I was in my memory, I couldn't risk getting a number wrong, so I wrote them down on a piece of paper.

The easiest thing to do was to take Kunkel's phone with me, but I couldn't after a long debate in my head. If I were searched for some reason, having Kunkel's phone would jeopardize everything. And its absence from the room would raise suspicion. It wasn't imperative that Kunkel's death look like natural causes, but it sure made things easier in the long run.

Excitement pulsed through me as I considered the options, but it was quickly followed by a wave of fear. How could I get this information to Jamie without putting her in danger? Even worse, how tragic would it be if I died with this crucial information in my head?

My first instinct was to call or email Jamie from my phone right away, but that wasn't secure. Calling her on Kunkel's phone wasn't an option either. If I did reach out to Jamie on an unsecure line, not only would it compromise my own safety, but also hers.

But then again, was this information worth the risk? Maybe. It could be the key to finally taking down the facility and preventing a worldwide catastrophe.

Was sacrificing Jamie and Alex's cover and potentially implicating them in the plan really the best course of action? It seemed like a last resort, and we weren't there yet, even though time was running out and Mossad needed to act fast.

Conflicted and unsure of what to do, I stood frozen, torn between my duty and my moral compass. I finally decided that the only option was to escape the country and hand over the information to her by secure means.

For a brief moment, I considered sneaking out of the hotel and making an all-out effort to get out of the country right now. Steal a car or something. Hike across the desert and mountains if I had to.

After a lot of emotional turmoil, I came up with a plan. It wasn't perfect, but it seemed like the best option. The easiest thing to do was fly out on our plane. We'd have to make it look official or we'd get shot out of the sky.

I'd call Jerry in the morning, and he could drive us to the airport. The guard outside would know that Kunkel hadn't left my room, but I'd say he was still asleep and not to be disturbed.

For the next two hours, I combed through Kunkel's phone for any information that might be useful. The only thing I found was a text exchange between Jerry and Kunkel discussing me.

Kunkel had started the conversation by expressing doubts about me after looking me up on the INWA website. Jerry reassured him that my story checked out.

"I'm supposed to meet her at eight tomorrow night at her hotel," Kunkel wrote.

"Do you want me to be there?" Jerry replied.

"No need, I can handle her. If she's not who she claims to be, I'll see right through it. And if she tries something, she'll regret it."

I chuckled as I looked over at Kunkel's lifeless body. "Who regrets it now?" I said with a smirk.

"She looks American," Kunkel continued.

"According to her bio, she was born in Bavaria," Jerry answered. "Maybe one of her parents is from America."

Then came an unsettling question from Kunkel: "Any chance she's CIA?"

Jerry responded, "Anything is possible, but I highly doubt it. I can spot a CIA operative a mile away."

"So can I."

I felt smug that I had fooled both of them.

The next few parts of the thread were lewd remarks about how sexy I was and what Kunkel was going to do to me. I wanted to walk over to his dead body and smack him again.

Jerry commented on my appearance since he had seen me and told Kunkel how lucky he was.

"She's half your age," he wrote.

"That'll make it more fun. No offense, but the dating prospects aren't that great here in Iran."

Adultery and fornication were a crime in Iran punishable by death, even though it was rarely carried out. Neither of them seemed concerned about breaking the law.

The text took another confusing turn, when Jerry began discussing someone named AP in America and their plans for Israel and potentially the US.

My curiosity was piqued; who was AP and what were they planning?

"When do I get to meet him?" Kunkel asked.

"He has to win first," Jerry replied.

Win what? I didn't understand what they were talking about. That seemed to be on purpose. Like Jerry was talking in code.

The next words left no room for doubt about their intentions.

"First we destroy Israel," Kunkel wrote, "Then America."

"Inshallah," Jerry texted, which meant God willing. Or if God wills. Meaning if Allah wills.

I desperately tried to piece together their intentions, but my mind couldn't handle the weight of such evil and I had to push those thoughts aside for now. I needed to focus on getting the information I had to Jamie and worry about the identity of AP later.

Slamming Kunkel's phone shut, I couldn't help but feel dirty from being so close to him earlier that evening. I quickly rid myself of my clothes and stepped into a scalding hot shower, scrubbing away at my skin like I still had remnants of him on me.

But even after washing away the physical remnants of Kunkel, when I stepped out of the shower his taste still lingered on my lips from where he kissed me earlier. Feeling sick with disgust, I repeatedly gargled with mouthwash until it burned the back of my throat.

And then it hit me like a slap in the face.

A-Rad.

I had promised to call him when Kunkel was taken care of. I walked back into the bedroom and dialed his room number letting it ring once before hanging up. It was our code that the deed was done.

But as soon as I hung up, guilt consumed me. A-Rad would be furious with me for letting Kunkel kiss me and even more furious that I hadn't called right away. Tomorrow, I'd have to beg for his forgiveness with apologetic groveling.

"I'm sorry, A-Rad," I said, as I hung up the phone.

I put on the clothes I intended to wear tomorrow and packed my belongings. I picked up Kunkel's clothes and folded them neatly and sat them on the chair. I returned his phone to the pocket.

Then slumped into a chair by the window, my mind racing with adrenaline from the night's events.

Had we pulled off the perfect crime for a second time?

There's a good chance they'd think Kunkel's death was from natural causes. That's the reason I struck him on the vagus nerve. In an autopsy, it'd look like he had a stroke.

Two missions, two kills.

And we had successfully evaded detection from both North Korean and Iranian authorities. I reminded myself that we hadn't gotten away with killing Kunkel yet and certainly hadn't evaded Iranian authorities. Not until we were out of the country safely.

Still, Alex and Jamie would think this was too easy even though it felt anything but easy.

As I waited for morning to come, I considered other options for our escape until my head hurt. At some point, I finally drifted off to sleep.

When morning arrived, I called Jerry and told him we were ready to leave and that our work was finished. He didn't sound at all suspicious and didn't ask any questions. He said he'd have a car outside our hotel door in thirty minutes.

When the time came, I put a "Do Not Disturb" sign on the door and told the guard that Kunkel was asleep and that he wasn't to be disturbed. The guard took a wary look at the door, but that was all. He followed me down to the lobby, since he was tasked with staying with me at all times.

A-Rad was already in the lobby and we exchanged knowing glances.

Jerry was early with an SUV to escort us to the airport. When I got into the car, I couldn't shake off the eerie sense of déjà vu from when we first arrived only two days ago. We were so close to getting away with it, but I feared that something could still go wrong.

With every passing moment, my anxiety grew as we approached the airport. Jerry remained silent, his demeanor distant and unreadable.

I was shocked that he didn't say anything about Kunkel's visit to my room. I thought about thanking him for setting up the visit but decided to leave well enough alone.

We passed through the familiar gates of the airport security once again and parked next to our plane, which sat in the same spot where we'd left it. As A-Rad hurriedly loaded our bags onto the plane, I kept expecting a confrontation that never came.

The goodbyes were terse and emotionless as we quickly boarded the plane. A-Rad immediately shut the door behind us and we were ready for takeoff. As we taxied away from Jerry and the SUV, I couldn't help but wonder if we had truly made it out unscathed or if this was the calm before the storm.

As we ascended into the sky, I felt a mix of relief and sudden tiredness from being up all night, but I wouldn't completely relax or close my eyes until we were out of Iranian airspace. I settled into the copilot's seat, glancing at A-Rad, who nodded in silent acknowledgment. We maintained silence until we were out of Iranian airspace, since we didn't know if the cockpit was bugged.

"We're clear," A-Rad said, less than an hour later when we were finally out of Iran.

I sank back in my chair in relief.

As much as I looked forward to that moment, I also dreaded it. A-Rad would have questions for me about last night and I was prepared to answer them.

To my surprise, he didn't ask me anything. He didn't even seem jealous or upset.

I had to give him credit for his trust in me. He knew I did what I had to do to get the job done. And even though I didn't call him right away after killing Kunkel, I'm sure he realized what happened as soon as he saw that I was alive. He knew I'd never let Kunkel touch me once we were in the room alone together.

Once we arrived back in South Korea, I would make it up to A-Rad and reaffirm my love and loyalty to him and him alone. That sounded good. After days of tension and stress, I eagerly looked forward to returning to our yacht and truly unwinding.

A few minutes later, I sent Jamie the coordinates of the secret facility along with an urgent message: CALL ME! ASAP!

When I got back in the cockpit, A-Rad had the strangest look on his face.

"What's wrong?"

"I was going over the flight plan. It has us landing in North Korea, not South Korea."

I couldn't believe the words coming out of his mouth.

"There has to be some mistake."

14

The confusion was evident in my voice as I asked, "Why are we going to North Korea?"

I stared at the lights on the control panel trying to make sense of A-Rad's words. The soft hum of the airplane's engines seemed unusually loud in the silence that followed.

"I have no clue," A-Rad responded with a frown, as he double-checked the instruments. His fingers danced over the controls with practiced ease, the subtle movements betraying the unease in his voice.

"Before we left Iran, I filed a flight plan to Germany. Once we were safely out of Iranian airspace, I expected Alex to work his magic and switch our destination to South Korea, while still making it look like we were heading to Germany in case someone is tracking us."

If we wanted Jerry to believe the ruse, we needed him to think we were headed back to Germany. In reality, now that we were out of Iran, it didn't really matter anymore. We weren't even sure Jerry was tracking us at all. But we'd gone to a lot of trouble to make things look a certain way, and I had hoped things would continue to go smoothly.

I didn't fully comprehend this new complication. My thoughts swirled as I tried to piece together the puzzle. The more I thought about it, the more elusive the answers became.

I gazed out the cockpit window, watching as the bright blue sky merged with the horizon. The sun was fully awake now, casting a golden glow across the clouds below.

"Are you sure?" I asked. "Check it again. What if it's an instrument mal-function?"

A-Rad's voice broke through my doubts. "Kaley, see for yourself."

He was pointing at the navigation display, his brows furrowed in concentration. The screen glowed softly in the light, displaying our flight path as a thin line cutting across the map.

"The flight plan is off course," A-Rad said, tracing the path on the screen with his finger. "We're definitely headed toward North Korea."

"That can't be right. Why would we go there?"

I leaned closer to the display, my eyes narrowing as I tried to make sense of the data.

"I don't know," A-Rad replied, his concern evident in the tightness of his voice. His usual calm demeanor was cracking, just enough for me to see the worry beneath the surface.

"Maybe Alex entered North Korea instead of South Korea by mistake," I said.

He shook his head, rejecting that possibility. "That doesn't sound like Alex. He's always meticulous about details."

I knew that to be true. Alex's attention to detail was one of the things that made him the best in the world at what he did. He wouldn't make such a careless mistake.

"He could've been in the middle of something important, or using a remote system," I countered, though I wasn't completely convinced myself.

"I'll change it back," A-Rad said, reaching for the instrument panel.

Instinctively, I reached out and grabbed his arm, stopping him. "If you do that, we risk exposing ourselves. Whatever Alex did to keep us hidden from Iran could be compromised."

The thought of losing the cover Alex had so carefully crafted for us sent a wave of dread through me. We were so close to safety. I didn't want to do anything that might jeopardize that.

A-Rad hesitated, his hand hovering over the controls.

I continued to plead my case. "We still have to cross some hostile territories to get back to that part of the world. What if Jerry found Kunkel's body and realized we weren't who we claimed to be? He could still try to take us down."

A-Rad's pulled his hand back.

"Are we heading south or north?" I asked.

Both directions posed their own sets of challenges.

"South," A-Rad said, his voice steady, but with an undercurrent of indecision.

"South makes more sense," I said, trying to remember my global maps and thinking through the possible routes.

I was relieved to hear that we were headed in that direction. South was the safer option. Although safe in that region of the world was relative.

Heading north would take us towards Russia. South would have us crossing over Afghanistan, Pakistan, and India, then stopping in Malaysia to refuel before heading to Seoul.

That seemed more like what Alex would plan.

East was the most direct route, but that was through China. That wasn't happening.

The picture in my mind of the landscape below us shifted in my mind as I imagined the journey ahead. The vast deserts, the rugged mountains, and sprawling cities. Filled with millions of people who hated us simply because we were Americans.

What if Iran told one of its allies to force us to land?

Before I could voice my concerns, the secure phone at the back of the plane rang, its sharp tone cutting through the silence. The sound was jarring and unexpected.

Only Alex and Jamie had that number.

We exchanged a quick glance before rushing to answer it.

A-Rad pressed the speaker button so we could both hear.

"Are you taking us on a sightseeing trip, Alex, or have you finally lost your mind?" he joked, though his tone was more strained than usual.

"Good to hear your voice," Jamie's voice crackled through, a hint of concern coloring her words. "Are you two safe?"

"We're clear of Iran," A-Rad confirmed, glancing at me as he spoke. "But we've got an issue with our flight plan. It's taking us to North Korea. We thought it might be a mistake."

His words were measured and careful. I wanted to shout the same thing into the phone except with more urgency. If we were going to adjust the flight plan away from North Korea, we still had time, but I felt like Alex needed to switch the plan right now, if only for my peace of mind.

"It's not a mistake," Alex's voice cut in, firm and reassuring. His calmness was like a lifeline, something to hold onto in the midst of the confusion. "We're sending you back there on purpose."

A-Rad and I exchanged puzzled glances, my mind racing with questions.

"Why? What's going on?" I asked.

Jamie's tone softened, becoming more empathetic, almost apologetic.

"Before we get into that, Kaley, I need to know what happened in Iran. You sent me coordinates with urgency. I assume they're important."

"Extremely."

"Tell me what they mean."

I took a deep breath as I prepared to recount everything. The memories were still fresh, vivid, each one etched into my mind like something in my past too important to forget. I never in my wildest dreams thought I'd be relaying information of such worldwide importance.

I began to speak, my voice steady as I detailed how we found Kunkel, killed him, and then discovered the coordinates to a secret nuclear facility. With each word, the tension inside me began to slowly unwind, like a tightly coiled spring slowly releasing its energy.

When I finished, there was a brief silence on the other end of the line, as they processed everything I had just revealed.

"Good work, Kaley," Jamie said finally, her voice filled with genuine admiration. "Finding those coordinates is huge. I'll pass them along to Mossad immediately. They'll know what to do."

"You two are amazing," Alex added, his tone warm and reassuring. "Let's hope Iran buys that Kunkel died of natural causes. Even if they don't, they won't be able to find you in North Korea."

"About that!" I exclaimed, unable to hold back the anxiety bursting inside of me. "Why are we being sent to North Korea?"

The question hung in the air, heavy with uncertainty.

Alex's voice remained calm and measured as he explained.

"There's been a significant development in the region. After you killed Yang and his sister, the situation in North Korea changed dramatically. With both of them dead, a power vacuum was created."

"We thought that might happen," I said, though the reality of it still felt surreal.

Alex's voice grew more excited as he continued, "It's even better than we expected. The U.S. saw a huge opportunity and took it. North Korean forces were leaderless and in disarray. South Korean and American forces crossed the border, and surprisingly, without meeting any resistance."

I felt my eyes widen in disbelief. "Are you saying we control North Korea now?"

The idea was so far-fetched, so impossible, that it took a moment to fully register.

"I wouldn't use the word 'control,'" Alex clarified. "We're helping facilitate a peaceful transition of power to a more democratic system. The people of North Korea are celebrating in the streets and welcoming this change. The oppressive regime is finally over. There's even talk of unification between North and South Korea. People are traveling freely between the countries. I never thought I'd see it in my lifetime."

"You mean the border is open?" A-Rad asked.

"Wide open," Alex confirmed. "The entire world has rallied to send humanitarian aid. It's a delicate situation, but right now, it's the safest place for you to be. No one will be looking for you there. You can stay at Momma-son's diner or the yacht or go back and forth."

"I prefer dry land," I said.

The idea of finding refuge in a place that had once been so dangerous felt like a strange twist of fate.

A-Rad leaned back in his seat, his mind clearly trying to process the information.

"That's incredible," he said. "It'll feel good to act normal again."

"What about the West? Is the CIA still after us?" I asked, the question slipping out before I could stop it. The thought of being hunted, of always looking over my shoulder, had become second nature to me.

"They suspect you're behind what happened in North Korea," Jamie said. "If anything, Brad is cheering you on."

"Does that mean we can come home?" A-Rad asked, though I could tell he wasn't expecting a simple answer.

"Not exactly," Jamie replied, her tone regretful. "I doubt that'll ever be possible. But at least you don't have to constantly stay on the run. Alex has basically erased your identities from the internet. There's no evidence you ever existed."

"Why does that not make me feel happy?" I muttered, the words slipping out before I could catch them.

"Considering where things were a few weeks ago, this is better than we could've hoped for," Alex said.

"I suppose," I conceded reluctantly.

"You should still be careful," Jamie warned. "But you don't need to go dark in the traditional sense. North Korea, or what used to be North Korea, is the last place anyone would think to look for you. Momma-son's diner is the perfect cover because you won't need one."

I felt a strange mix of relief and disbelief. The idea of finding sanctuary in a place that had once been synonymous with danger felt almost too good to be true.

Jamie added, "For now, take a breath, regroup, and get some rest. But be ready. We've got another mission coming up, and this one's going to be even more challenging."

A-Rad arched an eyebrow, a hint of curiosity flickered in his eyes. "What's next?"

Jamie's voice dropped, serious and filled with gravity. "Russia."

"That's another reason we want you in North Korea," Alex interjected. "It'll be a good staging ground for a mission to Russia. You can cross the border through one of the CIA entry points. The Colonel is already working on a plan."

The line went silent, leaving that single word hanging in the air.

Russia.

We all knew our work was far from over, but the thought of heading into the heart of a nation known for its complexities and dangers set me back on edge. The vast, cold expanses of Russia would send a chill down anyone's spine. It was a land of intrigue and danger, where one wrong move could mean the difference between life and death.

"We'll be ready," A-Rad finally said, his voice steady and resolved, breaking the silence.

"Good," Jamie replied. "We'll be in touch with more details soon. Stay safe."

The call ended, and we both collapsed into our seats, the reality of what lay ahead sinking in and dampening our spirits. Reality hit like a tidal wave, threatening to drown me in fear and uncertainty.

This was our life now. No time to relish in victories and thrust into another situation where failure meant death.

At least for now, North Korea, of all places, was our sanctuary. While Russia loomed on the horizon, I intended to try and enjoy what little time we had before we were thrown back to the wolves.

"You okay?" A-Rad asked, his voice cutting through my thoughts, grounding me.

I nodded slowly. "Just trying to wrap my head around it all."

A-Rad gave me a small, reassuring smile, his presence a comforting anchor. I don't think I could do all this without him. In fact, I knew I couldn't.

"This is what we signed up for," A-Rad said. "To make an impact in the world. The unification of North and South Korea is huge. Not to mention stopping Iran's nuclear program in its tracks. It doesn't get more impactful than this."

"You're right," I agreed, a sense of purpose slowly returning. "We are changing the world, one dead dictator at a time."

15

Russia

Yuli Belov was a man of great influence in Russia, though his power did not come from traditional means. Unlike the billionaire oligarchs or military generals, Yuli's power came from a more subtle and innate ability—a unique gift and instinct that propelled him from obscurity to the inner circles of Russia's elite.

His education and connections played a part, but it was his unique skill of perception that truly set him apart along with his friendship with President Nikitin Kuzman that spanned decades.

Over thirty years ago, before Kuzman became the President of Russia, the two were merely students at a Soviet university, living on meager meals and youthful dreams. While Kuzman had a clear sense of purpose and political ambitions, Yuli possessed a talent for understanding what people wanted to see and believe.

This caught Kuzman's attention, and as he rose to power, he brought Yuli along with him as his trusted advisor.

For thirty years, Yuli had been the silent architect behind Kuzman's public persona. His job wasn't to make Kuzman look good; it was to make him look powerful—unstoppable, even. The world and the people of Russia didn't need to love Kuzman, they needed to fear him.

Yuli understood this better than anyone. He meticulously crafted every speech, every appearance, and every carefully choreographed military demonstration to portray Kuzman as the one man who could restore Russia to its former glory.

The collapse of the Soviet Union had left Russia fractured and broken, but Kuzman refused to let it stay that way. Unlike leaders of the past whose

ambition led them to make fatal mistakes, his ambitions were more calculated and less grandiose.

He didn't want to rule the world, rather he wanted to bring back the
former Soviet states under Russian control, reclaiming territories that had
once been part of the Russian Empire.

It had been a long and difficult journey, filled with battles fought on
multiple fronts. But Kuzman persevered, slowly and methodically achieving
his goals. One by one, the states fell back under Russia's shadow.

Kuzman's ambitions didn't end there. He had his sights set on Poland
and East Berlin, territories that had slipped through Russia's fingers after
World War II. Reclaiming those lands would mean challenging America and
its allies head-on, a challenge Kuzman welcomed.

America had responded to the threat with defensive measures, arming
threatened nations in an attempt to deter Kuzman's expansionist campaign.
But Kuzman intended to press on undeterred, aided by Yuli's manipulation
of public perception which portrayed Russia as far stronger than it truly was.

The Americans, cautious of a full-scale war, eventually backed down and
had allowed Russia to rebuild its strength. With the resources of the former
Soviet states at his disposal, Kuzman's Russia had emerged as a formidable
force.

The world could no longer ignore its resurgence. The country's wealth
from oil, gas, and uranium reserves had been funneled towards building up
its military might to the point that it was second to none.

Russia had less than half the population of the United States but had
developed a superior military. More importantly, they had a greater resolve.
The American people didn't have the will to stop his advances and Kuzman
knew it.

All he had to do was maintain power in Russia. Despite the suffering
and sacrifice by its citizens, they remained fiercely loyal to Kuzman thanks
in large part to Yuli's propaganda campaigns promising a reunified and dominant Russia on the world stage.

The plan was working. The people were united in their belief that Russia
was on the cusp of greatness. The only obstacle left was America, but it was
only a matter of time until it fell.

America grew weaker by the year. Floundering in massive debt and bloated government, it was a mere shell of its former self, crumbling from within. All America needed was a catalyst and it could be destroyed forever. Relegated to the ashes of past former world powers like the Roman Empire, the British Empire, and others who were once the world's largest powers but now only littered the history books with their failures.

Kuzman had a secret plan, one that had been in the works for more than forty years. Yuli didn't know the details—few did, except Kuzman himself and a small inner circle. This level of secrecy only added to the intrigue and power of the plan.

Yuli trusted that when the time came, this plan would be the final piece in Kuzman's puzzle. He'd be free to take back Poland and East Berlin and America would be powerless to stop him.

Yuli hoped they both lived long enough to see it. Both men were pushing seventy.

In the meantime, Yuli was to keep doing what he had been doing.

One of his greatest ideas was the Power Parade, an annual event that showcased Russia's military might to the world. It also served as a symbol of unity, a message to both allies and enemies that Russia should not be underestimated.

The parade was considered a national holiday with schools and businesses closed. Over one million people gathered at the Red Square in Moscow to witness the spectacle, which was broadcasted globally, serving as a reminder to the world that Russia was once again a powerful nation.

The day of the parade was bitterly cold, even for Moscow standards. The sky loomed with heavy gray clouds, hinting at snow but never actually delivering it. The air had a sharp chill, nipping at the cheeks of the spectators who filled the square. Despite bundling up in heavy coats, a mix of excitement and pride permeated through the crowd.

Yuli had insisted on a wintertime parade. He believed it made the people of Russia and the military on display look tougher. The bleak sky made the display seem more ominous and added to the overall intimidating effect.

Yuli observed from the command center, situated high above the square. From this vantage point, he could oversee everything—the masses of onlookers, the parade route, and even the viewing stand where the president and top generals were seated.

He had meticulously planned every aspect of this day down to the smallest second; it was his masterpiece, a demonstration of his undeniable expertise.

The parade commenced with a thunderous boom of piped-in drums, their deep rhythm reverberating through the square. The first columns of soldiers marched in perfect unison, their heavy boots pounding the pavement in synchronized steps. More than twelve battalions took turns showcasing their strength before the viewing stand.

They stopped in place while the president inspected them from the viewing stand. They didn't dare move until he waved them on with his approval.

Following them were the tanks, armored vehicles, and missile launchers—all symbols of Russia's military prowess and power. The crowd erupted into cheers as each group passed by, the volume growing louder with each passing moment.

The crowd gazed in awe as twelve intercontinental Russian nuclear missiles were rolled past the viewing stand one at a time. Each one armed and ready to serve their one purpose for that day—to strike fear in the heart of their enemies.

Kuzman had privately proclaimed to Yuli that those missiles would one day land in twelve different American cities. He didn't see how that was possible, but Kuzman seemed confident in this secret plan.

Yuli was relieved when that part of the parade was over. He had always worried about a terrorist attack at that moment. Some enemy setting off one of the nuclear weapons. The generals had assured him that couldn't happen, but that didn't keep him from worrying.

On cue, parachutists descended from the cloudy sky, their colorful canopies unfolding against the gray backdrop like blooming flowers. With impeccable precision, they touched down on the ground in front of the viewing stand carrying large Russian flags.

The ecstatic roar of the crowd shook the foundations of the city, drowning out all other sounds in a deafening symphony of approval.

Yuli's heart swelled with pride as he watched his creation, his vision brought to life before his eyes. Everything was going off without a hitch. The president was pleased. He said as much as he stood and delivered a message to the crowd with the vim and vigor of a man half his age.

These military parades energized Kuzman. The crowd, too, seemed to draw strength from them. The pride and national unity of this particular crowd was at a fevered pitch.

Yuli quickly regained his focus on the main event as the president concluded his remarks. The true highlight of the parade was about to come. The grand finale. A confluence of the most elite soldiers and the most proficient pilots.

One hundred handpicked men were chosen for their skills and unwavering loyalty. They were there to pay homage to the president with a traditional 21-gun salute, a display of utmost respect and reverence for their commander.

This year, Yuli had added a special twist. As the soldiers took their positions, five fighter jets were already in the sky. Out of sight but making their way to the square for a flyover. Each one had taken off from a different airbase and flew solo for several minutes before joining together in formation.

They flew so closely together it seemed as though they were touching wings. The crowd collectively gasped in awe as the jets appeared on the horizon, zooming towards the square at breathtaking speeds.

The timing had to be perfect. The soldiers raised their rifles and fired the first shot at the exact moment, causing a wave of cheers from the crowd who were watching with great anticipation.

The jets grew closer, their engines roared and could be heard now off in the distance.

The soldiers continued to fire, each shot echoing through the square like a pulse.

Ten shots.

Fifteen.

The tension was building, the anticipation mounting for Yuli who had been planning this moment for months. The twentieth shot rang out just as the jets neared the viewing stand; the twenty-first shot signaled a victorious finale.

The president was standing as was everyone in the crowd. He had a rare smile on his face, clapping along with the rest of the enthusiastic throng, basking in the adoration of the cheering masses. Yuli directed one of his drones into position so he could zoom in and capture the look on the president's face.

But then, something happened. Something that wasn't planned.

Yuli's sharp eyes saw it first. A flicker of something out of place.

As the fighter jets roared overhead, everyone else was too enthralled to notice. But Yuli's gaze was fixed on the president, watching his reaction and ultimately his approval.

The president's smile turned to confusion before he collapsed to the ground, his hand swatting at an invisible force.

Yuli's heart stopped as he realized what had happened.

He zoomed in closer, horrified to see blood pooling around the president's head, staining the pristine stone floor beneath him.

The president had been shot.

For a moment, no one in the viewing stand could comprehend what was happening. They stood staring at the president, frozen in shock as the crowd continued to cheer and clap oblivious to the events unfolding right before them.

Panic surged through Yuli's body like an icy wave, paralyzing him with terror. He wanted to scream for help, but his voice failed him. The world seemed to slow down, every sound fading into distant echoes as he struggled to make sense of the nightmare before him.

He raced down to the viewing stand. By the time he arrived, a medical team had gathered around the president. They worked furiously on him.

A deathly hush fell over the crowd as they realized something was horribly wrong. Panic gripped the generals as they began to bark orders to the troops, barely audible above the chaos. They frantically commanded their men to spread out, desperate to find the source of the shot that had shattered their peace.

Yuli realized that he should've stayed in the command center. He might've been able to use the cameras to help them search for the assailant. Although, the killer could be anywhere by now, blending into the dense crowd with ease.

The medical team worked on the president for several minutes before loading him into an ambulance and transporting him to a local hospital where he was pronounced dead two hours later.

Yuli couldn't believe it. The president was assassinated in the middle of the most important day of the year.

This was supposed to be his day, his moment of triumph. But instead, it had become a scene of unspeakable tragedy and loss. As he looked out at the chaos and devastation around him, he knew his show would never be remembered for its grandeur or artistry but would be forever tainted by this brutal act.

Yuli didn't go home that night. His hands shook as he went through the footage from the day's events. His cameras had captured every angle, and it didn't take him long to find the assailant.

A man in the group of one hundred loyal soldiers performing the twenty-one-gun-salute had turned his rifle towards the viewing stand and fired a single shot. No one saw it because everyone was looking up at the sky at the fighter jets.

As Yuli zoomed in on the blurry figure, his mind was full of questions. How could this have happened? How did no one notice this traitor among their ranks?

A sickening realization struck him. Something was off in the formation. He couldn't pinpoint what it was, but it looked different from when they had practiced it.

He counted the number of men. He couldn't believe what he was seeing. There were one hundred and one soldiers, not one hundred. The attacker had infiltrated the formation undetected, and now the entire nation was reeling from the consequences.

Who was this man? Was he Russian?

Whoever it was had just taken down the most powerful man in the world and changed history with a single bullet.

16

Six months later

After six months of blazing a trail of dead dictators, A-Rad and I had finally been given a much-needed break. With six successful kills under our belts, the initiative had exceeded everyone's expectations.

North Korea had become our base of operations—the last place anyone expected to find the ghosts responsible for taking out some of the world's most powerful men.

Surprisingly, I liked where we were. Momma-son's diner was starting to feel like home.

A-Rad and I never talked about our missions once they were over. They'd gone so well, we didn't want to jinx them. It's almost like we'd be testing fate or triggering bad luck if we discussed them.

That didn't stop me from constantly reflecting on them.

Our mission in Russia had been the most daring with Iran coming in a close second. A-Rad deserved the credit for killing the Russian president during a military parade, a feat few would have dared to attempt.

We weren't your average assassins. We had a purpose and drive that pushed us to take risks others would avoid.

Next was Venezuela, a country ruled by a tyrant who had been in charge for more than two decades. Despite his claims of holding free and fair elections, the reality was far from it. In the most recent election, polls showed that over seventy percent of voters chose his opponent. However, he changed the results on the voting machines and declared himself victorious.

With his iron grip on power, he became our target.

Pretending to be part of his security detail was easier than it should have been. His arrogance made him careless, and his blind trust in those around him led to his downfall. I still remember his look of realization as A-Rad pulled the trigger and ended his life with a single shot between the eyes.

Another tyrant down; another mission complete.

But we didn't stop there. The Cuban president was foolish enough to travel to Russia, seeking to strengthen ties and secure his own power. He thought he was safe in a luxury hotel suite with layers of security between him and the outside world.

But we were already inside, waiting in the shadows of his room. The poison we slipped into his dinner was undetectable, leaving no trace for the autopsy. By the time his aides found him, we were long gone, blending into the crowded streets, like two strangers simply passing through.

Laughingly, the Russians got the blame, since they were known for their history of poisoning enemies. No one could articulate a motive as to why they'd kill one of their allies, but the west didn't need one to propagate the theory.

It left a power vacuum in Cuba which was exactly what we wanted. We had to wait to see who rose to power. If he wasn't an improvement, we'd take him out as well.

We might have to kill a second Russian president. That remained to be seen. It'd be more difficult this time, since he was wrapped up in security tighter than a newborn in swaddling clothes.

The whole adventure was exhilarating in a twisted way. Each mission was a high-stakes game of cat and mouse where we were always one step ahead. The world was starting to notice the pattern, the series of mysterious deaths that were too perfectly timed to be coincidences.

According to Jamie, there'd been numerous articles written about it. We were oblivious. We didn't watch the news. A-Rad and I were content living in our own little bubble, our own fantasy world we escaped to. We only ventured out of the cocoon when necessary, long enough to kill a dictator, then we'd retreat back until duty called again.

In a way, A-Rad and I were the two most powerful people in the world at that time. Deciding who lived and died. The best part was that the world didn't know who was behind the killings.

Not yet, anyway.

Somehow, we had managed to avoid detection by staying off security cameras and covering our tracks. Along with a little bit of luck along the way. Jamie warned us not to get too cocky. If we thought we were invincible, that's when things would go wrong.

On this particular morning, we were discussing plans for a trip to Pyongyang. It felt weird choosing to take a vacation in a city with such bleak landscape, gray worn out concrete, and lifeless streets. But in some ways, it seemed like a fitting backdrop for the life A-Rad and I had been leading, which might be why we chose it.

Things had improved in the cities of North Korea, but it'd take a generation for the country to fully recover. We wanted to go there and do our part by spending some money to help the economy.

We weren't that far into our discussions when the call came.

The secure phone in our small apartment in Momma-son's basement rang loudly, causing A-Rad and I both to jump. It didn't matter how many times it happened, hearing that noise sent a rush of adrenaline through me.

It usually meant that Jamie had a mission for us, and I was far too aware that the next mission could potentially be our last. A-Rad was on the other side of the room. He looked up as I answered the call, his eyes narrowing when he heard the tension in Jamie's voice.

"Kaley," Jamie said before I could say hello. "We have a problem. Is A-Rad there?"

"He's right here," I said.

"Hello Nuna," A-Rad said. The North Korean word used when a male was addressing a senior female. It didn't exactly fit, since it was meant for an older sister, but A-Rad didn't particularly care about the strict meaning.

"A problem? You don't beat around the bush, do you?" he added. "The least you could do is say hi?"

"Annyonghaseyo, A-Rad," Alex chimed in with his own informal North Korean greeting. "Do you want to play golf with me today?"

"Sure, what time?" A-Rad replied with a perfectly straight face.

"Neither of you even play golf," Jamie quipped.

It's comforting that we could still banter, even though the words, "we have a problem" lingered over the room like a foul odor. My stomach clenched at Jamie's words, and it didn't ease up even when A-Rad and Alex attempted to lighten the mood.

Problems in our line of work usually meant one thing: someone was onto us.

"What kind of problem, Jamie?" I asked, keeping my voice steady.

"I sent something to your email. Did you see it?" she answered.

"No," I said, as I immediately clicked off the website for a hotel in Pyongyang and logged into our email. "But I'm doing it now."

I clicked on the attachment which was a link to an article from a British tabloid. The headline was bold and screamed at me:

ARE THESE TWO THE WORLD'S DEADLIEST ASSASSINS?

Beneath it was a photo of A-Rad and me, our mug shots taken when we were arrested in Norway for killing the crown prince. I remembered the moment all too well—the flash of the camera, the cold steel of the handcuffs around my wrists and the irons around my ankles.

We had escaped with Alex and Jamie's help, but the damage was done. Our cover was blown, and we could never work undercover with the CIA again.

"I'll give you a second to read it," Jamie said.

A-Rad moved a chair next to me and we read it together. The article was short on facts, but it laid out a compelling circumstantial case that tied us to the string of mysterious deaths of political leaders around the world.

According to the article, the man who shot the Russian president was about A-Rad's height. A man and a woman who matched our descriptions were spotted outside the hotel the night the Cuban president was poisoned. A man and a woman posed as security and killed the president of Venezuela who refused to cede power after he lost the election.

The article even praised our actions as vigilantism and as doing the world a service, which I read aloud in disbelief.

"Then why are you outing us!" I shouted angrily at the computer screen.

"I know, right," Jamie said.

"It doesn't matter why," Alex said. "What matters is that it's done and out there for everyone to see. This will go viral and major news outlets will pick up the story. Eventually, it may die down, but your face will always be associated with this."

"Which means we aren't safe anywhere," I said.

"That definitely complicates things," A-Rad said. "There might even be people in North Korea who can connect the dots."

"Ironically, that's our fault," I said. "When North Korea was a closed country, this kind of information never made it to the masses. Now, everyone is getting more access to the world and is more informed."

"The cost of freedom," Jamie said.

I muttered a groan under my breath, scanning the article a second time. It was all there, piece by piece, a puzzle that someone had taken the time to put together. The picture they painted was dangerously close to the truth.

"Let's talk about who might use this information to go after you," Jamie said.

"Norway," A-Rad said.

"I don't think so," Alex replied. "For obvious reasons. They don't want the information about the prince and his sex trafficking to get out. I don't even think they're looking for you anymore."

"I doubt Cuba or Venezuela are either," Jamie said. "Russia is a different story. I'm sure they'll take this information and start tracking you like dogs."

"Maybe not," A-Rad said. "Let's not get paranoid here."

"There's also a fairly good size reward out for you," Alex said.

I knew better than to hope for uncertainty in this business. This kind of exposure meant our days of operating in the shadows were over.

"I don't think we're being paranoid, A-Rad," I said. "With this kind of exposure, we'll be hunted, not just by governments, but by every mercenary and wannabe hero looking for a payday."

"So, what's the plan?" A-Rad asked, his voice steady but with an edge of concern. "I assume you have one, Jamie, since you called us."

Jamie posed a question out of the blue. "Do you want to stop what you're doing?"

I answered right away. "There are more people to kill on our list. I don't want to stop."

"Me either," A-Rad said. "We're doing too much good in the world to stop now. We'll just have to deal with it. We knew the risks going in."

"I agree," I said.

"Hold on guys. Don't speak so quickly," Alex said. "Maybe you two should get out while you still can. You could take the yacht to our island and hang out there indefinitely. I wouldn't think less of you if you did."

"Nah," A-Rad said, shrugging his shoulders. "I'd get bored after a week."

"I feel the same," I said. "I want to keep doing what we're doing. Like A-Rad said, it was already risky. It's not like it's going to get that much worse."

"I have a different idea," Jamie said. "But you may not like it."

"What?" A-Rad and I said the words in unison.

Jamie hesitated briefly, then said, " I want to send you both to India."

"India!" I exclaimed. "They don't have anybody on our list to kill."

"Not on a mission," Jamie said. "I've arranged for a top-notch plastic surgeon in Mumbai who can completely change your appearances."

"Are you talking about reconstructing our faces?" I asked, my mind racing with conflicting thoughts.

"You're right. I don't like the idea," I said.

My initial reaction was that undergoing such a drastic change was terrifying. What if I didn't recognize myself afterwards? I didn't want to completely lose my identity. It'd be weird looking at myself in a mirror.

"We need for the people in that picture to disappear, Kaley," Alex said. "Both of you. It's too dangerous if you don't do something different."

On the other hand, changing our appearance sounded like a good solution to our problem. We could travel freely again. We could walk around any city in the world without anyone recognizing us.

I exchanged a look with A-Rad. It was drastic, but what was the alternative? Staying the same could mean certain death.

"I think it'll be an improvement for A-Rad," Alex added, with humor clearly behind the words.

That did make me laugh, but it didn't change my mood.

"Very funny," A-Rad said. "Do I get any say in what I look like? Will the surgeon in India have pictures for me to choose from?"

"Probably," Jamie said. "You can ask him when you get there."

"I want to pick out your face," I said to him.

"Why? Don't I get a say?" he retorted, roughly.

"I'm the one who has to look at you."

"Then I get to pick out what you look like."

"That's not happening."

We both had wide smiles on our faces, so we knew each other was kidding.

"How soon do you want us there?" I asked, already calculating the logistics in my head.

"As soon as possible," Jamie said. "Take the yacht, though. It's too dangerous to fly."

I took a deep breath. Despite the attempts to lighten the mood, it felt like I'd been punched in the gut. I wanted to protest, to come up with another plan, but my mind was blank.

We were out of options. Up to now, our mission had been clear-cut and our targets easy to identify. But now, we were the targets, and the world was closing in.

"Okay," I finally said. "We'll do it."

But as soon as the words left my mouth, doubt crept in. Was this really our best option?

I voiced my concerns. "What if we get the surgery and then new pictures surface of us with our new identities? It's nearly impossible to pull these things off without being seen. Isn't it just a matter of time until new pictures of us with the new look are out there and we're having this same conversation again?"

"We'll cross that bridge when we come to it," Jamie said. "For now, let's take it one step at a time. You get the surgery and we're back in business."

Her reassurances did little to ease my worries. A-Rad's stoic expression mirrored my own inner turmoil.

"All right," I said, reluctantly. I still didn't like it, but it didn't seem like we had any other choice.

"I'll send you the address," Jamie said.

As the call ended, I looked over at A-Rad. His face was impassive, but I knew him well enough to see the tension in his eyes.

"Plastic surgery," I said, my voice softer now. "What do you think?"

He sighed, running a hand through his hair. "You're right, it's a gamble. Our cover could easily get blown up again. But it's the only play we've got."

"Oh well. Look how many kills we got under our belt before our cover was blown the first time. We figured it'd happen after the first one. Maybe it won't happen for a while."

Deep down, I knew it was just wishful thinking. The reality was that every move we made now came with a high-stakes gamble, and there was no telling when our luck would run out for good.

Jamie always said that luck was when opportunity met skill. But luck was a fickle thing. It could turn on us in an instant, leaving us exposed and vulnerable. And in our line of work, vulnerability was a death sentence.

"Will you still love me even if I change my appearance?" I asked, with a forced smile on my face.

"I'll get used to it," he said, nervously, not matching my lame attempt at humor.

"Do you want me to get a boob job while I'm at it?" I asked.

This time he laughed. "No. I don't want you to get a boob job. But I have always wished my nose was smaller."

"I love your nose. It matches your head."

I pushed my cheeks up on both sides.

"I could use a face lift," I said. "I've seen a wrinkle or two in the mirror lately."

A-Rad stood and walked over to me and leaned over me, kissing me hard.

"Nothing will change between us," he said, after sending my heart spinning. He still had that effect on me.

"We're in this together. For better or for worse. Like Alex said, maybe I'll look better afterwards."

"You'll always be the same A-Rad to me."

"And you will always be Kaley to me."

The moment passed and A-Rad abruptly stood and began packing.

I sat frozen in the chair, contemplating this turn of events that had rocked my world. Plastic surgery felt so final. Once I changed my looks, I'd never be able to go back. It's like I was losing a part of myself.

What would it be like to look in the mirror and see a different person staring back at me? Alex had already erased any evidence that we ever existed. Our birth certificates, social security numbers, even high school yearbook pictures were all wiped from existence on the internet.

Now, the identities we'd worn like armor would be a thing of the past.

In a few days, I'd be someone completely different.

But A-Rad was right. I was still Kaley, and I still had one mission left: to survive.

17

India

Somewhere between South Korea and India, it felt like we crossed an invisible line, one we could never come back from—a proverbial line in the sand.

We sailed there on the yacht, and the weather was perfect. We couldn't have asked for more idyllic conditions, but a heaviness hung over us like a shadow, as if we were on our way to serve out a lifetime sentence of hard labor in an underground coal mine.

"I think we're making too big a deal out of it," A-Rad said at one point, trying to cheer me up. "We're still going to be the same people inside. What we look like on the outside shouldn't matter."

"I know. It's going to be good once it's done. We'll be free to move around again. We can even fly commercial if we need to."

"I've gotten used to the private planes and this yacht," he said, with a slight chuckle.

"I'm just saying that things will be different."

"Different but better."

"I hope so."

It took two weeks to reach India, and by the time we passed Sri Lanka and finished going around the tip of India, I had come to terms with what was about to happen. Soon, the faces we'd worn like masks, the identities given to us by God and that defined us as recognizable human beings, would be gone forever.

I kept staring at A-Rad, memorizing every detail of his face as if I might somehow forget it. He eventually caught me doing it.

"Quit staring at me," he said. "You're weirding me out."

"I can't help it. I want to remember everything about you. We don't have any pictures of each other. All I have are my memories."

CIA operatives avoided pictures like they avoided a run-in with a cobra. We went to extraordinary lengths to keep our faces off of cameras and especially off the internet.

In a lame attempt to lighten my mood, A-Rad started telling plastic surgery jokes, claiming he made them up himself. I suspected he looked them up online but didn't contradict him.

"Did you hear about the husband who gave his wife ten thousand dollars for plastic surgery?" he asked one day.

"No," I replied.

"He decided he wanted his money back but couldn't find her."

"That's funny," I said, flashing him a fake smile.

Time would pass between jokes. He'd spring them on me at different times. Maybe when he sensed I was at a low point.

"Do you know what the best thing about plastic surgery is?" he said on a different day.

"What?"

"You can pick your nose."

I had to admit that joke was a little funnier. One night when we were getting ready for bed, he said, "What do you call a model who has plastic surgery?"

"I don't know, but I have a feeling you're going to tell me."

"A remodel. Get it?"

I chuckled, letting him know I understood the play on words.

We made love that night and every night of the trip. Almost as if I felt like these would be the last times. I didn't know how I'd feel the first time I made love to him after the surgery.

Would it feel like cheating?

One morning at breakfast, A-Rad popped another joke.

"What did the plastic surgery support group leader say?" he said, with a broad smile on his face.

I humored him because it seemed so important to him. To me, changing our faces was no laughing matter.

"What did the plastic surgery support group leader say?" I replied.

"I see a lot of new faces here today."

I gave him an obligatory laugh and the jokes started coming more frequently. The last one was the funniest. The day before we were to arrive in Mumbai when the tension for me was the highest.

I wasn't in the mood. All I wanted to do was to turn back and return to North Korea. To Momma-son's diner. Even though I knew deep down this was the best thing for us, I couldn't shake the feeling that our lives were about to change forever.

A-Rad must've sensed my struggles, even though I bit my lip and kept the inner turmoil hidden as much as I could.

He wore a sly mischievous grin on his face as he prepared to tell me his joke. He looked so cute. I wanted to freeze that moment and lock it into my memory.

"People used to frown at plastic surgery and Botox," A-Rad said, slowly for effect. "Now, they don't even raise an eyebrow."

I burst out laughing. I wasn't even sure where that desire to laugh came from.

Then I started giggling. I snorted, making me laugh even harder. A-Rad started laughing. It was contagious and made me laugh that much harder. Within seconds, I had tears in my eyes and we were practically rolling on the floor.

It's exactly what I needed. I felt the tension leave my shoulders and the pit in my stomach disappear. Things were going to be okay. As long as we were together, that's the only thing that mattered. We were resilient. We'd always found a way to make the best of a bad situation. In this instance, the advantages far outweighed the disadvantages. At least that's what I kept telling myself.

The next day, we dropped anchor in the bay and rode our small craft over to the marina.

Jamie had arranged everything. A car was waiting for us. As we drove towards our destination and the start of our unknown future, the doubts started to creep back in.

This is really going to happen.

I kept staring at A-Rad again, making him uncomfortable, but I didn't care. His face, as familiar to me as my own, would soon be altered beyond recognition. I wanted to reach out and keep touching his face, to reassure myself that he would still be the A-Rad I knew and loved.

Would things change between us? I couldn't stand the thought.

Would he like the new me?

I didn't want things to change. I liked who we were together.

But Alex's words echoed in my head: "We need those people in that picture to disappear."

Disappear.

The word lingered, almost haunting me. I had always been good at disappearing, slipping into the shadows, blending in with the crowd. It's a skill that served me well as an operative.

But this was different. This was erasing the very essence of who I was and replacing it with something new, something foreign.

The driver took us to a secluded villa on the outskirts of Mumbai. The villa was luxurious, with sprawling gardens and a pool that sparkled under the hot sun. I couldn't appreciate any of it.

It felt more like a prison.

From the outside, you couldn't tell it was a medical clinic.

Was this even legal? It almost seemed barbaric. Like something out of a Frankenstein novel.

Dr. Bhattacharya, the surgeon Jamie had arranged for us, was one of the best in the world. I had no idea how much she was paying him, but I imagined it was a lot. He was known for his skill and discretion, the kind of man who worked miracles in secret and never spoke a word about it.

When we arrived, he welcomed us with a calm demeanor and a heavy accent. A small, wiry looking man with tiny glasses that matched his appearance perfectly.

"I am pleased to meet you," he said along with some other initial pleasantries.

"I understand what you're asking for, and I want to make sure you understand what this means. This isn't just a physical change. It's a transformation. Once we begin, there's no going back."

"We understand," A-Rad said, his voice steady.

I nodded in agreement, though my heart raced. I didn't intend to say much. I'd let A-Rad take the lead.

Dr. Bhattacharya led us to a small consultation room that used to be a bedroom. There he showed us a series of digital renderings.

"These are potential new faces for you," he explained, scrolling through the images on a large television screen mounted on the wall. "You can choose the one you prefer, or we can make adjustments to suit your needs."

The images were surreal—a collection of faces both familiar and strange. Based on our own features but altered in subtle ways. Different noses, different eyes, different jawlines. Eyebrows could be adjusted in any number of ways by the click of the mouse.

They were us, but not us.

I carefully studied each face, trying to imagine myself with it. I wished I could pull them off the screen and try them on like a mask.

"This one," I finally said, pointing to a face with softer features, a smaller nose, slightly fuller lips, and higher cheekbones. I'd always had extremely thin lips and had wished they were fuller.

Now was my chance.

The woman I chose was more attractive than me. She wasn't the most gorgeous option. Jamie had taught me the art of blending in. It helped in undercover work to be unremarkable. Like me, she had said.

I wasn't offended. I was pretty in my own way, but I wouldn't be the first person men noticed in a bar. Which was fine by me.

Of course, Jamie was the most beautiful woman alive in my book. One of the images on the screen matched her beauty. This was my chance if I wanted to take it.

I resisted the urge. I could hear the AJAX team making fun of me. I chose a more modest looking girl. It was a better version of myself, and it felt right. "I'll definitely take this one."

A-Rad seemed to agree.

I liked his choice as well but mostly kept quiet letting him choose it. I didn't want him to be angry at me later if he didn't like it. The man on the screen had a more rugged look with a stronger jaw and a different hairline.

It was close enough to A-Rad's current face that he wouldn't be unrecognizable to me, but different enough that no one would ever connect him to the man he was now.

"Very good choices," Dr. Bhattacharya said, making notes. "The surgeries will take several hours, and the recovery process will be intense. But I assure you, when it's done, you'll be completely new people. No one will recognize you."

The day of the surgery arrived quickly—too quickly. The next morning, actually. There was no time to second-guess our decision, no time to back out. We were fully committed now.

They prepared us for the operations in separate rooms, though I wished we could have been together. The last thing I wanted to see before I went under was A-Rad's face—the face I knew so well, the one that would soon be gone.

But they kept us apart, and the last thing I remembered before the anesthesia took hold was the sterile smell of the operating room and the bright lights above me.

I woke up in a haze, drifting in and out of consciousness, my mind swimming in a fog of drugs and pain. There were moments when I could hear voices, distant and muffled, and what felt like the sharp sting of needles pricking my face.

It all blended together and felt like a nightmare I couldn't wake up from.

When I finally came to, I was in a dimly lit room with the curtains drawn. My face was wrapped in bandages, tight and uncomfortable. I could barely see through small slits in the bandages. Couldn't move, couldn't speak without sending an excruciating pain through my body.

Panic surged through me, but I forced myself to stay calm. This was part of the process, the nurse assured me. I had to trust her.

The days that followed were filled with discomfort and agony unlike anything I'd ever experienced before. The bandages were oppressive, suffocating, and I longed to have them removed.

But Dr. Bhattacharya was adamant, "You must give it time to heal properly," he said. "The bandages will come off when the time is right."

I couldn't see A-Rad, but I could hear him in the room next to mine. He was going through the same thing and knowing that we were in this together was the only thing that kept me sane.

Eventually, we were able to sit with each other. "Like two mummies in a horror movie," A-Rad quipped.

After ten days of torture, the bandages were ready to come off. I was both eager and terrified.

What if I didn't like what I saw?

18

Dr. Bhattacharya started with me and worked slowly, carefully unwrapping the layers of gauze around my head and face. I could feel the cool air on my skin, which felt good to me. The feeling of freedom stoked the excitement pulsing through my veins.

When the last of the bandages were removed, he stepped back with his arms crossed to admire his work. I watched carefully for a frown or grimace that never came. He seemed satisfied.

He handed me a mirror.

"Take your time," he said gently. "It may be a shock at first."

I hesitated, reminded myself to breathe before slowly lifting the mirror to see my reflection.

I gasped, even though I didn't mean to.

The person staring back at me was a stranger.

I don't hate it, was my first reaction.

I'm pretty, was my second thought.

I don't think I'd ever had that thought when I looked in a mirror before. My features were softer, more refined, but it was still me—just different. I couldn't explain it if someone forced me to try.

The eyes were the same, but the nose was smaller, the lips were fuller, just like the lady I'd seen on the screen when we first arrived at the clinic. I could be her twin. This doctor was amazing.

She looked strangely like me. It felt like I was looking at an alternate version of myself, one that had been crafted with careful precision.

An improved version. Sculpted by a master artist.

I reached up and touched my face, feeling the unfamiliar contours. It was strange, but it wasn't horrifying. It was just ... different. Not as bad as I expected.

I could live with this.

A-Rad had no reaction, although he couldn't really see me. Not until his bandages were off.

I turned to Dr. Bhattacharya, who was watching me closely. "It's ... it's good," I said, my voice shaky. "It's better than I expected. Thank you."

He grinned, a small, but satisfied smile.

"You look beautiful my dear." he said. "I'm confident you'll be even happier with the final results after the swelling comes down. Once the stitches are out, we'll color your hair and complete the transformation."

I nodded, still in shock as I stared at my reflection, trying to come to terms with the fact that this was really me.

A-Rad was next.

I put down the mirror and watched nervously as they removed his bandages, my heart in the back of my throat. When they finally handed him a mirror, he gazed at it for a long time, devoid of emotion.

Then he looked up at me, and a slow smile spread across his new face.

"You look beautiful, my love," he said after he studied me closely. I smiled, although it felt weird to do so. My face was tight, and it felt like it'd crack in several places if I smiled too big.

"I don't like mine," A-Rad said, looking directly at the doctor. "Can you change it back to how I looked before?"

Even Dr. Bhattacharya, usually serious, cracked a smile.

"It's different," A-Rad admitted, "but I think I can get used to it."

"I like it, too," I chimed in.

I really did. I stood from my hospital bed and walked over to him and extended my hand. "Hello, my name is Natasha, what's yours?"

"Sorry to disappoint, Natasha," A-Rad joked back. "But I'm already taken. Has anyone seen my wife?"

He looked around the room, pretending to be searching for me.

We all shared a good laugh, but it hurt me to do so, and I let out a cry of pain.

"Perhaps you should lie back down," the doctor said. The nurse led me back to my bed.

The room was freezing cold, but my heart was warm. A-Rad's voice and dry humor were comforting. I could see my A-Rad behind the man across the room who was now telling his plastic surgery jokes to the doctor.

The next few days were spent recovering and adjusting to our new appearances. It was a strange feeling at first, almost like wearing someone else's skin. Every time I caught a glimpse of myself in the mirror it was jarring, but I was slowly coming to terms with it.

A-Rad was going through the same thing. He would stand and stare at his reflection, tracing his fingers over his new features as if trying to commit them to memory. But there was also a lightness about him, a sense of relief that we had made it through this ordeal.

We decided to dye my hair a sandy blond and A-Rad went with a salt and pepper look. It was a good choice because it made him look older and less recognizable.

I didn't think anyone would be able to connect us to our old identities. In some ways, I was even starting to leave that part of my life behind and focus on our new path forward.

Our new passports arrived in the mail with our updated pictures and new names. We'd be leaving the villa soon and could get back to work.

One evening, A-Rad and I sat by the pool watching the sunset. The heat had dissipated, and the air was filled with the sweet scent of honeysuckles. The moment was peaceful, calm amidst all the chaos we had endured over the past few weeks and months.

"You know," A-Rad broke the silence, "I think this might be the best thing we've ever done."

I looked at him, his new face becoming more familiar with each passing day. "Yeah," I agreed, "I think you're right."

We were different now, changed in ways that we were still trying to understand. We even decided to call each other by our new names from now on, so it'd become second nature to us, and so we wouldn't slip up in the field.

It felt like Kaley and A-Rad were dead and we were given a new life, to start over. I was excited about the new beginnings. Our future was bright.

We might even live long enough to see it.

* * *

Iran

Jeric Beri sat at his desk in a cramped office in Tehran, where he had been working for years. As part of his morning ritual, he had already finished two cups of Sharbat and was now on his third, which he insisted on brewing himself. Being quite the tea connoisseur, Jeric enjoyed discussing and trying various types.

Today's choice was a distilled Thyme Sharbat, but he liked to mix it up with peppermint, sour orange, rosewater, distilled furnitory, or occasionally dog-rose and pussy willow, although those were not his favorites.

As he scrolled through the dense intelligence briefing on his desk, as he did as the first priority each day, something caught his eye. An article from a British tabloid. But it wasn't the sensational headline or the juicy gossip that drew him in.

It was a photograph. The image was crystal clear and the faces instantly recognizable to him. His heart rate spiked, and he could feel his blood pressure rising as he read on.

The picture showed a man and a woman, who he had encountered in Iran not that long ago. According to the article, they had been arrested in Norway for killing the crown prince. He vaguely remembered hearing about this story but hadn't paid much attention to it at the time.

They had escaped and were on the run. On a killing spree unmatched in human history.

Now that he saw their faces once again, he remembered them clearly and things were starting to make sense to him. They had arrived at the airport in Tehran, and he had personally greeted them with open arms.

She introduced herself as Dr. Mina Volk, an expert on nuclear energy sent by INWA to inspect the facilities. She had all the necessary credentials and spoke the lingo fluently, exuding a quiet confidence that made him trust her.

The woman had mentioned Dr. Kunkel, a German engineer working on Iran's nuclear program. She said she'd had a liaison with the doctor in Germany. It seemed strange at the time causing alarm bells to go off in his head. She requested a private meeting with Kunkel, which made him even more uneasy, but he had arranged it.

Kunkel didn't remember the woman but didn't seem as concerned as Jeric had been and agreed to meet the woman. When Kunkel was found dead in Dr. Volk's hotel room, Jeric immediately suspected foul play. But the coroner's report stated that Kunkel died of natural causes and found no evidence to suggest otherwise, so he let it go.

But now, looking at that photo, all his old suspicions came flooding back. They weren't suspicions anymore. The woman killed Kunkel. No doubt about it. He didn't care what the coroner said. She somehow made it look like natural causes.

The explosion at the nuclear facility three weeks later, which had obliterated years of work, made it all fit together too neatly.

He'd been played, and he knew it.

The woman must've gotten the location of the secret nuclear bomb making facility from Kunkel's phone.

"The fool," Jeric said out loud. "Taken in by the oldest trick in the book. The wiles of a woman."

His hand shook slightly as he logged into his computer. He needed more proof. With a few clicks, he pulled up the INWA website and typed in Dr. Mina Volk's name.

Nothing came up. Not a single result. Jeric tried different variations but got the same empty search results. There was no record of Dr. Mina Volk.

A lump formed in Jeric's throat as he scrolled through the list of staff members. Her name was noticeably absent, and her photo, one he distinctly remembered seeing before, was gone as well.

He had a photographic memory, one that had never failed him. He knew what he had seen, and now it was missing from the website's records.

He picked up the phone and dialed the INWA headquarters in Vienna. After being transferred multiple times, a professional voice answered.

"How may I assist you at the International Nuclear Watchdog Agency?"

Jeric attempted to sound calm. "I'm trying to reach Dr. Mina Volk. She conducted an inspection in Tehran a few months ago. Can you connect me with her?"

There was a pause that felt longer than necessary. "I apologize, sir, but we have no record of anyone by that name."

Jeric's grip tightened on the receiver. "Are you certain? She's a nuclear energy expert."

"I am positive, sir. We do not have a Dr. Mina Volk on our staff."

The receiver slammed down before Jeric could stop himself. Anger and frustration flooded through him. They had deceived him, entering and leaving Tehran without his knowledge, and he had been completely unaware.

He felt a sense of dread as he realized the chaos left behind by the couple could potentially lead back to him. It was his responsibility to vet the inspectors and he had failed.

Jeric didn't know what to do with this information. He read the article again, searching for more details. According to the report, the couple were responsible for multiple assassinations targeting world leaders, including allies of Iran.

They were cunning and still at large, meaning they would continue killing until stopped. Jeric had to take action. He needed someone who could track them down without asking questions and eliminate the threat before it connected back to him.

His hand hovered over his phone, fingers hesitating for only a second before dialing a number he knew by heart. It rang twice before a gruff voice answered on the other end.

"It's me," he said without preamble. "I've got a job for you."

The voice on the other end chuckled in a diabolical tone, a sound that always sent a chill down Jeric's spine. "I'm listening."

Jeric took a deep breath, steeling himself. "I need you to find two people. I'm sending you their images. I want them dead. A million dollars each if you succeed. Half now and half when the job is done."

He knew this man could be trusted to finish the job without question. He'd never let him down before.

"Who are they?" the killer said in a more sinister tone.

"Why does it matter?" Jeric snapped. "They're a threat. That's all you need to know."

There was a pause, then the voice responded, "Understood. Send me the details."

Jeric hung up and attempted to steady his trembling hands as he transferred the images from the tabloid onto his phone. Once completed, he attached them to a message and sent it to the number he had just called. As he waited for the message to deliver, Jeric leaned back in his chair and stared at the screen in front of him

The wheels were in motion now, and he knew the kind of man he had just hired. The assassin was one of the best—efficient, discreet, and ruthlessly effective. If anyone could find these two and make them disappear permanently, it was him.

But as Jeric sat in his office, the tension in his chest refused to ease. He had always been careful, methodical, never taking unnecessary risks. Yet here he was, gambling everything on a last-ditch effort to clean up a mess he hadn't even realized he'd made.

For the first time in a long time, Jeric felt a sliver of fear. Not just for what he had done, but for what might happen if this plan failed. More importantly, what would happen to him if his bosses ever found out he was responsible for the destruction of the Iranian nuclear weapon's program.

The woman in the photograph had already proven herself to be dangerous. She couldn't be underestimated. If she could kill the Russian president, she could kill anyone. Including him. He had no doubt that if she realized he was coming after her, she wouldn't hesitate to strike back.

But Jeric pushed the fear aside. He had no choice. He couldn't afford to let them live. His only hope now was that the assassin would be quicker, smarter, and deadlier than his targets.

All he could do now was wait.

19

CIA headquarters
Langley, Virginia

Jamie adjusted the belt around her waist for the third time in the reflection of the tinted window. Since she had twins, her stomach pooched more than in the past and she still wasn't used to it.

Most people would consider her fit, but there was a time when she was in peak physical condition. At one point, she was in such good shape that she won a gold medal at the Winter Olympics.

Those days were long gone and she was fine with it. The cost of her figure was her two babies, and she wouldn't trade any level of vanity for them.

The soft morning light filtered through the glass of the original headquarters building of the CIA, casting a somber glow over the room. Jamie could see Alex in the corner of the room, his hands in his pockets, his jaw set in a hard line.

He always looked stoic at times like this, but she knew better. Beneath that tough exterior was a man who felt every loss deeply, and today was no exception.

The CIA headquarters was quieter than usual, the normal hum of activity stilled by the weight of the occasion. Today, they were gathered to honor Sean O'Connell, a fellow operative and good friend, who had been killed in the line of duty.

The Memorial Wall ceremony was something every agent hoped to never attend, especially not for someone they considered family.

Jamie walked over to stand by Alex, slipping her hand into his. He glanced down at her, his eyes softening slightly as their fingers intertwined. They didn't need words; the silence between them was filled with shared grief and understanding.

As they made their way to the courtyard where the ceremony was to be held, Jamie caught sight of the Memorial Wall—a beautiful white marble slab etched with stars, each one representing a life lost in service.

The sight of it always sent a chill down her spine. There were too many stars already, and now they were adding one more.

The acting director stood at the podium, his voice steady as he spoke of Sean's bravery, his dedication, and his ultimate sacrifice. Jamie felt a lump in her throat as she listened, tears welling up which she fought to contain.

Sean had been one of the best—clever, resourceful, and brave, always willing to go the extra mile. They had worked together on several missions in her early days, and she could still hear his contagious laugh and see the mischievous glint in his eyes whenever he had a new idea.

Now, all that remained were those memories. A star in his honor was carved on the white marble wall and another would be added to the book of honor sitting in a glass case in front of the wall.

Sean's actual name wouldn't be in the book. The identities of the unknown stars were kept secret, because of the delicate role they played as spies.

It reminded Jamie of the thankless nature of their job. Even in death, they couldn't receive proper recognition for their sacrifices. They served the country on the front lines of wars that few people knew about or would understand.

Sean deserved to be honored by a nation, but ultimately, the only people who would remember him were his wife and son, and a few people who worked with him.

It confirmed to Jamie that she'd done the right thing retiring when she had her twins. As much as she had been willing to sacrifice her life for her country, she couldn't risk the kids growing up without a mother.

That's a sacrifice she wasn't willing to make.

When the director finished his remarks, they returned inside and stood in front of the wall. He unveiled the newly added star and tears once again threatened to spill over. She could feel the collective sorrow of everyone gathered; a heavy, suffocating presence that pressed down on everyone in the room.

After the ceremony, they stayed for a while, exchanging quiet words with others who had known Sean. Jamie hugged his widow even though they had never met.

The CIA was a competitive agency, but in times like this, there was a strong sense of camaraderie and unity of purpose. A bittersweet gathering—comfort found in being with people who understood the loss. It also reminded the operatives in the room of their own mortality once again in a cruel way.

Jamie and Alex eventually made their way to the car. The drive home was quiet at first, the two of them lost in their own thoughts. It wasn't until they were halfway home that Jamie finally broke the silence.

"You know, I'm surprised we aren't on that wall," she said.

"We came close," Alex agreed with a nod. "More times than we'd like to admit."

As soon as the words escaped her mouth, she could hear Curly yelling in her head. He was her trainer with the CIA. A hard nosed son-of-a-gun who also trained Alex. He wouldn't tolerate such negative thoughts and would reprimand her harshly for voicing them if he were there to hear them.

Curly was gone now, but always in her head. He died from a heart attack while on a mission to Costa Rica. He didn't have a star on the wall since he died of natural causes, although Jamie thought he deserved one. The rigors of the mission might've been what killed him.

Regardless, Curly was huge on positive thinking. He often said that negative thoughts could get you killed and had no place in the CIA.

"I don't want to do this again," Jamie said, her voice barely above a whisper.

Alex glanced over at her, frowning slightly. "Do what again?"

"I don't want to attend another ceremony like that," Jamie clarified. "Especially not for Kaley and A-Rad."

She saw Alex's grip tighten on the steering wheel.

The mention of their friends brought a fresh wave of anxiety for both of them. Kaley and A-Rad had cheated death several times already and were living on borrowed time.

"I don't think I could stand it," Jamie said softly, reaching over to place a hand on Alex's arm. "We're the ones sending them into these dangerous situations. It's only a matter of time until—"

She caught herself and stopped mid-sentence. She shouldn't allow her mind to go there, even though it already had.

"It's what they signed up for," Alex said. "They know the risks."

He was trying to sound convincing, but his words lacked conviction.

"That's because they had no choice," Jamie argued. "After what happened in Norway, which wasn't their fault, they had to go on the run. The entire world was looking for them. Even the CIA wanted them dead. But things are different now. With their new identities, they can never be found as long as they don't take on any more missions."

"I tried to talk them out of it. You heard me. It's their decision. They're adamant. And I know you well enough to say that you would make the same decision if it weren't for the kids. So would I. We're wired differently than most people."

She shook her head. "I don't know. I'm not as foolish as I used to be."

"I understand what you're saying," Alex said. "I've been thinking about it as well. We need to be more careful with them. We can't stop what they're doing. They're too good. They're doing such amazing things that are changing the world. But there's got to be a way to minimize the risk. I just can't think of one. Not yet, anyway."

Jamie bit her lip, considering his words.

"They are good at what they do, Alex. They're the best of the best. But we can't just hope they'll be okay. We need to be proactive. If they won't think logically, we'll have to do it for them."

His gaze remained fixed on the road ahead. "About that. I was thinking— "

"How many times have I told you not to think without consulting with me first?" Jamie teased, her smile as broad as possible so he'd know she was kidding.

This had always been their pattern when they discussed difficult topics. One of them introduced humor to release the tension before it became intolerable.

Alex pursed his lips in a mock expression that said, "very funny."

"As I was saying," he continued. "I was thinking that I could talk to Colonel and see if there's anything we can do to protect them. Maybe change their assignments, keep them off the front lines for a while. Take away some of the risk."

"Be careful?" I said incredulously. "I drilled 'don't be careful' into Kaley until I was blue in the face. Like Curly drilled that into me. I can't very well go back and say forget what I said and be careful now."

"I know. Careful will get you killed."

Jamie rubbed her face roughly.

"It's not just about being careful, it's about being smart," she said. "You and I both know that Kaley and A-Rad aren't the kind to sit back and play it safe. They'll fight us every step of the way if we try to pull them from the action. We'll have to be more subtle. They depend on us. They can't act unless we tell them to."

"They'll be mad if we put them on the shelf," Alex said.

"I'd rather have them ticked off at us and safe, than the alternative."

"We can't. The next target is Russia. We have to consider that. Kuzman is dead, but his replacement is worse. We need to send them on that mission, sooner rather than later."

"I know."

"Maybe we could buy a cruise missile and launch it into the Russian presidential palace," Alex said, half-heartedly. "We have the money. All we need is a missile launcher."

"That's all."

"I'm just saying."

"Good idea, Alex. Let's start world war three," she said in her most sarcastic tone.

A huge grin came on his face, which seemed out of place considering the topic. It was obviously his turn to bring down the tension.

"Remember when Russia had those mobile missile launchers pointed at America and you turned them around? When they went off, they hit Moscow instead." He chuckled as he said it. "We could do something like that."

"It's not a bad idea."

"I did have another idea. Do you want to hear it?" Alex asked excitedly, with his eyes lit up like lights on a Christmas tree.

He told her the idea before she could answer.

"I'm going to start recording videos and posting them on the internet. Videos of A-Rad and Kaley making all kinds of threats. Taking credit for all their kills. And sending dire warnings to the dictators of the world."

"How are you going to do that? Are you forgetting that A-Rad and Kaley had their faces altered?"

"I'm going to use their old images and voices."

"How?"

"Are you forgetting about that new AI software I created? I can do amazing things with it. I can take previous images of them and their voices, enter them into my software and it'll create realistic videos. I've been recording all of our recent conversations. It'll look like it's them talking. No one will ever be able to tell the difference. I'm going to post them on the internet for everyone to see. I'll call it 'The Fugitives.'"

"Do you really want to draw that much attention to them?"

"That's the beauty of it. It's not about them specifically. I want everyone in the world to be looking for Kaley and A-Rad. I want a full out manhunt like the world has never seen before. A-Rad and Kaley don't exist anymore. They'll be chasing ghosts. Our enemies will waste resources searching for two people who don't exist."

Jamie smiled faintly, her heart warming to his idea. "You truly are brilliant, Alex."

"And you said I shouldn't think without your permission! See what we'd miss out on if I listened to you."

"I'll make an exception this time," she quipped. "But don't get used to it."

"I won't."

"I do think that's a great idea. Every time there's a kill, they'll think the old A-Rad and Kaley did it."

"Exactly."

A smile tugged at the corner of his mouth. Jamie could see the wheels spinning in his computer-like mind. It really was a clever tactic, but only if they could keep the new Kaley and A-Rad free from suspicion. If their new identities were linked to another murder, it wouldn't take long for someone to connect the dots and realize they had changed their appearances.

They could keep going under the knife, but when Jamie talked to A-Rad and Kaley the day before, they both insisted they weren't doing the plastic surgery again. The process was too painful.

They drove in silence for a while before Jamie spoke again, her tone more serious. "You're right, Alex."

"Wow!" he exclaimed. "I can feel my head getting bigger. First you give me permission to think, now you're saying I'm right about something."

"If your head gets any bigger, your right ear will be in a different time zone from your left," she quipped.

He made a silly face at her and twisted his lips playfully.

"Tell me what I'm right about, because I don't know what it could possibly be," he said in a mocking tone.

"You are right that we have to find a way to keep A-Rad and Kaley safe."

"I plan on speaking to Colonel and seeing if he has any suggestions. He's currently working on the plan for Russia. Maybe there's a way we can involve them without constantly putting them in harm's way. The idea of launching missiles might be worth exploring."

"That's a good idea."

"I'm not sure how to handle all these compliments you keep giving me."

"Okay, okay. I'll stop," Jamie conceded.

Instantly, she noticed the worry return to Alex's face. It was something that would not easily go away. They were well aware of the dangers A-Rad and Kaley faced since they'd been in the field for years. The recent death of their colleague Sean and his memorial service only reinforced what they already knew but had been out of their minds for a while.

As they pulled up to their home, Jamie turned towards Alex with a softer expression. "All kidding aside, I know you care about A-Rad and Kaley as much as I do. You'll figure something out, Alex. You always do."

He looked at her with intensity, but the love and trust they shared over the years was behind his gaze. "Yeah, we will."

Alex squeezed her hand, silently conveying his own promise.

They didn't have a solution yet—but it was a start. And sometimes, that's all they could hope for.

20

Russia

Yuli Belov stood on the control stand, his gaze fixed on Red Square below. The ancient cobblestones glistened in the fading sunlight, and the majestic spires of Saint Basil's Cathedral were almost eye level to him from his high perch.

Normally teeming with the daily activity of citizens living their lives, the square was now occupied by rows of uniformed military personnel standing tall and proud, while citizens waved Russian flags in unison. The atmosphere was charged with anticipation, for today was a momentous day in Russian history—a day that Yuli had meticulously orchestrated.

The newly elected president of Russia, whose ascent to power had been swift and unpredictable, was about to be sworn in. Yuli felt a surge of pride. Everything was perfect, exactly as he had planned it.

The massive stage in the center of the square was flanked by enormous screens displaying the state emblem, while the grandiose facade of the GUM department store served as a magnificent backdrop, illuminated by carefully placed lights.

The main stand was packed with dignitaries, both from home and abroad. In the distance, Yuli could make out the shapes of news crews, their cameras pointed towards the stage like unblinking eyes.

Yuli's hand rested on the control pad that monitored his drones. Over a dozen of them hovered silently above, blending into the sky with their sleek metallic bodies. Each one was equipped with high-definition cameras, capturing every moment from multiple angles to ensure nothing was missed.

These drones were Yuli's pride and joy, a testament to his ingenuity and foresight. They weren't just machines; they were an extension of his will, allowing him to control and shape the narrative.

The earpiece in his ear crackled with updates from his team. "All drones are in position. Cameras are live. Audio levels are optimal."

The voice was calm and professional, as he expected. Yuli had personally chosen each member of his team, making sure they were the best of the best.

There could be no errors today. The disaster at the military parade was a distant memory but still a reminder that something could still go wrong.

After losing one leader, Russia couldn't afford to lose another, and security preparations were unprecedented. Every precaution had been taken to avoid a repeat of the disaster that had shaken the nation to its core.

Yuli scanned through the feeds on his control pad, switching between views from different drones. The images were stunning as the president's motorcade slowly made its way through cheering crowds, banners waving in the wind, soldiers standing at attention.

Everything was going according to plan. As the president's armored limousine pulled up to a position beside the stage, Yuli couldn't help but smile slightly in satisfaction.

The man who emerged from the vehicle was the epitome of power and authority. Towering and muscular, the newly appointed president of Russia exuded confidence with every calculated step he took. Yuli knew that this man had been trained for this moment, and he was certain that under his leadership, Russia would enter a new era.

As the president made his way towards the stage, his confident strides echoed in Yuli's ears as he climbed the steps. The crowd erupted into thunderous applause, their cheers resonating through Red Square and bouncing off the ancient walls of the Kremlin.

Acknowledging the crowd, the president raised his hand and flashed a rare smile. Yuli's eyes narrowed as he watched the president behind the bulletproof glass, a precaution put in place after Kuzman's assassination. No risks were being taken.

Through the loudspeakers, the president's booming voice filled the air as he addressed the nation. His words were commanding and full of promise, assuring a resurgent Russia would once again hold its rightful place on the global stage.

Yuli listened intently to every word, nodding in agreement with each statement made. The president spoke of building upon Kuzman's initiatives but also pledged to accelerate them, taking bolder actions.

His eyes shone with passion as he outlined his vision, beginning with Poland, then moving on to East Berlin. The crowd hung on his every word, completely captivated by his fervor and determination.

The president's speech reached a fevered pitch, and Yuli's attention was drawn to the drone capturing the scene from a unique angle. It hung over the stage, providing a breathtaking view of the president as he delivered his words. The images it transmitted were nothing short of spectacular, guaranteed to dominate news cycles for weeks.

But suddenly, amidst all the chaos and excitement, something caught Yuli's sharp eye. A flash of movement on the screen that didn't belong.

He leaned in closer, his brows furrowed in confusion. One of his drones had deviated from its assigned position, accelerating towards his favorite drone. The one above the president.

Yuli's hand trembled over the control pad as a knot of unease formed in his stomach. "What's happening?" he muttered urgently under his breath.

His fingers flew frantically over the controls, desperately trying to regain control of the rogue drone. But it refused to respond to his commands, its ID not matching any in his fleet.

A cold sweat broke out on Yuli's forehead as realization dawned on him like a punch to the gut. This was not his drone.

"No, no, no," he shouted at the screen in a mounting panic. He hammered on the control pad with renewed vigor, desperation taking hold as the drone steadied itself ominously next to his lead drone.

Its camera was now locked onto the president with chilling intent.

Yuli's heart pounded in his chest, a wild, frantic rhythm that drowned out everything else.

The voice of the president continued in his earpiece, but he could barely process the words as his eyes remained glued to the screen. The rogue drone descended with calculated precision, its mechanical body aiming straight at the president.

Yuli's breath caught in his chest as time seemed to slow down. He could see the dark maw of the drone's barrel pointed directly at the hapless leader. Without warning, the deafening crack of gunfire shattered the air, cutting through the electric atmosphere like a blade.

The crowd erupted into chaos as Yuli watched in horror, helpless to do anything as the first bullet tore through the president's chest. Blood sprayed out in a violent burst, staining his pristine white shirt with a grotesque pattern of red.

Before Yuli could even process what was happening, two more shots followed in quick succession, each one finding its target with deadly accuracy. The president's head snapped back violently, like a marionette cut loose from its strings. His limp body collapsed behind the supposedly impenetrable bulletproof glass that had failed so miserably to protect him from the merciless rain of bullets from above.

As if in a daze, Yuli's hand slipped off the control pad, his entire body going numb with shock and disbelief. The realization hit him like a physical blow—the president was dead. Murdered before the horrified eyes of thousands of onlookers and millions more watching from screens around the world.

For the second time in only a few weeks.

The once jubilant square was now a vortex of pandemonium and terror. The deafening cries of the crowd had turned into blood-curdling screams as they frantically fought to flee the chaos, trampling over one another in their desperate attempts to escape. The honor guard, trained for discipline and order, stood frozen in shock at the horror unfolding before them.

High above, the killer drone hovered for a moment longer, a malevolent eye surveying the destruction it had unleashed. And then, without warning, it shot off into the sky, vanishing into the darkening sky. Yuli's eyes followed its path until he could no longer see it, his mind racing with disbelief and fear.

Who was behind this heinous attack?

How had they managed to bypass all his security measures?

The questions spun in his head like a cyclone, each one more frantic than the last. The panicked voices in his earpiece only added to the chaos, orders for backup and emergency response.

Yuli could barely process any of it. His world had just been shattered before his very eyes, and all he could think about was that it happened on his watch.

He knew what fate awaited him.

The screen in front of him showed the aftermath—guards rushing to the stage, the lifeless body of the president being dragged away on a stretcher, blood staining the pristine floor of the stage.

Trembling, Yuli reached out to turn off the control pad. He couldn't bear to see anymore. Taking a step back from the balcony, his legs suddenly felt weak and wobbly. The full weight of what had just happened crashed down on him like an avalanche, filling him with an overwhelming sense of dread.

This was supposed to be his moment of triumph, a display of his power and influence. Instead, it had turned into a nightmare of epic proportions.

The assassination of the president would send shockwaves through the government, throughout the entire country, for a second time. The power struggle after Kuzman was killed had threatened to divide the nation.

When the dust settled, a leader had risen from the ashes. Now he was dead.

Yuli knew that there would be consequences. He had not been blamed for Kuzman's death. He would be for this one. A drone had delivered the fatal blow.

If he was lucky, they'd hang him quickly. If he wasn't, he'd spend years of torture rotting away in a prison cell, or worse, forced into hard labor in Siberia where even polar bears hated the weather.

His heart raced to dangerous levels as he turned away from the balcony, his mind already processing through the implications. The investigation that would follow, the inevitable scapegoating, the questions about how such a breach had been possible.

He'd be called a traitor. That he was somehow involved.

His hands trembled with fear and anger as he thought about how some-one had outmaneuvered him. Someone had known exactly how to exploit the one weakness he hadn't accounted for.

He needed to get to his office, to access the deeper layers of the security network, to find out who launched the drone. Every second felt pained as he forced himself to move, his body not over the shock.

He combed through hours of footage, his eyes burning with exhaustion and determination. But no matter how much he searched, there was nothing. Whoever it was had gotten away with it unscathed.

He knew who it was. The infamous couple who were on a killing spree. The pair who were on a mission to win a war that even the massive armies of the west could not win.

21

Three months later

Our luxury yacht was anchored off the coast of a Mediterranean island, the sun was at its peak, casting a shimmering golden glow across the calm waters. I lay on the deck in my bikini, letting the sun bask on my already deeply tanned skin.

The past three months had been a whirlwind of fun and exciting vacations, with a few precision strikes and covert operations sprinkled in, each one as daring as the last.

The world had been shaken, its balance of power tipped by a series of drone attacks that left dictators and terrorists alike fearing the silent predators in the sky. I lifted my head up and took a sip of my drink, savoring the cool, tangy taste, then laid my head back down continuing the opportunity to revel in our success.

This was what we were fighting for—a world where the wicked were no longer untouchable.

The drones had been Colonel's idea. They never said it, but I got the impression Alex and Jamie were trying to keep us out of harm's way as much as possible, and I wasn't complaining.

Now that our new identities were unknown except to only a chosen few, A-Rad and I had settled into a somewhat normal routine. If you could call killing world leaders occasionally, normal.

When we weren't on a mission, we had the freedom to travel wherever we pleased. We made sure to visit all the places on our bucket list in record time. The missions themselves were less nerve-wracking with the help of advanced drones that allowed us to keep a safe distance from danger. These high-tech machines could be controlled from hundreds of miles away or in close proximity to the target.

The bold moves sent shockwaves through the corridors of power worldwide, and I can still vividly remember the chaos that had ensued when we took out the biggest fish for a second time. The Russian president.

Russia was thrust into turmoil, the desired effect, and it didn't take long for leaders across the globe to stand up and take notice. Our message was loud and clear. Step out of line, and we'd take you out when you least expected it.

The installation of a more moderate leader in Moscow brought a sense of relief and hope that the era of dangerous authoritarianism was coming to an end. For now, the threat to Poland and Berlin seemed to have passed.

I could hardly fathom that we were having this much impact on the world. It felt exhilarating and deeply satisfying at the same time.

My mind wandered to the other successful targets we had taken down. Next on our list was the president of Pakistan, a tyrant who had oppressed millions. Under the cover of night, we used a drone to launch a missile through his bedroom window with pinpoint accuracy. The explosion was contained within the room, sparing the rest of the building and protecting innocent lives.

The western world received the news with a mix of shock and grim approval. Another dictator had been removed from power without a single innocent life lost.

Kaley and A-Rad claimed responsibility for the attack in a video released only hours later. Alex came up with the clever idea to use AI-generated images of our previous identities and post them online. Every time we struck, we took credit and sent a warning to everyone that no one was immune to our reach.

No country could be blamed which made retaliation impossible.

We were making progress on our list of targets and in need of new ones. Anyone who posed a serious threat to global stability, such as arms dealers or terrorist financiers, were fair game.

On one particular mission, we didn't even have to leave our yacht. Our target was hosting a lavish party on his nearby yacht, surrounded by beautiful women and a few friends. We could have destroyed everything with the push of a button, but since there were innocent bystanders, we focused on taking out our main target: an infamous arms dealer who was too busy celebrating his latest deal to notice the silent drone closing in on him.

We commandeered the drone and gave it commands from the comfort and safety of our own yacht. As we expertly navigated it through the dark night sky, its barely audible hum went unnoticed amidst the noise of the party. It came within inches of the man before we gave the signal for it to strike.

Shock and fear were evident in his eyes, seconds before we snuffed out his life. I can't think of anything more satisfying than to see him finally get what he deserved.

All we had to do was simply direct the drone back to our yacht and store it until we were ready to use it for another mission. A new modus operandi that made catching us nearly impossible.

Our next target was a terrorist leader lounging by the pool of his opulent mansion on a private island. Our drone flew above undetected by his security team, delivering a precise strike that left him dead in his lounge chair.

A drone carried and delivered a bomb to the doorstep of a Columbian drug dealer's house. The drone even pushed the doorbell. Another drone dropped a similar bomb on another drug dealer's car in Mexico as he drove in his convertible with the top down.

The operations had been flawless, executed with the kind of clinical efficiency that made us proud. We were rewriting the rules of warfare and the world was taking notice.

Each video of our successful missions garnered millions of views, with the one taking credit for killing the Russian leader surpassing a whopping billion views.

Alex assured us that the videos were untraceable back to him and that anyone who tried would be sent on a wild goose chase around the world wide web, hitting countless dead ends that even top-notch computer hackers couldn't unravel.

As I started to drift off with my thoughts, my phone buzzed on the table beside me. I thought it might be A-Rad, but it was Alex calling. With a smile on my face, I answered the call.

"Hey, Robin," Alex's voice came through the speaker, filled with uncontainable excitement.

We used our new names at all times now, out of an abundance of caution. We didn't want anything to be tied back to the internet couple creating a world-wide stir.

I chose Robin, because I considered myself a real-life Robin Hood. Less the stealing money and giving it to the poor part. What we did was even better. We were systematically freeing millions of people from the tyrannical control of dictators.

"You won't believe the news I've got," Alex said, excitedly. It sounded like Jamie wasn't with him, since he didn't say the news *we've* got.

I sat up straight up, the calming gentle rocking of the boat that had almost put me to sleep seconds before, was forgotten now as a surge of adrenaline coursed through me.

"What is it?" I asked, my inside's now brewing with my own excitement.

"First of all, can you believe how successful you've been? I mean, you're literally changing the world, one drone strike at a time. Everyone's talking about it—governments, media, the CIA, even the people on the streets. They're calling it the war to end all wars."

I couldn't help but laugh. "All thanks to you and Jamie. And Colonel. We couldn't do it without you. It's been a wild ride."

"Listen, that's why I called. I found something. Or rather, someone."

My curiosity was piqued. "Oh? Who did you find?"

There was a brief pause on the line, and I could hear the sound of papers rustling in the background, as if Alex was gathering his thoughts. Then he spoke, his tone more serious now.

"I found Jash's father."

A-Rad had chosen the name, Jash, for himself. Jash was short for Jashobeam the Hakmonite, one of David's mighty men in the Bible, who used a spear to kill 800 enemy warriors in one battle.

"I have an address and phone number, and I've confirmed he still lives there," Alex added.

My mind struggled to process the words as my heart seemingly stopped beating for a moment. "What? How? I thought he was dead."

"That's what Jash thought too," Alex said. "But I was doing some digging online, just trying to piece together more of Jash's past, and I came across some old records. An old copy of his birth certificate that I had missed earlier. I searched for his father's death certificate but couldn't find one. I did find his mother's death certificate."

Mentioning A-Rad's mother sent a sad arrow into my heart, even though I'd never met the woman and A-Rad never talked about her. At some point in his past, A-Rad experienced that loss, and I felt it in that moment.

"I started digging and found him. His father is alive, Robin."

I felt a surge of emotion, a mix of disbelief and a deep, protective instinct for my husband. A-Rad's past had always been a sensitive topic, one that he rarely spoke about.

I knew almost nothing. Since he didn't want to talk about it, I didn't bring it up and had imagined the worst.

"Does Jash know you found his father?" I asked, my voice softening with concern.

"Not yet," Alex replied. "That's why I was calling. You two are usually together. Sounds like he's not there with you."

"No. He went to the mainland for supplies."

Now I wished he was there. The responsibility of telling him was going to fall on me.

"I don't know how he's going to take it," Alex said.

"Yeah, this is ... a lot. He's always been so closed off about his past. I think it's his way of coping, you know? He doesn't want to deal with the pain, so he just locks it away."

"I get that," Alex said. "But I thought he deserves to know. His father might be a part of him that he's been missing all this time."

After taking a deep breath, I thought about the potential consequences of revealing this information to A-Rad. It could either bring closure or open old wounds.

"Where does his father live?" I asked, my voice steadier now.

"He's living in California," Alex answered. "He's been there for twenty years, remarried and he has a family. He seems to be doing well. I guess he never tried to reconnect with Jash."

I felt a pang of anger at the thought of his father abandoning A-Rad.

"So he just walked away and started a new life, huh?" I said, bitterly, as if it had happened to me. That's how it felt since A-Rad was as much a part of me as my arm and leg.

"That's ... that's horrible."

"I know," Alex said, his tone somber. "But maybe there's more to the story. We won't know until Jash calls him."

"You said that you have an address. What if Jash wants to come to California and confront him?"

"That's not a good idea."

"I didn't think it was either. I'm just asking."

"If I can find his birth certificate, someone else can as well. For all we know, there could be someone watching his father's house. Probably not, but we can't be too careful. If he wants to talk to his dad, you'll have to convince him just to call. Even that will need to be on a secured line that can't be traced. In case his phone line is bugged. You guys have made a lot of enemies around the world. They don't know who you are and I want to keep it that way."

I was standing now, pacing on the deck as I attempted to process the ramifications of the information. "Okay. I'll talk to him tonight. He'll be back soon."

"Thanks, Robin," Alex said, relief evident in his voice. "I'm glad we're on the same page. And hey, Jamie and I are really excited about how everything's been going. We're proud of you."

I smiled, feeling a sense of appreciation for the kind words. "We'll be back in touch."

We said our goodbyes, and I ended the call, my mind now swirling with thoughts of A-Rad. I stood and walked to the edge of the yacht, looking out at the horizon searching to see if he had started back to the yacht.

How do I tell him?

Things were going so well. Could he handle it?

The future suddenly felt uncertain.

Were there now personal battles to be fought, demons that couldn't be defeated by drones or bullets?

22

The night was still, with only the faint rustle of the wind against the flags flying on the masts and the gentle lapping of the ocean waves hitting the hull of the yacht. The stars had begun to twinkle in the darkening sky, a blanket of tiny lights that seemed to stretch infinitely above me.

I stood on the deck, leaning against the polished wooden railing, my eyes fixed on the horizon, searching for any sign of A-Rad. The ocean's vast expanse mirrored my swirling thoughts, deep and tumultuous.

A-Rad had called and said he was running late, but he'd be home soon. I wanted to see him so badly, but I also dreaded the conversation that would be difficult—perhaps one of the hardest we'd ever had.

But it was necessary. A-Rad had a right to know about his father. As much as I dreaded opening up old wounds, I would be there for him, to offer my unwavering support as he always had for me.

He returned to the yacht within the hour, looking more exhausted than usual. His eyes, typically sharp and alert, were clouded with fatigue.

"I'm tired and have a headache," he said wearily, as we unloaded the supplies together.

"Are you hungry?" I asked.

"No. I ate something earlier. Give me a few minutes. I'll feel better after I take an aspirin and get a short nap."

It didn't seem like the right time to burden him, so I let him go below to rest.

As I stayed on the deck, I rehearsed in my mind how I would break the news to him.

What words could possibly convey the gravity of what I was about to reveal? I wanted to be gentle, as if I could somehow cushion the blow, but I also needed to be direct. A-Rad deserved the truth, unfiltered and whole, no matter how painful it might be.

Time passed, and the sky deepened into an inky black, as the clouds blocked all the light. It matched my mood.

Finally, I decided it was time.

The lower deck was dimly lit, the soft hum of the yacht's systems provided a comforting backdrop as I approached the main cabin where A-Rad was resting.

I hesitated for a moment outside the door, gathering my courage before gently pushing it open.

A-Rad was sitting up in bed, a book in his hands, looking better than before. He had obviously taken a shower and his hair was still wet. His face immediately lit up with a smile when he saw me.

"Hey, Robin," he said, his voice still carrying a hint of weariness. "Everything okay?"

He must have sensed something in my demeanor, a nervousness I couldn't quite hide. I crossed the room and climbed into bed beside him, reaching out to take his hand in mine.

The warmth of his touch was familiar, connecting me to him in the moment.

"Yeah, everything's fine," I said, my voice gentle but steady. "But there's something important we need to discuss."

He sat the book down on the nightstand next to the bed. His brow furrowed slightly in concern, but he didn't pull his hand away.

"What is it?"

I took a deep but shaky breath, clinging to his hand for reassurance, more for myself than for him.

"Alex called while you were out."

"Is everybody okay?" His eyes searched mine for answers.

"Yes. Yes. Everyone's fine," I stammered. "He said he found your father."

I just blurted it out. Like ripping off a band aid.

The words hung in the air between us, carrying the weight of all that they implied.

For a moment, A-Rad didn't react, his expression frozen in time. Then, slowly, his eyes darkened, a storm of emotions flickered across his face—anger, confusion, pain.

His gaze bore into mine, searching for any hint that this might not be true.

"He found my father?" he repeated, the words catching in his throat as if they were foreign to him. "He's ... alive?"

I nodded silently, my heart aching for him as I saw the turmoil playing out on his face.

"He's living in California."

"How ... How did Alex find him? Why was he even looking for him?"

"Alex found your birth certificate while searching the internet, trying to make sure there was nothing in your past that could be traced back to you."

A-Rad's face twisted in a grimace that became a snarl of agony, a mix of emotions that were almost too painful to watch.

"He left us, Kaley."

Interesting that he used my old name now. I guess that's what made him feel the most comfortable—the person he had the most trust in and history with.

"Alex thought you might want to talk to him," I said, gently.

A-Rad's jaw tightened, his eyes narrowed as he let his anger show. "He left my mother and me to fend for ourselves. Why would I want anything to do with him now?"

I hesitated, searching for the right words. "How old were you when he left?"

The question seemed to bring a fresh wave of pain over him. His expression hardened as he recounted the past, the words spilling out like a confession.

"I was only six. My mother was an addict, and we barely made ends meet even with my father there. I had a younger sister who I was basically raising ... to the extent a six-year-old boy could."

His voice grew quieter, tinged with a sadness that tugged at my heart.

"One day, my father patted me on the forehead and said he was going to work. He never came home. My mother told me he was dead, but . . . I didn't believe it. I knew he had abandoned us."

I could see the pain etched into every line of his face, the burden he had carried for so long.

"So you didn't really know that he was dead."

A-Rad shook his head, his eyes distant again. "He was dead to me," he said bitterly, "but in the back of my mind, I always wondered if he might still be alive."

"Have you ever thought about trying to find him?"

His response was immediate, almost forceful. "No. I thought about trying to find my sister. In fact, I did try. But I had no luck."

His voice faltered slightly, and I felt a pang of sadness for the little boy who had been left alone, fending for himself and his sister, in a world that was far too cruel.

"What happened to your sister? How did you get separated?"

I never even knew he had a sister. That's how closed off he had been about his past.

"My mom . . ." He took a deep breath. "She couldn't take care of us."

He continued, his voice taking on a hard edge as he delved deeper into the painful memories.

"She was strung out on drugs all the time. One day, she loaded us in a wagon—she didn't have a car; my dad took it—and she rolled us down to a church at the corner and left us there. She stood at the corner across the street and watched until someone came."

His words hit me like a punch to the gut; the rawness of his pain tore at my heartstrings. I could only imagine what it was doing to him. This was one of the saddest things I'd ever heard in my life.

"The people at the church called the cops. They asked me where we lived. I showed them our house. They arrested my mom. My sister and I went to a foster home."

I decided to stop asking questions and let him speak at his own pace now that he was finally opening up.

"One day, a family came, they adopted my sister. They didn't want me. I still remember it vividly . . . her screaming for me as they put her in the car and drove away. I never saw her again."

His hand gripped mine so tightly it hurt, the pain of the memory evident in the tension of his muscles. I didn't complain, offering silent support as he continued.

"I went from foster home to foster home. When I got old enough, I looked for my mother. I learned she passed away from an overdose. I wanted to find my sister, but I didn't know where to look. Eventually, I joined the Air Force. I told them I was eighteen, but I was really sixteen. I think . . . I didn't really know. I've never even seen my birth certificate. I'm surprised Alex found it."

A single tear escaped from his eye, trailing down his cheek. I reached up, brushing it away with my thumb, ignoring the tears that were now escaping from my own eyes.

He had been carrying this story inside of him for years, but it had been too painful for him to share it. Now, as the dam finally broke, the emotions poured out, raw and unfiltered.

"I blame my dad," he said in a bitter tone. "He abandoned us."

"I know, A-Rad. I know he hurt you, and I can't begin to understand what that must have been like. But maybe . . . maybe talking to him could bring you some closure. Maybe there's more to the story that you don't know."

A-Rad looked away, his jaw clenched as he grappled with the conflicting emotions swirling inside him.

"I don't want to hear his excuses. I get why he didn't want to be with my mother, but there's no excuse for abandoning your kids like that. I don't need closure. I have it. I've spent my whole life trying to forget about him."

I leaned in closer, my voice soft but firm. "You don't have to make any decisions right now. Think about it. And whatever you decide, I'll be here with you. You're not alone in this."

His eyes met mine, and for a moment, the mask of the hardened operative slipped away, revealing the vulnerable man underneath. He nodded slowly, his hand tightening around mine again.

"I don't need to think about it."

"That's fine. I'll support you no matter what."

I stood up and opened the window. I felt suddenly flushed, hot and uncomfortable. The cool sea breeze was immediately refreshing.

I climbed back in bed, and we sat in silence for a while, the sound of the sea provided a soothing backdrop to my thoughts. No matter what happened with A-Rad's father, we would deal with it as we always had—side by side.

As the night wore on, the gentle sway of the yacht became more pronounced. I turned off the lights, and we lay down together, my body naturally curling into his as he wrapped his muscular arm around me, holding me close. His warmth was comforting, a reminder of the unbreakable bond we shared, despite the challenges we had faced.

We stayed there in silence for what felt like hours but was probably only an hour or two. I wasn't going to fall asleep until A-Rad did. The rhythmic rise and fall of A-Rad's breathing told me he was still awake since it hadn't slowed. I could feel the tension in his body slowly ebbing away being replaced by a quiet resolve.

Finally, in the darkness, his voice broke the silence. "I want to talk to him."

I sat up slightly, my heart suddenly pounding in my chest. "Are you sure?"

"Yeah," he said, his voice steady. "I want him to know what he did to us."

I nodded, though uncertainty gnawed at the edges of my mind. "Okay. Alex said he'd arrange a call."

A-Rad shook his head. "Not on the phone. I want to see him in person. I want to see his face when I tell him I'm the son he abandoned."

"You mean ... go to America?"

"Yes."

The thought of him confronting his father in person made me uneasy.

"Okay," I said finally, my voice soft. "If that's what you want, then that's what we'll do."

I wanted to sound supportive, but deep down I wasn't sure this was such a good idea.

23

California

We didn't tell Alex and Jamie that we were going to California to confront A-Rad's father. When the subject came up, A-Rad simply told Alex, "Thank you, but I have nothing to say to him."

Alex sent us the address and phone number in case A-Rad changed his mind. They didn't bring it up again, but it didn't keep me from talking to A-Rad about Alex's concerns.

A-Rad was adamant that we were going no matter what. He was almost rude about it. Ever since I told him his father was alive, he'd been on edge and short with me. When he opened up, he coped by shutting down emotionally, putting up a tough front. Maybe that's why he pushed me away.

I tried not to take it personally.

"Jamie and Alex can't tell me what to do," A-Rad had said harshly. "This is my decision."

"I know. But Alex thinks it might be dangerous."

That caused A-Rad to laugh.

"I stood in line with a hundred Russian soldiers, killed the president, and got away without getting caught. This won't be more dangerous than that."

"Okay. Dangerous might not be the right word. There are some logistical problems going to America," I said.

"Like what?"

"For one thing, we can't take the yacht or the AJAX plane without Alex and Jamie knowing. Without Brad knowing for that matter."

"We'll fly commercial."

"We'll have to get through security."

"We have passports. They work everywhere else."

"What about fingerprints and DNA? Alex said we couldn't come back to America, because the CIA had those on file. There's no way Alex can delete them."

"You're being paranoid now. Why would anyone fingerprint us or run a DNA test? Customs won't. As long as we don't get arrested, we'll be fine."

I didn't mention someone possibly watching his father's house. That seemed far-fetched to me. There were people looking for A-Rad and Kaley, but they didn't know our names. Without our names, they couldn't find a birth certificate. Without a birth certificate, they couldn't find A-Rad's father.

All they had was a picture of us from before. They wouldn't recognize us now. That's why we went to all the trouble to change our looks.

The day couldn't come soon enough. We told Alex and Jamie we were taking a break from missions and moored the yacht at a Greek island before flying to Rome. From there, we took a flight to Miami and then caught an overnight flight to Los Angeles.

The only anxiety came at Miami customs, but as A-Rad predicted, our passports worked. I was unnecessarily worried that the CIA knew our new identities and flagged them.

I probably was being paranoid, but if anyone in the world knew we had changed our appearances, it was Brad. As Assistant Director of the CIA, he knew when a mosquito crossed the border from one country to another.

When we landed in Los Angeles, we didn't even bother to check into our hotel before heading straight to A-Rad's father's house. He wanted to get it over with as soon as possible.

A-Rad was distant and didn't say much as we drove over.

I could only imagine how he was feeling.

We arrived at a modest house in a middle-class neighborhood on the outskirts of Los Angeles, unsure if his father would be there or not. A-Rad had insisted on surprising him, wanting to see his reaction first-hand.

I understood his desire to gauge his father's feelings towards him in the spur of the moment. Would his father welcome him with open arms or act as if he couldn't care less? Would he seem nervous? Did his new family even know he had another family in his past?

My biggest fear: Would he reject A-Rad again and want nothing to do with him?

As much as I wanted to shield A-Rad from any potential pain, I knew I couldn't protect him from the unknown. So many questions swirled in my mind and it wasn't even my father.

I could relate though. I'd grown up without my parents who had died when I was young.

Our little AJAX group had suffered a great deal of childhood loss. Alex's parents died in a car accident when he was a teenager. Jamie lost her mother to breast cancer at seventeen. Her father was an astronaut she never had the chance to meet in person. She talked to him once right before he blasted off on a mission to the ends of the universe, never to be seen nor heard from again.

I didn't even know the entire story, but it sounded heartbreaking, and Jamie clearly felt the loss of growing up without a father as did I. According to Jamie, the CIA specifically sought out operatives with no family ties. They wanted the agency to become our family instead.

I couldn't help but feel that our CIA family had abandoned us as well.

As we prepared to exit the rental car and approach the house, A-Rad revealed the emotional turmoil he was experiencing inside. "This is a lot nicer house than where we lived!" he said, angrily.

I nodded and let him vent out all of his emotions. It didn't even matter if he took it out on me. I could handle it. All that mattered was keeping him from physically taking his anger out on his father. After all, he had been trained to kill a man with his bare hands in a hundred different ways, and I didn't want to take any chances.

As we walked up to the front door, each step felt heavier than the last. A-Rad raised his hand to knock, hesitating before finally rapping his knuckles against the wood. Footsteps sounded from inside, and I braced myself for what might be on the other side of the door.

What if it was the man's wife? What if it was one of his kids? What would A-Rad say if it wasn't his father who answered the door?

If I was this nervous and filled with uncertainty, A-Rad's anxiety level had to be off the charts.

The door opened and an unkempt man in his fifties appeared, holding a can of beer and looking annoyed at our presence. I recognized him instantly as A-Rad's father, but he didn't seem to recognize his own son at all.

Why would he? If we hadn't had the plastic surgery, his father would've recognized him immediately. As it was, we were nothing more than a couple of strangers interrupting his day.

A-Rad stayed silent as he studied intently the familiar features of the man who had abandoned him years ago. His father's expression remained indifferent.

"If you sellin' something, you wastin' your time with me," his father said gruffly.

Finally, after another moment of tense silence, A-Rad croaked out a weak, "Dad, it's me, Arnold."

I never knew A-Rad's real name. He'd always been A-Rad to me. I was told it was a nickname given to him because of his radical nature. His wild and fearless nature seemed to fit the moniker.

Arnold. I like A-Rad better.

Time stood still.

Neither of them spoke, the years of silence between them hovered over us like those drones we used to kill dictators.

Recognition came over the man's face, even though he still seemed confused.

"Son," he said, more as a question than a statement.

"Yeah, I'm your son."

The father became self-conscious and awkwardly ran his hand through his thick hair in the same way I'd seen A-Rad do it a thousand times. He looked down at his tee shirt and wiped his hand on it. He reached out his hand but then abruptly pulled it back, realizing it wasn't an appropriate greeting to a son he hadn't seen in years.

Instead, he stepped aside and opened the door wider. "Come in," he said, his voice still harboring disbelief. "Please, come in."

A-Rad hesitated before stepping inside. When he finally did, I followed closely behind. The man eyed me closely as I passed by him, our eyes met briefly.

The house was small but cozy. It wasn't well kept but wasn't filthy either. Lived in was how I would describe it. It had a few family pictures on the wall, displayed in various places.

A-Rad noticed them too, and I could sense his anger growing. Those were images of a life that didn't include him.

How could he not feel resentment?

I wanted to remind him why he was there. For answers—for closure, but I was determined to only speak when spoken to.

His father led us into a dimly lit family room that had a television as the centerpiece, blaring something about yesterday's presidential election result. Apparently, a man named Andrew Pash had been declared the winner.

I didn't even know that an election was taking place or who was running. That's how out of touch we were with our own country that no longer felt like home.

An uncomfortable silence settled over the two men, like it would two combatants getting ready to square off in an octagon. I stayed close to A-Rad's side as we sat on the couch while his father took his obvious usual spot in a well-worn chair that seemed to fit his body perfectly from sitting in it for years.

In that way, they were nothing alike. A-Rad was muscular and could be on the cover of a fitness magazine. His dad was out of shape and overweight. Big boned like A-Rad but that was the extent of it.

A-Rad's facial reconstruction made it difficult to see any resemblance between them. It must have been confusing for his father. Did he wonder if the man standing in front of him was really his son?

"Well, this is unexpected. I never thought I'd see you again," his father said. "I lost track of you."

A-Rad clenched his fists, the anger he had kept buried for so long threatened to spill out at the first words.

"You didn't lose track of me—you left!" A-Rad's voice cut through the room. "You abandoned us. Why?"

"You're right, I did," he said too casually. "I regret it every day, but at the time, I thought it was the best thing. Your mother—"

"My mother is dead. She died shortly after you left."

He nodded in acknowledgment.

"I figured as much. She was spiraling out of control, and I had no choice but to leave."

"You did have a choice."

"I was weak, Arnold. I'm not proud of it, but I couldn't stay. I thought you'd be better off."

"Better off?" A-Rad's voice rose, his anger finally breaking free from its leash. "How could we possibly be better off? No, you thought you'd be better off! All you cared about was yourself."

"That's not true," his father argued. "I loved you."

"Then why didn't you take us with you?"

"Children need to be with their mother."

A-Rad shook his head violently from side to side.

"That's just an excuse. If you loved me, you wouldn't have left me in that horrible situation. I needed a father. Do you know what your leaving did to me?"

"I do," his father said, his eyes filled with guilt for the first time as he grimaced slightly. "I know I failed you, and I'm sorry for that, Arnold. I really am. I don't expect you to forgive me, but I want you to know that I'm sorry."

"It's too late for apologies."

The father's jaw tightened in anger. "Is that why you went to all the trouble to find me? To say that?" he seethed. "Do you feel better now?"

"Not one bit!"

"Then save your breath! It's been years. It's time for you to grow up and move on from the past. You seem like you're doing just fine now."

"No thanks to you."

I felt every muscle in A-Rad's body tense. It took all of his self-control to keep from standing and smacking the man across the face.

I wanted to stand up and strike the man myself.

But something on the television screen had caught my attention, pulling me away from the argument at hand. The news channel was playing clips of the president elect's victory speech. I was angry at myself for letting it distract me at a time when A-Rad needed me the most.

"I don't expect you to understand," his father said. "You were just a boy."

"A boy who needed his father."

"Yeah, thems the breaks. I said I was sorry. Get over it."

I couldn't believe how insensitive his father was being. This wasn't how I had pictured it going down. I had naively hoped that A-Rad's father would take one look at him, and they would embrace each other warmly, like long lost family members. But it was clear that wouldn't be happening anytime soon.

Even though his father had apologized twice now, it felt hollow. Not fake, but certainly not genuine either. There was a wall between them that couldn't be broken down, a harsh exterior they both shared.

It's like his father was sitting in the room with a stranger, not his own flesh and blood, and he really didn't care. He'd like to get back to his television show.

The volume on the television was still too loud, odd considering the tension between them. Maybe his father thought it would provide a buffer, something to distract them from their issues.

How could they truly address their problems with such a noisy distraction? They were both shouting now, and it felt like a mistake to be having this conversation if this was how it was going to go down.

In the midst of the chaos, my attention kept drifting to the presidential election, which had been close last night according to the news. Overnight, millions of votes were counted flipping the election to Pash. He now won by an electoral college landslide.

The opposing candidate refused to concede, claiming the election had been stolen.

What was it about the story that kept drawing me in?

Then it clicked. Kunkel's phone. The night I killed him in Iran. The message flashed in my mind.

I struggled to remember the exact words he had sent to Jerry. The context had to do with setting off nuclear weapons in Israel, then America.

When do I get to meet AP? Kunkel wrote.

He has to win first, had been Jerry's reply.

Win what had been my first question. A presidential election?

AP. Andrew Pash. He did win.

Was that AP? "Is that what Jerry meant?

The argument with A-Rad's father didn't seem important anymore.

24

The air crackled with fury as A-Rad and his father's argument escalated, reaching a boiling point. Each word was a weapon, sharp and pointed, aimed at the other's heart.

Then something happened. Something unexpected.

"I said I was sorry," his father repeated in a softer tone, "and I meant it. I hope you'll find it in your heart to forgive me."

And there it was. A small, flickering flame of something else—something I hadn't sensed since his father opened that door.

Hope.

Was reconciliation possible? I sure hoped so, for A-Rad's sake.

I didn't expect them to leave with their relationship completely restored—that was unrealistic. But I hoped they could part on better terms, with A-Rad having said what he needed to say and finding some peace in it.

"I don't know that I can forgive you right now," A-Rad said honestly, his voice steady but not as combative.

And just as fast as it appeared, hope dissipated like a puff of smoke from a cigar.

"Then why did you come here?" his father sneered, the venom in his voice sounded like acid meant to burn through A-Rad's defenses.

His father's face contorted with anger and self-righteousness as he didn't wait for A-Rad to respond. "Do you think I care if you forgive me? If you think you can shame me into feeling guilty, well think again, son."

His voice rose to a deafening roar as he continued to berate A-Rad, acting like a father correcting a son, even though this man had forfeited that right years ago.

A-Rad refused to back down. "I don't need to shame you," he said, his voice now cold and resolute. "You did that all on your own when you walked out on us."

"What did you hope to accomplish by coming here, Arnold?" he said, his words dripping with vitriol. "Did you think you were going to show up and we were all of a sudden going to be one big happy family?"

"No! I wanted you to know what you did to us. Obviously, you don't care."

"So you wanted to make me feel guilty. Well, I don't. I did what I had to do, and I'd do it again. I don't need you showing up on my doorstep trying to make me feel regrets. I felt them long before you walked through that door. But it's not what you think. I regret ever meeting your mother. That was the worst mistake of my life. If you want to blame someone, blame her."

With those words, I knew all hope for reconciliation was gone.

A-Rad bolted to his feet, muscles coiled like springs ready to unleash fury. I reacted immediately, grasping his arm tightly to hold back the violent force within him. His father's words, disparaging his mother, had dug deep into a raw wound, setting off an inferno of rage that could easily consume us all.

I couldn't let A-Rad lose control. Not now, not in this place. I knew too well the danger that lurked beneath his calm facade, the same danger that made him one of the most feared assassins in the world. I had to stop him before things spiraled out of control.

Thankfully, A-Rad reluctantly sat down again, struggling to regain his composure. "You're right, Dad," he spat out through gritted teeth. "I was better off without you. I made something of myself despite your absence. You, on the other hand, are still the same despicable excuse for a man you were back then."

I kept my grip on his arm. Better to attack his father with words than with fists.

His father chuckled darkly. "Who are you to come into my home and judge me?"

A-Rad paused, choosing his words carefully. "Do you want to know how I know you haven't changed and aren't worth a second of my time?"

His father didn't respond and refused to meet his gaze, looking away dismissively.

"Because not once have you asked about your own daughter, my sister." A-Rad's voice shook with emotion.

His father's response was almost sarcastic. "How is your sister?"

I thought A-Rad was going to explode as he jumped to his feet again.

"This was a mistake," he said, loud enough for everyone to hear.

To my surprise, A-Rad walked toward the door.

His father remained seated, making no move to stop him. I glared at the man as I walked past his chair.

A-Rad was out the door before I could react—not that I would try to stop him. He got what he needed. I'm sure he realized, as I did, that while he might not have been better off because his father left, the man wasn't worth pining over now.

We drove a few blocks in tense silence before A-Rad spoke. "I'm sorry you had to see that."

"I'm sorry you had to go through it."

"I don't know what I expected, but I didn't expect that," he said with a slight chuckle that was filled with disgust.

"At least now you know."

"He didn't even ask your name," A-Rad said.

I noticed that too but wasn't going to say anything. This wasn't about me.

A-Rad continued. "Can you believe that? My own wife is standing right there, and he doesn't even acknowledge her," A-Rad fumed. "It's so disrespectful."

"I know."

"What kind of man doesn't even care about his own daughter?" A-Rad questioned bitterly.

"You know exactly what kind of man he is."

He reached over and took my hand in his, squeezing it tightly. "I need to focus on what I have, not what I never had."

"I agree," I said sweetly.

"Colonel has been more of a father to me than he ever was," A-Rad said, his voice cracking with emotion. "Jamie has been like a sister. And you ... you're the best thing that ever happened to me."

Tears welled up in my eyes as he held onto my hand so tightly, like he was afraid of losing me.

That would never happen.

"I need to be thankful for what God has given me. It's much better than what I lost."

"You're an incredible man, A-Rad," I said, my voice shaking with its own emotion. "I'm so, so proud of you. Despite everything you've been through, you've come out a strong and compassionate person. That's all you. You deserve all the credit. Don't let the past change who you are now that you've overcome it."

"I won't."

We didn't say anything more for a good ten minutes.

"You have to forgive him," I finally said, as gently as possible.

"I know, but it's hard," A-Rad admitted, his voice heavy with pain and hurt, but at least the anger had subsided.

"You don't have to trust him or let him back into your life," I said. "But forgive him and move on," I said firmly. "You'll feel better once you do."

"I will," he replied, and I could see the determination in his eyes even though I wasn't sure what was behind the look.

"If you need any help, just let me know."

Out of nowhere, he began singing a Beatles song, which was completely unexpected given that I'd never heard him sing before. The lyrics to "Help" filled the car.

And just like that, the old A-Rad was back. An emotional switch had been flipped. I didn't question it because we were trained to do this, move on from missions once they were completed. We didn't dwell on them.

I joined in the song. We sounded like a couple of hoarse canaries and laughed the rest of the way to the hotel.

A-Rad had fulfilled his mission to confront his father, and now he could compartmentalize it. He could bury it deep within himself and move on. I had no intention of bringing it up again.

Jamie had an insightful perspective on it. She said that people in the real world made a mistake by constantly dwelling on their past. So many let their past traumas consume their present reality. As operatives, we couldn't afford to dwell on past missions other than to learn from them.

I wouldn't be surprised if A-Rad never mentioned it again, and that was perfectly okay with me. There were more pressing matters at hand; something that would immediately take A-Rad's mind off his father.

The new President of the United States, Andrew Pash.

What was his connection to Jerry and Iran?

* * *

Iran

Jeric's body ached with exhaustion, but sleep was a distant memory since the brutal assassination of Kunkel and the devastating destruction of the Iranian nuclear weapons program. The chaos that had consumed the entire Iranian government had also consumed him, leaving a good night's rest an unattainable luxury.

Known for his meticulous nature and ability to anticipate every move of his enemies, Jeric prided himself on staying three steps ahead. But these past weeks had been a relentless assault on his carefully curated plans.

The couple who masqueraded as nuclear inspectors had outsmarted him, manipulating him like a puppet on strings. And in their wake, they left behind a trail of devastation beyond comprehension.

The location of Iran's most secretive and heavily guarded nuclear facility was no more, thanks to the cunning tactics of these imposters. Before anyone could even see it coming, an Israeli air strike reduced years of construction to nothing but rubble.

Adding to the nightmare, the mastermind architect behind the program was dead. In a calculated move, the woman posing as a nuclear inspector, killed Kunkel in her hotel room and made it look like natural causes. It was only by chance that Jeric stumbled upon her picture in a British tabloid, otherwise he would have never suspected her involvement in this catastrophic chain of events.

Iran had struck back, launching a barrage of missiles at Israel, but their retaliation was futile. They were no match for the combined might of Israel and America. Not without a nuclear bomb to offset them.

Amidst the chaos and tension, Jeric found himself in the crosshairs of an investigation. He had been interrogated as authorities tried to discover how this happened. They suspected a traitor had given away the secret location.

The investigators bore down on him like a crushing weight, threatening to suffocate him with guilt and fear. They'd leave no stone unturned in search of a scapegoat.

In a desperate attempt to cover his tracks, he hired an assassin to eliminate the two individuals responsible. But weeks had passed, and he hadn't heard anything from the killer, the uncertainty gnawing at his sanity.

So when his phone rang in the dead of night, jerking him awake with its shrill call, Jeric's heart raced with anticipation and dread. He knew this call could be his chance to regain control and fix his mistake, or it could be the killer calling to say he couldn't find them.

Fully awake now, he answered it. "Talk to me," he said urgently, his voice barely above a whisper.

"I've found something," came the calm yet excited voice of the assassin on the other end. Jeric could hear the faint hum of a car engine in the background.

"I'm in America," the paid killer continued. "Outside a house. I think I may have discovered the identity of the man. I'm pretty sure I located his father. Two people just entered the house. I've sent you a picture, take a look."

Jeric quickly pulled up the image on his phone, studying it intently despite the darkness of his room. At first glance, the figures in the photo didn't resemble their targets at all.

"That's not them," he stated hesitantly.

But as he scrutinized their stature and build, a chill ran down his spine causing him to shudder.

"But then ... they're exactly the same height, same build."

The assassin hesitated for a moment before asking, "Could they have changed their appearances? You know, they got some kind of plastic surgery on their faces."

Jeric's heart thudded against his ribcage like a trapped animal. The possibility that his enemies could be unrecognizable was something he had never considered. But these were no ordinary criminals. They were highly skilled operatives who had the means and resources to change their identities at will.

It might explain why they hadn't been caught.

A cold sweat broke out on Jeric's forehead as he studied the photo once more, his mind racing with terrifying possibilities. The figures in the image moved with an undeniable sense of purpose, with a lethal confidence in their manner, a familiarity with how they carried themselves that made Jeric second guess his first reaction.

"Follow them," he commanded, his voice laced with steely determination. "Confront them and find out for sure. And if they are who we believe them to be, eliminate them."

The assassin's response was a simple but ominous, "Understood."

The line went dead, and Jeric could sense it in his bones; it was them. And they wouldn't get away this time. They had been too arrogant, too sure of their ability to remain hidden. That overconfidence would be their downfall.

He moved towards the window, carefully pulling back the curtain to peek out into the dark night. Every shadow seemed to hold a potential threat.

But he still had the ultimate plan, one that he had been meticulously crafting for four decades. The killers hadn't done anything to stop it from unfolding.

Things were finally in motion. Andrew Pash had won the American election by a landslide, claiming to have earned the most votes.

Jeric chuckled at how naive and gullible the American infidels were. They used voting machines connected to the internet to count their votes. Changing a few numbers in key states was easy enough to secure the outcome he desired. They'd been doing it for years in countries like Venezuela, Nicaragua, and Russia.

In reality, Pash lost by about seven percentage points. They made it so he won by seven. The election was never in doubt in his mind. They could've flipped more votes if they had to. The American media had done their part, making sure the fake polls showed a close enough race that the results wouldn't be questioned.

Once Pash was in power, they could set everything else into action.

For now, he needed to focus on the task at hand. The assassin he hired was reliable. One of the best in his line of work. Jeric specifically chose him for his discretion and efficiency. If these were indeed his targets, the assassin would take care of them quickly, without leaving any traces behind.

Tonight was the night that would shift the balance of power back to him. If his suspicions were correct, Jeric would have a chance at redemption and the Iranian government would get their long-awaited retribution on America.

He picked up his phone again and opened the picture, studying the faces of the two individuals who had done so much damage to his years of hard work. His finger hovered over the screen, zooming in on their expressions.

They looked familiar, in a way he couldn't quite place. It was something in their eyes, something in the way they held themselves.

A cold smile formed on Jeric's lips. Soon enough, he would have confirmation.

Jeric settled back onto the bed, feeling some tension ease from his shoulders. He knew better than to hope, but this time he allowed himself a moment of anticipation. If everything went according to plan, he would be one step closer to gaining back the control he desperately needed.

And then, perhaps, he could finally sleep.

25

Back at the hotel, the tension from A-Rad's confrontation with his father had dissipated, becoming a distant memory. We didn't discuss it—not because it wasn't important, but because that was our way of handling things.

My mind was still occupied by something else that had been bothering me since we left Iran. I had put it off because I couldn't make sense of it.

"Do you remember the message on Kunkel's phone I told you about?" I asked A-Rad after we settled into our hotel room.

He shook his head.

"He asked Jerry when he could meet AP."

A-Rad looked at me quizzically. "AP? Yeah, I vaguely remember. Why?"

"Jerry told Kunkel that AP would have to win first."

"Win what?"

"That was my initial question as well," I said. "Did you see who won the US election yesterday?"

"Nope. I haven't been paying attention."

"Neither have I. A man named Andrew Pash won."

A-Rad furrowed his brow, trying to connect the pieces. His eyes widened when he figured it out. "So you think Andrew Pash might be AP?"

"I don't know," I admitted. "Their initials match, and he won an election."

"Why would Kunkel care about meeting a US presidential candidate?"

"A more important question is why would a presidential candidate want to meet with Kunkel and why would Jerry be in charge of making it happen?"

"He wouldn't."

"I didn't think so either. The whole text chain was in the context of dropping a nuclear bomb on America. Jerry specifically mentioned destroying Israel first, then America. That's what they were going to do once Iran had the bomb."

"Even with the bomb, Iran wouldn't have the capacity to hit the United States. We would blow them off the face of the earth if they tried."

"That may be true, but what if they had the president in their pocket?"

It sounded silly as I said it. I hoped A-Rad didn't take the opportunity to mock my foolishness.

He didn't.

"Well, that's a moot point since Israel took care of that issue. Iran doesn't have the bomb now."

"That's true. But what if Andrew Pash really is AP? If he's some kind of secret agent, then he's still dangerous."

"Are you saying that Iran flipped a presidential candidate into an asset who's working for them?"

"I don't know what I'm saying."

I had my phone in my hand searching for the origin of the name Pash.

"Listen to this. Pashia is a Persian name."

"I thought you said his name was Pash."

"Pash, Pashia. Pretty similar."

"I think you may be grasping at straws here."

I turned on the television and saw that the election coverage was still ongoing. The news anchors were practically gushing over Pash's victory. It didn't take long for an image of him to appear on the screen.

"There!" I exclaimed. "He definitely looks Iranian to me."

A-Rad leaned back in his chair, arms crossed as he studied the information on the television. This was our dynamic. I was impulsive, while A-Rad was thoughtful and strategic. He wouldn't speak until he had fully processed his thoughts.

I could almost hear the gears turning in his head, each idea carefully dissected and examined, before being put back together again.

"I'm not saying you're incorrect, Robin," he said, using our new names that we had used throughout the entire trip. "AP could be anyone. Perhaps Kunkel was trying to gain favor with someone he believed would be beneficial to his work."

"Someone who had to win an election first."

"All Jerry said was 'win first.' He didn't specify an election."

"Maybe," I admitted, but doubts still lingered in my mind. "Kunkel was a scientist. He didn't make casual connections. He wasn't talking about winning a friendly game of softball. He was talking about winning a nuclear war. And very few people have the capability to help Iran achieve that. One of them is the President of the United States."

"The President of the United States is planning to launch a nuclear war against his own country that he is now in charge of running?"

I rubbed my forehead, trying to eradicate memories of past mistakes when I had impulsively made leaps and connections that weren't there. Despite my doubts, if I was correct about this theory, ignoring it could result in handing over the keys to a potential nuclear disaster.

"I know. It sounds ridiculous when you put it that way. Still, there has to be a reason why Kunkel would mention Pash."

A-Rad shrugged his shoulders. "He didn't exactly mention Pash."

I started to provide a retort, but he raised his hand to silence me so he could finish his thought. "But let's assume for a minute that AP is Pash. What does it really mean?"

I paused to carefully choose my next words. "Pash might be a pawn in a larger scheme involving Kunkel."

"Kunkel is dead."

"He wasn't when he sent the message. And Jerry and Pash are both still alive."

"Sometimes a cigar is just a cigar; sometimes it's a piece of candy."

I laughed. "What does that mean?"

"Have you ever had a candy cigar?"

"No. I have no idea what you're talking about."

"It's a cigar-shaped piece of candy. I loved them as a kid."

I stood and went behind A-Rad and rubbed the back of his neck when he tried to stretch his shoulders to relieve the tension. I realized that I may have made a mistake bringing up such a serious subject after all he'd been through that day.

"I still don't understand what you're talking about," I said, as I struggled to penetrate the tight muscles in his shoulders.

"It's like how something may look one way, but in reality, it's something else entirely. You can't be certain that AP is Andrew Pash. In your imagination, you're making connections that may not even exist. That's all I'm saying."

"It's not just in my imagination!"

I reminded myself not to get defensive. A-Rad was making a good point.

"The message was a real cigar, not a piece of candy," I argued. "Kunkel and Jerry were talking about the annihilation of America. In that context, Kunkel wanted to meet AP."

"Pash might be a piece of candy."

"Or he may be the cigar," I said a little more forcefully.

I would've preferred to move on to a different analogy but couldn't think of one off the top of my head.

"I'll give you that AP may only look like a cigar," I continued. "AP could be anyone."

"AP can't be anyone," A-Rad countered, making it sound like he was taking the other side of the argument. "He can't be me. My initials are AR. He can't be you. Yours are KP. Close but not a match. So I'm not saying you're crazy for making the connection."

"I'd advise you, for your own health, to never say I'm crazy about anything," I said in a joking tone.

"You're crazy about me."

"Well, that's true."

"You may be right," he said. "All I'm saying is that we don't have any solid evidence to support it. And even if we did, what could we do about it? We don't have the resources to investigate a president. Maybe Alex could help. He's the only one I know who could do it."

"Oh no," I said. "No way I'm telling Alex. Not without more proof. He'll definitely think I'm crazy."

"He wouldn't think you're crazy. He'd just say we don't have enough proof," A-Rad replied.

"I know," I conceded, my frustration evident in my voice. "I only have a gut feeling, and that doesn't hold much weight in our line of work."

"So we drop it," A-Rad suggested, though there was reluctance in his tone. "It's a moot point now anyway. Iran's nuclear program is destroyed. It'll take them years to rebuild it, if they even can. The INWA will be all over them, trying to save face after missing such a big threat right under their noses. This is above our paygrade. Let someone else figure it out."

I nodded in agreement, knowing he was right. "You're right. We've got enough things to worry about."

"Are you hungry? Want to grab dinner?" A-Rad asked while rubbing his stomach.

"Sure," I said.

Together, we made our way down to the hotel restaurant where the sounds of conversations and clinking silverware provided a soothing contrast to the tension of the past few hours. The smell of grilled meat and fresh bread filled the air, momentarily making me forget about our situation and feel like any other guest at the hotel.

But that fleeting sense of normalcy shattered the moment we entered the lobby.

A-Rad and I both noticed him at the same time.

A man sitting casually in one of the plush chairs near the entrance. But there was nothing casual about his intense gaze that scanned the room with a predatory hunger.

My muscles tensed as I felt A-Rad stiffen beside me.

I could tell from the man's demeanor and deliberate observations he was not to be taken lightly. He may have appeared unassuming in his expensive suit and trimmed beard, but every fiber of my being screamed danger.

As a seasoned agent, I could spot a trained killer from a mile away. This one was Russian, a fact confirmed by his facial features. He was some kind of operative based on his subtle movements and calculated mannerisms.

When his eyes locked onto us and a look of recognition crossed his face, I knew we were in trouble.

Without hesitation, I took A-Rad's arm and guided him towards the door. We needed to get away from the crowded lobby before this man made his move. Away from the innocent civilians.

I also knew we were at a severe disadvantage without weapons, so our best option was to level the playing field or escape and regroup. Easier to make that happen if we weren't in a confined space.

Stepping outside, I positioned us strategically to block the exit. The man wouldn't risk walking out while we were there, and he couldn't shoot us from inside the hotel.

As my mind raced through possible scenarios, one thought stood out above all else: we weren't running. We were trained to face danger head-on, and if this man wanted a fight, we would give it to him on our own terms.

A-Rad's voice broke through my thoughts, low and steady. "I don't know how, but he's definitely looking for us."

I nodded grimly, steeling myself for what was to come. "How do we play it?"

"I say we don't run."

Interesting how we were thinking the same thing. A-Rad was considering the same options that had popped into my head.

"We need to find out who he is and what he's after," A-Rad said. "I don't want to be looking over my shoulder again. Let's deal with the threat now."

I nodded, my mind racing through those options. We needed to isolate him somewhere we could control the confrontation.

"Let's take a walk," I suggested, trying to sound nonchalant as I pointed south.

The air outside the hotel was thick with the scent of hot pavement, mingling with the exhaust fumes from passing cars. Every noise felt amplified—the bustle of pedestrians, the distant honk of a horn, the soft thud of footsteps behind us. We strolled pretending nothing was amiss.

The man had exited the hotel shortly after us, confirming our suspicions even more.

I felt a prickling at the back of my neck, an instinctual warning that we were being followed.

The killer was too far away for me to literally hear his footsteps, but I heard them in my head. It's how I calculated the distance between us and kept adjusting it based on how far we made it down the street.

I could feel the man's gaze burning into our backs as he followed us, his presence like a shadow.

"Let's cross the street," I whispered urgently, then took A-Rad's hand, looked both ways, taking off without hesitation.

We jaywalked through the busy traffic, the rush of cars and honking horns providing a brief moment of cover. It bought us a little time and allowed us to keep an eye on the man without having to turn back to look.

We continued to walk with forced nonchalance, allowing the man to tail us at a safe distance. We didn't want him to know we were onto him.

He was good—but not good enough. I had to believe that we were better.

After a few blocks, I spotted a small clothing store with display racks on the sidewalk. I stopped to browse, giving me a chance to see how far away he was. He immediately turned and looked into a shop window. Trying to act like any other tourist.

He wasn't as good as I thought he was. Which would work to our advantage if we wanted to lose him but would still make it difficult to trap him. He wouldn't react like a trained operative. This man was a stone-cold killer. A hired hand, not a spy with training in these sorts of things.

I exchanged a glance with A-Rad, and he gave a subtle nod, understanding my plan without words.

"I'll duck into the store," I murmured. "You keep going."

A-Rad didn't need any further instructions. "Stay sharp."

"You too."

I slipped inside the store, the jingle of bells announcing my arrival. I feigned interest in the trinkets on display, while keeping a watchful eye on the man outside. He hesitated for a moment, scanning the street for signs of me before deciding to follow A-Rad.

Good.

I waited until the man had disappeared from sight, then darted out of the store, staying close to the buildings as I followed him. My senses were on full alert and ready for action.

A-Rad led the man into an alley behind the same store I had just been in, the perfect spot for a confrontation. The narrow passage was growing darker as the sun had started to set, the distant hum of city life muffled by the looming buildings.

My steps were silent as I closed the distance between us. I intended to sneak up on the man and take him out while A-Rad distracted him.

Stop now, A-Rad.

He stopped a couple of steps later, as if he heard me say the words that were in my head.

Turn around and face him.

A-Rad turned, his posture calm but ready.

It was as if A-Rad and I were one, acting in perfect synchronization.

I moved toward the man fast, my breath steady, my mind focused. The killer still didn't know I was there which gave me the element of surprise.

He reached into the back of his pants. My heart skipped a beat as I saw the glint of metal in his hand—a gun.

I was close, but not close enough to prevent him from getting a shot off at A-Rad.

A-Rad was also too far away to stop him.

Panic struck me as I realized I may have given him too much room.

I let out a sharp scream to distract him, buying myself a few seconds. He turned toward me, surprise evident on his face.

It was a trap and he had fallen right into it.

Our eyes locked, both filled with determination. Time seemed to slow down as we sized each other up, the gap between us shrinking as I moved quickly now.

I felt satisfaction that A-Rad was now out of harm's way. If the man killed me, A-Rad would kill him before he could turn and get off another shot.

His finger twitched on the trigger, and I launched myself forward in the air, knowing this was my only last chance.

Him or me. Kill or be killed.

26

Iran

Jeric leaned back in his office chair, the oppressive heat outside doing little to diminish the icy chill of anxiousness spreading through his veins. The flickering shadows cast by the sun shining through the partially closed curtains danced across the room, but his focus remained on the phone in his hand.

It had not left his sight in the last few hours. The digital glow illuminated his face as he stared at the screen, waiting for the one message that would determine his destiny.

He'd never been so nervous.

Not since his hired assassin sent him the picture of the two people who he was certain were behind Kunkel's murder and the destruction of Iran's nuclear facility. His lifetime of work, up in flames within seconds.

Jeric's fingers drummed against the desk. He was generally an optimistic person, but the silence gnawed at his composure. For a brief moment, the thought of failure wrapped itself around his mind, tightening like a noose.

He was old enough and had seen enough disappointments to know that this could go either way. His assassin was good, but so were the two killers he was chasing. After all, they had already gotten away with killing more than a dozen world leaders, penetrating some of the tightest security in the world.

They could not be underestimated.

He frequently reminded himself that they had killed two Russian presidents on Russian soil, right under the noses of thousands of armed soldiers and had gotten away with it. An unprecedented act of savagery that seemed impossible for only two people to accomplish.

If the stakes weren't so high and so personal, he might even admire the resourcefulness of the duo. But it's when he thought of these things, that the doubts became overwhelming.

Why would he think his assassin could do what no one else had been able to do?

The longer time passed, the more certain he was that his man had failed. He might not ever get a call which sent a fiery dart into his heart causing him to feel the agony of failure. If the assassin was dead, the two killers would make his body disappear and he'd never know what happened to him, other than that he had not succeeded.

Jeric had no idea what he'd do then.

His phone vibrated, the sound cutting through the stillness like a gunshot. He almost jumped out of the chair. His breath caught in his throat as he glanced down at the notification and saw it was from the assassin.

It's done.

A wave of relief washed over him, followed by a surge of euphoria. He quickly opened the message, his hand shaking almost uncontrollably from the excitement.

Two images loaded, one after the other.

The first picture showed one of the targets lying on the ground, a bullet wound to his head. The second brought him even more joy. The woman, also on the ground, with a single, precise bullet hole in the center of her forehead.

The assassin had done his job with clinical precision. There was no mistaking it: they were dead.

Jeric exhaled slowly as the tension that had gripped him for weeks finally released its hold. The threat was gone, neutralized in a way that left no room for doubt. He'd known the assassin would come through—he chastised himself for ever doubting.

Seeing the proof, those images, gave him an unspeakable joy beyond words. The problem was solved, and now, everything would fall into place.

He leaned forward, his fingers brushing across the screen as he studied the photos one last time. It was over. The people who had threatened his plans, the ones who had cruelly taken Kunkel from him, were no longer a problem. And no one would be able to connect them to him now.

Jeric had already started to weave the narrative, setting up the pieces that would exonerate him and point the blame squarely on the two killers who were now dead. He'd use their deaths to his advantage, tying them to a man who had worked at the secret nuclear facility. Someone who had conveniently died when Israel struck it.

The employee, who Jeric had carefully painted as a traitor, would be posthumously linked to the two operatives.

The evidence was already in place—an altered email here, a fabricated bank transfer there. Jeric had been meticulous, ensuring that every detail pointed to a grand conspiracy between the employee and the two operatives.

The story would be that he had given the pair the location of the facility, they had immediately betrayed its location to the Israelis who destroyed it, and now all three have paid the ultimate price for their treachery.

Thanks to Jeric's decisive action.

He'd be hailed as a hero, the man who had rooted out the traitors and protected Iran's interests. The investigation would be closed, the loose ends tied up neatly, and Jeric would be free to focus on the next phase of the plan.

He smiled to himself, savoring the moment.

The destruction of America was imminent, and with Andrew Pash poised to take office, everything was aligning perfectly. Once Pash was in power, they could execute the next part of the plan.

The groundwork had been laid, and soon, the world would witness the fall of a superpower.

Jeric's phone buzzed again, jolting him from his thoughts. He glanced at the screen, expecting another update, but it was just a mundane notification. He set it aside, his mind already racing ahead to what came next.

He logged into his desktop computer and immediately sent the second payment to the assassin. Then texted him back telling him the transfer was done.

He decided he had reveled in the demise of the two operatives long enough. There was still work to be done. He needed to ensure that Pash kept his end of the bargain, that the strings he'd pulled to get him into power remained taut.

Russia had to do their part as well. The new Russian leader was skeptical at first, but he had come around and could now see the opportunity for what it was. The chance to destroy America once and for all.

Jerry had convinced him that the two people in the British tabloid were behind the killings of the two Russian presidents and that the pair worked for the CIA. The Russian president had dismissed the theory out of hand, but Jerry convinced him it was the only explanation that made sense.

Now, the pictures of the two dead operatives would add to his credibility. He'd tell the Russian president that he found proof on their phones that they had been planning on coming for him next. At the direction of the CIA.

That should solidify his support once and for all.

The plan counted on Russia unleashing its nuclear arsenal on America, with such overwhelming force that it destroyed the country for good. Simultaneously, they'd launch nuclear bombs at Israel, and Iran's mortal enemy would be wiped off the face of the earth.

He felt a twinge of bitterness.

None of this would've been necessary, had he not been so careless and let the two operatives into Iran and let them get close to Kunkel. He would've loved to have the satisfaction of using Iranian bombs to destroy Israel and America.

That wasn't possible now, so he'd have to count on Russia to follow through with their commitment. While he didn't like not being in control, it's the only play he had left.

There could be no mistakes, no missteps now that they were so close. Everything had to go according to plan.

Doubts started to creep in again. But then, in the distance, the call to prayer echoed through the city.

It had to be a sign.

He smiled at the timing and his hope was restored. The plan was going to work.

History was about to change, and he had lived long enough to see it. The pieces were in place, the players were on the board, and the game was his to win.

27

Andrew Pash was about to become the most powerful man in the world, ready to fulfill his predetermined destiny.

He stood behind a thick oak door, momentarily separating him from the buzzing crowd on the other side of it. The faint hum of voices could be heard, an electric mix of anticipation and excitement.

Inhaling deeply, he placed his hand on the cold metal doorknob and waited for his cue. The solemnity of the moment sat heavily on his shoulders, but underneath his calm facade, his mind raced with exhilaration.

The weather was unusually chilly for an inauguration, with a biting wind whipping through the air. The sky was a vibrant shade of blue though, free of clouds, a fitting backdrop for the ceremony that would cement his place in history.

He checked his red tie, made sure it was centered, and smoothed out his jacket. Everything had to be perfect, just like the plan.

Forty years of careful scheming had led to this exact moment. Decades of manipulation and intricate webs woven so tightly that no one could ever untangle them.

He was the embodiment of a vision conceived by those who had foreseen the future. They somehow understood that true power did not lie in military might or economic prowess, but in strong leadership.

Interestingly enough, he wasn't focused on the speech he was about to give. The teleprompter would guide his every word. Instead, his thoughts drifted back to the day when his parents revealed the truth to him.

On his 30th birthday, they had gathered in his parents' penthouse apartment in New York City. His father, a man of few words but with a commanding presence, said unexpectedly that he had something important to share with him.

As he felt his father's intense gaze upon him, he couldn't help but feel as though he had done something wrong. In contrast, his mother, always more affectionate but just as intense, took hold of his hand and assured him that his father was about to disclose secrets that had been kept hidden since before he was born.

The revelation left him stunned, struggling to come to terms with the fact that his entire life had been orchestrated by forces beyond his control.

His parents, along with five other couples, had been carefully selected by the Iranian government for their intelligence and ability to seamlessly assimilate into American society. They had migrated from Iran to the United States under the guise of seeking a better life, but in reality, they were on a secret mission.

Each couple had been given a specific task: to have a child in America, provide them with the best education money could buy, and groom them for greatness. No expense was spared as Iran funded their children's private school tuition and tutors and helped them gain admission into prestigious universities.

"You have been chosen for such a time as this," his father had said. "You are a savior to the world."

The words sounded so nonsensical he couldn't wrap his mind around it. *Savior.*

He was an overachiever. Head of his class at Harvard, editor of the Law Journal, recipient of numerous awards. Yet he was still struggling to find his place in the world. Hadn't even found a wife yet.

The fact that the Iranian government had specifically chosen him and invested millions of dollars into his grooming was hard for him to grasp. Was it even legal? And what did they expect from him in return?

Pash had always felt a strong sense of purpose and entitlement, though he never quite knew why. Things started to make more sense the longer his father spoke of things that had been hidden from him all these years.

He was drawn to politics and fascinated by the power held by those in office. Looking back, he realized that his parents were the ones who had instilled this obsession in him.

For the first time, his father revealed his deep-seated hatred for America and his undying affection and loyalty to Iran. Even his normally soft-spoken mother used terms like infidels, oppressors, and terrorists when she referred to America and its citizens.

He was shocked to the point of disbelief that these words were coming out of their mouths.

"The blood of the oppressed will not be forgotten," she said, bitterly.

At first, he didn't know how to feel. He had grown up as an American with Iranian roots, but his parents had always made sure he assimilated into American society completely. His initial drive to enter politics stemmed from a desire to improve the world.

He could now see the underlying contempt his parents held for capitalism and the depraved lifestyle of Americans. He shared some of those feelings too. Deep down, he harbored a disdain for America and its excesses. The rampant capitalism, inequality, and arrogance of a nation that believed it was superior to all others, grated on him.

That's why he aligned himself with the political side that advocated for change and railed against those things. But he never expected it to go this far. He always believed America could change and make things right.

But seeing this hate from his parents revealed a different level of conviction. They truly believed America was beyond redemption. Their solution was to destroy it and rebuild it entirely, replacing it with a new global order where one country did not impose its values on the rest of the world.

Doubts swirled in his mind as he listened to the words, but he kept quiet. His father's wrath was not something he wanted to face by questioning him.

Despite this, some of the things his father said made sense to him. He believed in a world where American dominance was no longer necessary, and wars were avoidable. It troubled him that so many people lived in poverty while others lived in excess.

Pash shared his parent's hatred for the Jews. That's something they had always been open about. He had never been able to put these thoughts into words like his parents were doing right then.

"What do you mean I've been chosen? Chosen for what?" he finally asked, after his father finished speaking.

"You will become the President of the United States," his father stated confidently.

Pash wanted to laugh at the absurdity of the statement but bit his lip instead. He would never show such disrespect towards his father.

But how could that be possible?

He was just a community organizer, a low-ranking member among party leaders who didn't even know his name. He was a political novice, and he knew that the presidency was only available to a select few individuals backed by a powerful machine, a shadow government that controlled everything from behind the scenes.

"You will first become a senator," his father continued. "Then you will secure your party's nomination for president. And you will win."

"How is that even possible?" he finally mustered the courage to ask, despite the screaming doubts in his head.

"God wills it."

He buried his skepticism from that day and went back to work. It wasn't until things started to almost miraculously fall in place that he realized sources beyond his imagination were pulling the strings.

A wife was chosen for him. A child of one of the six couples. A stunningly gorgeous woman who he felt privileged to marry after meeting her. While they weren't in love, the arranged marriage seemed right. She was the perfect woman to be by his side and help him achieve the goals his father had laid out for him.

Somehow, his father's plans began coming true. Pash rose rapidly through the ranks, each victory bringing him closer to the ultimate goal. Within five years, he became a senator from New York. No one was more shocked when he secured the nomination against more formidable foes who stepped aside and ceded it to him.

Even then, he thought becoming president was an impossibility. Or at least out of his reach for thirty or forty years. The older generation controlled the party and determined the line of succession.

His father had insisted, and Pash threw his hat into the ring and began to campaign for the presidency. Money flowed, although he never really knew the source of the funds. Against all odds, he won the nomination and eventually the election.

In his wildest dreams, he never thought it possible. His own internal polling showed him behind. Yet somehow, he garnered the most votes in the election, winning every swing state by the smallest of margins, with enough votes to secure the popular vote and the electoral college majority.

That's when more of the truth was finally revealed to him at another meeting in his father's penthouse. He really didn't have time for that meeting. The next few months would be a whirlwind as he had to prepare for the transition into the presidency. But when his father called him, he had no choice but to comply.

"There's someone I want you to talk to," his father had said. He had a phone in his hand that Pash had never seen before.

"Who?"

"His name is unimportant."

"At least tell me where he's from."

"He's a leader in Iran. He's the one who chose you to become president."

Pash objected.

"I can't be caught having a phone call with an Iranian official," Pash said. "I'm not the president yet."

"Don't worry," his father said. "The line is secure."

How did his father have a secure satellite phone?

The man on the other line was direct while being ambiguous.

"You will choose Tarik Hannan to be your chief of staff," he said.

"I've already chosen someone to be my chief of staff," Pash retorted.

His father glared at him.

The man on the phone burst into a rage. When he calmed down, he said to Pash's father, "I thought you said he was ready to be president."

"He is," his father said. "You can trust him. You have my word."

Pash learned that Hannan was the son of one of the six couples. It made sense that they'd want him in his inner circle.

When they hung up the phone, Pash asked his father, "What if I don't go along with what he wants?" he dared to ask.

"Then your mother and I will die having failed."

His father didn't elaborate on what that meant, but he assumed the worst.

"You must do what he says," his father said, bluntly. "Where do you think all this came from?"

His father pointed around the luxurious apartment.

"Your education. Who do you think paid for that? You wouldn't be president had it not been for that man. You owe him."

Pash wasn't naïve. He knew how politics worked. Politicians were indebted to those who helped get them elected. In his case, he was a slave to unknown forces he'd never met.

"But what does he want from me?"

"All will be revealed in due time."

Before Pash left the apartment that day, he agreed to the plan. His father said that he'd be a world leader but not in the way that he expected. Not the leader of the free world secured by an election, but propelled into power by an organization who ran the world from behind the scenes.

Pash would be tasked with leading the world into a globalist system that provided equality to every man and country. Fear should have consumed him in that moment, but somehow, in all the craziness, he was emboldened by the idea.

Despite not knowing how he could possibly carry it out, he embraced it. He trusted his father implicitly and would have to do so one more time.

Now, standing on the verge of becoming president, everything was falling into place. He'd had one more conversation with the mysterious man from Iran. One of his first tasks as president would be to visit Russia, where the final phase of their plan would unfold.

Pash didn't know the specifics of the plan, but he was so far deep in the clutches of the man that he didn't question him.

A gentle tapping on the door interrupted his thoughts. It was time for the inauguration. He straightened his posture, lifted his chin, and opened the door to a deafening wave of cheers from the crowd outside.

Pash maintained a calm and composed expression as he stepped onto the platform, ready to take on the daunting roles of leadership and responsibility.

As he made his way towards the podium, he caught a glimpse of his parents sitting in the audience. Their faces glowed with happiness and pride. They had played their part in getting him to this point, but now it was up to him to fulfill his duty.

Tomorrow, they would return to Iran for some unknown reason.

"When are you coming back?" he had asked them.

"We aren't," his father said soberly. "We have fulfilled our mission."

He didn't understand but didn't question it.

With his hand on the Bible, he recited the oath given to him with a steady and strong voice. Despite the irony of his situation, he swore to defend and uphold the United States constitution.

He still didn't know all the specifics but felt like he was betraying his country in some way. He pushed aside any conflicting thoughts and focused all of his energy on the task at hand.

When the oath was complete, the Chief Justice stepped back and Pash turned to face the cheering crowd. In his inaugural address, he carefully crafted words meant to inspire hope and patriotism and unite a deeply divided nation. He acknowledged the obstacles ahead and stressed the importance of working together as a country.

His tone was genuine, and he made eye contact with many of those gathered before him.

He was determined to fulfill his destiny, the path chosen for him before he was even born. He wasn't sure how it'd all play out, but according to his father, the fate of the world rested on his shoulders, even though only a handful of people knew it.

As Pash finished his speech, the audience erupted in applause once again. He took a step back from the podium and acknowledged the cheering crowd with a wave.

Looking at his father's smile, a rare sight, Pash felt a sense of pride and accomplishment. He had finally made his father proud.

28

Russia

Two months later

The trip to Russia had been delayed. Most of President Pash's advisors were against it. For a number of reasons.

"Can the Russians guarantee your safety? They already have two dead presidents shot right in front of their eyes."

"That's why I have to go," the president had argued. "They think the United States is behind those killings. I have to assure the Russian people that we are their friends."

"Should I remind you that the two killers are still on the loose?"

His advisors didn't know that the two people behind those killings were dead. Pash had raised that concern with Jeric, the mystery man from Iran, who had given Pash proof that the two were killed by an assassin hired by him.

Jeric also revealed to Pash the real reason he needed to go to Russia: to execute a plan for the complete destruction of the United States with nuclear bombs.

At first, Pash was horrified by the idea, but over time he became convinced that it was the best course of action. His wife and chief of staff were already aware of the plan and helped him see why it was necessary.

While America as they knew it would be destroyed, the world would be better off. So would Pash. He would be responsible for ushering in the New World Order and become its leader. He could remake the entire world in his image.

That could never happen as long as America was the only dominant superpower in the world. The U.S. dollar was the primary global currency. After the nuclear bombs hit, the dollar would lose all of its value and the stock market would crash to zero.

A new form of digital currency was already being developed. Emerging nations were stockpiling and repatriating gold to support their buying power with something valuable to back their currency.

From the ashes would come a new monetary system that was fairer. A financial reset that was long overdue.

First, he had to convince his advisors without seeming overly anxious to travel to Russia. The entire time, he had been looking over his shoulder. Petrified that someone was going to discover his plan. The punishment for treason was death.

"We've detected an unusual amount of activity in the Russian nuclear arsenal," one of his generals had commented. "We have reason to believe that Russia may be planning a nuclear attack on America."

"That's impossible," Pash argued, even though he knew that's exactly what was going to happen.

"Why would Russia do such a thing?" he said. "We'd launch our missiles at them and that would ensure our mutual destruction."

Little did they know that Pash's chief of staff, Tarik, would see to it that the nuclear codes didn't match, rendering America defenseless.

"That's another reason I need to go," Pash said, convincingly. "I want to look the Russian president in the eye and assess his intentions."

Ultimately, he had the final say and after two months of planning, the trip was scheduled. The day had finally arrived for him to travel to Russia along with his wife and chief of staff who carried with him the nuclear football.

The previous administration had implemented new protocols for handling nuclear codes that would work to his advantage. The nuclear football, a black briefcase containing the launch codes, used to be carried by a member of the military. The decision was made that it'd be more appropriate for a member of the president's staff to carry it.

The chief of staff was chosen for this responsibility since they were almost always with the president. In instances when they weren't, such as overnight hours, one of their aides would stay outside the president's personal residence with the football.

In this instance, Tarik Hannan, the current chief of staff, was the only one he could trust to carry out their diabolical plan.

The plan itself was carefully crafted and organized down to the smallest detail. Inside the nuclear football were two important items: a plastic card known as the "biscuit" which contained a code to verify the president's identity at the National Military Command Center, and the launch codes needed to unlock nuclear weapons.

In order to prevent any potential security breaches, the biscuit was permanently affixed inside the briefcase after an incident when a former president lost it in his suit pocket and it ended up at the dry cleaners.

To further enhance security measures, the launch codes were now different from those held at the National Command Center, requiring both sets of codes to successfully activate nuclear weapons.

In the event that the president decided to launch nuclear missiles, he would open the case and read the numbers on the biscuit to his general, verifying his identity. Those numbers weren't changed. Pash wanted them to think he was on the other end of the call.

Once the president's identity was verified, he'd read the launch codes, and they'd unlock the missiles. Then he'd give the instructions on how to use them. If the codes didn't unlock the missiles, it meant the weapons could not be launched, as the generals didn't have the authority or the means to override them.

When Pash arrived in Russia, the plan was for Russian nuclear weapons to be unleashed on both the United States and Israel. Hundreds of missiles would target military bases and major cities, while ships and submarines with nuclear capabilities would also be targeted using non-nuclear intercontinental missiles.

America's leadership would be in disarray. No one had considered what would happen if the launch codes didn't match, or if the person carrying them decided to change them. But that's exactly what Tarik had done. He had switched out the codes in the case, so when the president read them, they wouldn't match, and America would be unable to retaliate.

There wouldn't be enough time to come up with an alternative plan. From the moment Russia launched its missiles, America only had eighteen minutes before Guam was hit, thirty-seven minutes before Honolulu was hit, thirty-eight minutes before Los Angeles was annihilated, and thirty-nine minutes before Chicago, New York, and Washington D.C. were obliterated. Even Alaska's major cities would be hit within twenty-nine minutes.

Pash refused to think about the destruction that would follow, lives lost, chaos reigning supreme, and a nation brought to its knees. But it was all necessary for the greater good. America had its time in power, and now it was time for a new system that would treat everyone fairly.

The aftermath of a nuclear attack would leave America crippled beyond repair and Israel would suffer the same fate at the same time.

Every detail was in place. Nothing, no one could stop those nukes from hitting America.

* * *

Moscow

Air Force One descended smoothly onto the runway of Moscow, the city below covered in a light dusting of snow. President Andrew Pash gazed out the window, taking in the sight of the country he'd never been to.

He felt an unusual sense of calmness as he landed. This was what everything had been leading up to, and there was no turning back now. He'd probably never step foot in America again.

The aircraft touched down gracefully on the tarmac, its wheels gliding over the pavement without causing so much as a ripple in his drink. Pash leaned back in his seat and closed his eyes for a moment.

The upcoming hours were crucial. The plan that had been set into motion decades ago was finally reaching its peak, and any mistakes could prove disastrous.

As the jet taxied towards a group of people waiting for them, Pash felt a slight twinge of unease in his chest. It wasn't fear. He had learned long ago how to suppress that emotion. It was more of a heightened state of alertness.

The jet came to a stop and the door opened, letting in a blast of cold Russian air that made Pash shiver despite his heavy coat. He straightened his tie and descended down the metal stairs onto the tarmac, where a row of black SUVs waited for him.

Two men in suits approached, one holding an umbrella to shield him from the light snowfall. "Mr. President," one of them said with a thick Russian accent, "welcome to Russia. President Orlov is waiting for you in the hangar."

Pash nodded and offered a polite smile. "Thank you."

He was guided to one of the SUVs, and the motorcade began its short journey to the hangar. The atmosphere was thick with anticipation, and Pash could feel it pulsing through every inch of his body.

As they arrived at the hangar, Pash spotted President Sergei Orlov standing near the entrance. Orlov was the new face of Russian power, having taken over after the second assassination, an event that had shocked the world but ultimately served their purpose.

To the western world, Orlov appeared to be a moderate leader, but that was just a facade. In reality, he was as power-hungry and determined as his predecessors, with a desire to restore Russia to its former glory and even surpass it. For his cooperation in the plan, he had been promised control over Europe, except for neutral Switzerland, where Pash planned to live as the leader of the New World Order.

As Pash stepped out of the SUV, he adjusted his overcoat and approached Orlov. The Russian president extended his hand, which Pash firmly shook. Their eyes met, conveying an unspoken understanding between them. They may not have become friends, but they were united by a common goal.

"Welcome to Russia, Mr. President," Orlov greeted fluently in English.

"Thank you, President Orlov. It is an honor to be here," Pash replied.

The two men stood in silence for a moment, their breath visible in the cold air. Then, Orlov gestured towards the hangar. "Shall we?"

Pash nodded and they walked together into the warmth of the hangar. Inside, a small group of aides and military officials awaited them with solemn expressions. Both men seemed tense from the gravity of what was about to be discussed.

Orlov led Pash to a private room where only Pash's chief of staff and one of Orlov's generals were allowed. A table sat at the center of the room with a large map of the world spread out on it. Red and blue lines crisscrossed the map, marking missile trajectories, potential targets, and strategically important areas. As Pash gazed upon the map, he realized the magnitude of what they were about to unleash.

Breaking the silence, Orlov spoke up. "All preparations are complete. The missiles are armed and ready. All that remains is for me to give the order."

Pash looked up from the map, meeting Orlov's gaze. "We are ready on our end," he said.

"And the codes? They've been changed?" Orlov asked.

Pash nodded to Tarik, who stepped forward with the black briefcase and placed it on the table.

"I can assure you that the codes have indeed been changed," Tarik said. "Our military response will be delayed, and we will not be able to retaliate."

"You have my word that no missiles will hit Russia," Pash said.

Orlov nodded in understanding.

Pash then asked, "When do we start?"

Orlov checked his watch. "First, we must make an appearance. The world is watching. Then ... we move forward."

Pash agreed with a nod. "Very well. It must appear as though I had no involvement in this scheme."

The two men shared one last look before exiting the hangar. As they stepped outside, the biting cold air hit him once again, but Pash barely noticed. His mind was focused and determined. A large crowd had gathered outside the hangar. Reporters, diplomats, and military personnel. all eager to catch a glimpse of the two leaders.

Pash and Orlov strode confidently towards the podium, greeted by a flurry of camera flashes. They had agreed to keep their speeches brief, knowing that this event was just a distraction from their true intentions.

Orlov spoke first, his booming voice addressing the crowd in Russian. Pash only caught fragments of his words, but it didn't matter. The message was clear: two major powers were standing together in unity.

Stepping up to the microphone, Pash felt the world's attention on him. He carefully delivered his speech of peace, cooperation, and a new era of understanding between their nations. An orchestrated performance meant to reassure the world that everything was under control.

But as he spoke, Pash's mind was elsewhere. He could see the plan unfolding in his head, the missiles hidden away in silos, the codes changed to leave America vulnerable, and the cities wiped off the map in an instant.

Yet there was no trace of guilt or remorse in Pash's demeanor as he stepped down from the stage to cheers and applause. Only a cold determination that this was necessary.

29

A few hours earlier

I crouched in the cramped, dark compartment beneath the floorboards of the AJAX plane, my knees aching from being in the same position for too long. It smelled like stale sweat and metal, a mix of fear and adrenaline that clung to the inside of the secret space.

Next to me, A-Rad's face was barely visible, his features contorted into a mask of intense concentration as we listened to the muffled sounds of boots moving inside and outside the plane. The Russians were searching, scouring the aircraft for anything suspicious, but they wouldn't find us. We were well hidden, and we'd made sure of that.

Flying into Russia only four days before the president's scheduled trip was a risky move, but nothing about this operation was safe. We figured that if we landed at the same airport, the authorities would allow our plane to be parked at a hangar out of the way but within the security perimeter.

The AJAX plane was equipped with a secret compartment precisely for situations like these. It wasn't the first time we had needed to transport sensitive cargo without it being discovered.

Sometimes, it was young girls rescued from human trafficking rings. We also had a similar compartment on our yacht, which could hold up to a hundred girls at a time while we brought them to safety.

Other times, we used the compartment to conceal weapons, fake passports, money, mission plans, and gear. Despite operating under the guise of an art distribution company, we knew that our planes and even our yacht could be searched by authorities at times, so we needed a way to hide our true activities.

In this instance, we were certain that Russian authorities would thoroughly search our plane ahead of the president's arrival. That's why we decided to hide in the compartment until it was time to make our move on him.

We were there to kill the Presidents of the United States of America and Russia.

A necessary measure after a series of alarming events that began in Los Angeles. After meeting with A-Rad's father, we were confronted by a hired assassin who had somehow managed to uncover our identities as the notorious killers from the British tabloid.

We confronted and killed him in an alley behind a store and disposed of his body in a dumpster. After we relieved him of his phone and ID, we found communications with Jeric in Iran, who had clearly hired him to kill us.

So we decided to pay Jeric a visit.

We sent him pictures from the assassin's phone pretending to be dead.

I'll never forget the look on his face when we confronted him in his home in Tehran. His initial reaction was surprise, then shock, followed by a sense of resignation as he realized his life was coming to an end.

"Who is AP?" we demanded, hoping to finally get answers.

Jeric refused to give us what we wanted, so we dragged him to his bathroom, shoved his head into the tub, and waterboarded him until he choked on his own lies. It didn't take long for him to tell us everything.

What we learned was beyond shocking?

President Pash was a carefully selected Iranian asset, groomed from birth for decades as part of a sinister plan. And now, he was moments away from betraying America and ensuring her utter destruction.

Jeric gave us all the details: how the nuclear codes would be changed, how Russia would launch hundreds of bombs, and how it would all be too late by the time anyone figured it out.

At first, we were skeptical. But Jeric gave up all the details when we threatened to waterboard him again.

In his office, he showed us where to find a trove of evidence; birth certificates, wire transfers, and forty years' worth of meticulous planning and work. On his phone were incriminating conversations with the President of the United States and detailed texts with the Russian president.

A massive conspiracy with global consequences.

In the end, we put a bullet in Jeric's head and took everything with us.

My mind had become so consumed with anger that I could barely think straight.

Rage that Jeric sent a hitman after us. Rage at Pash, the so-called leader of the free world, who was nothing more than a puppet dancing to Iran's strings. Rage that nuclear bombs were about to rain down on America while we were powerless to stop it.

But anger wasn't enough. It wasn't going to save America, and it wasn't going to save us. We weren't sure exactly what to do with the information.

We considered going to Brad, but he was now the CIA director appointed by Pash himself. We weren't sure if we could trust anyone in the American government, which was deeply entrenched with corruption and cover-ups.

We'd seen it over the years. Scandals were buried so deep within the government that the truths behind events from a hundred years ago were still buried. Classified information that should've been released to the public was so tightly locked in the vaults of the government that they might not ever be released.

We trusted Alex and Jamie but involving them could implicate them in our plan. I could envision them getting arrested. Jamie separated from her kids.

We had an ongoing rule that we lived by at AJAX. We never did anything to expose the AJAX cover or other operatives. Everything had to be protected at all costs.

So we found ourselves in Russia, alone, hoping that our risky plan would work.

We gave our success odds, known as the mission S.O., at twenty percent. It depended on a lot of factors outside of our control.

Assuming we could land at the same airport that the president would arrive at and that there wouldn't be a last-minute change of plans; assuming they wouldn't make us move our plane outside the perimeter; assuming that we could hide in the plane without being detected.

I could hear Jamie in my head saying, "Never assume anything!"

What choice did we have?

Even if we got past all of those obstacles, we still had to launch our drone and kill the president without someone shooting it down. Surely, the Russians would be more diligent since a drone had killed their last president.

And ... assuming we were successful and did kill the president, then what? How did we get out of Russia alive?

Our plan was to fire up the plane and fly out. Hoping that the element of surprise would allow us to get in the air before anyone realized it. If we got safely away from the airport, we had to get out of Russian airspace before fighter jets could scramble and shoot us down.

Twenty percent? That might be generous.

The sound of heavy footsteps faded and A-Rad nudged me, signaling it was time to move. We emerged from our hiding spot with silent steps, like shadows slipping out of the darkness.

The plane was now empty, but the stairs were still down. To avoid suspicion, A-Rad and I wore Russian uniforms, as we had when we killed their previous two presidents. Our disguises had worked then and we could only hope they would work again now.

A-Rad checked his watch. We still had a few hours until Air Force One arrived. Just enough time to prepare for our next move. I quickly lowered all the shades on the aircraft, not wanting anyone to see inside while we made our final preparations.

"Is the drone ready?" I whispered, scanning the area outside the cockpit window for any signs of movement.

My chest tightened with tension as I waited for A-Rad's response. He nodded grimly.

"As ready as it can be. I need to test it to be sure."

It had taken us hours to assemble the small but powerful drone in the confined space of the AJAX plane. It was loaded with enough firepower to take out our two targets, but when he tried to test it, nothing happened.

The screen stayed black, and the controls were unresponsive in A-Rad's hands. After troubleshooting for nearly an hour, he finally figured it out. The

Russians had jammed all radio signals after our last attack that took out their president.

Panic set in as we realized our primary plan had failed and we were running out of time.

"What are we gonna do?" A-Rad's voice was low but edged with frustration. I could see the anger in his eyes, the same fury that was clawing at my insides. "We can't just sit here and watch Pash start a nuclear war."

Now, as I stared at the lifeless drone in front of me, I realized we were right back where we started. Out of options, out of time.

"We have to think of something," I said, through gritted teeth. "We didn't come this far to fail."

A-Rad ran a hand through his hair, his eyes darting around the plane like he was searching for answers in the aircraft.

"We could try hacking into their system directly," he suggested, though he didn't sound convinced. "There must be a frequency open for their internal communications."

"That could take hours," I pointed out. "Assuming we even know how to hack into it."

"Maybe we should warn Alex and Jamie then," A-Rad proposed. "They might be able to stop it on their end."

Our initial plan was to send them all the information after the fact, so we could justify our actions. Everything was already compiled in a file, ready to be sent once A-Rad hit 'send'.

"How do we send him a message without incriminating them?" I asked.

"If those nukes detonate, will it matter?" A-Rad shot back. "They'll be dead anyway."

"We can't let those bombs go off," I stressed. "We have to stop the president."

"I have an idea," A-Rad said hesitantly. "But ... it's not a good one."

"I'm open to anything at this point," I replied.

"We could crash the plane into the president," he suggested.

"No way," I immediately protested, although it wasn't a horrible idea. It'd definitely kill the presidents but would also kill us in the process.

"Do you have a better idea?" he challenged.

"No."

We sat in silence for a good five minutes, trying to think of another plan.

"I'll try what I did before," A-Rad finally said. "Integrate with the troops and get close enough for a shot."

"They'll spot you immediately," I retorted, my mind frantically exploring every possible option. None of them seemed feasible or safe.

He didn't argue. We both knew the risks we were taking.

Glancing at my watch, I saw that Air Force One was scheduled to land in less than an hour. With each passing second, the countdown to disaster grew louder.

Then, a wild thought crossed my mind, reckless and dangerous, but it might be our last hope. I raised the window shade slightly and motioned for A-Rad to look outside.

"Do you see that building over there?" I pointed.

He nodded.

"If we can somehow get up there, we'll have a clear line of sight to where the president will be speaking."

A-Rad frowned. "It's probably heavily guarded."

"We'll overpower them if we have to," I declared. "Or maybe we can bluff our way through by saying we have assigned positions on that roof."

"That's suicide," A-Rad argued, his voice tense. "We'll never make it out alive. We'll be trapped on that roof."

"I don't care," I snapped, the words bursting out before I could stop them. "We either stop this, or we watch everyone we love burn. I'm not going down without a fight."

A-Rad glared at me, his jaw set in determination. For a moment, I thought he was going to argue, but then his shoulders slumped, and he let out a heavy sigh.

"Alright," he said. "Let's do it."

We moved quickly, grabbed our gear, and slipped out of the plane. Snow fell softly around us, creating a hushed blanket of white that muffled our footsteps as we walked with purpose towards the building.

Surprisingly, there were no guards in sight.

"How do we get up on the roof?" I asked, my voice low and urgent.

"Around back," A-Rad replied, his eyes scanning the area for any signs of danger. "There's got to be an air conditioning unit or a ladder."

We found what we were looking for and climbed onto the roof undetected. The sloped surface provided us with cover as we crept towards our vantage point, hidden from view until we had a clear shot at our targets.

"This is too easy," I muttered.

"A definite lapse in security," A-Rad agreed. "Somebody dropped the ball."

In the distance, Air Force One descended towards the runway in the morning light.

"It's early," A-Rad said.

"Good thing we moved when we did," I answered.

My heart raced with adrenaline as each beat seemed faster than the last. This was it. No turning back.

"Who gets to take out our president?" I asked.

"I will," A-Rad declared. "You kill the Russian president."

I watched as President Andrew Pash stepped out of the plane flanked by two others, a woman and a man carrying a black briefcase. His smug expression made my blood boil.

Everyone seemed oblivious to our presence. To them, we were invisible.

"I have a good shot," I said, as I zeroed in on him in my sight.

"We need to do it when he's with the Russian president," A-Rad whispered, his eyes fixed in that direction.

I nodded, tightening my grip on my gun as I mentally went over our plan.

"Where is he?"

"I haven't seen him."

As we spoke, the president got into an SUV and drove to a nearby hangar.

"The Russian must be in there," I said.

Then a horrifying thought entered my mind.

"What if that's where they're going to do it?" I asked, my voice trembling with fear and frustration.

"Nothing we can do about it," A-Rad said, pulling out his phone.

"What are you doing?" I asked.

"I'm sending Alex a text," A-Rad replied, his fingers typing rapidly on the screen.

"Warning him. I hope I'm not too late."

30

The biting cold wind cut through my stiff Russian uniform as I lay flat on the roof, watching through the scope as the Russian president stepped out of the building, followed by the American president.

Relief washed over me when I saw the two figures heading towards the main staging area. They hadn't initiated their plan in the hangar, which meant we still had a chance to stop them.

They were too far away to take a shot. Waiting until they were on the makeshift stage was the best strategy. I reminded A-Rad to take the wind into consideration when he took his shot.

He scowled at me for stating the obvious but kept quiet. This wasn't the time for dissension between us.

Despite being on a cold rooftop, it felt like we were in a foxhole. Jamie had said a thousand times that when the bullets start flying, to remember who the real enemy is and don't take our frustrations out on each other.

Snowflakes fell softly around us, each one a tiny reminder of the ticking clock that was running out on our mission. I could feel A-Rad's tension beside me, his breathing steady, but charged with the urgency of what we were about to do.

The wet snow was another problem to consider because it could build up on our rifle scopes and blur our vision. I didn't remind A-Rad of that this time avoiding another glare from him. He knew that fact as well as I did.

It'd also be problematic when we made our escape. Going down the sloped roof would be as difficult as going up it, if not more so. The roof had been slippery on the way up, and now we had to be extra careful not to slip and fall off.

We couldn't afford any injuries, especially a broken ankle, at this crucial moment. I knew we would have to move quickly and stealthily like deer evading a predator. Except, in our case, the predators were hundreds of armed Russian soldiers.

My gaze stayed fixed on the Russian president as he made his way towards the main area, surrounded by guards who seemed anxious yet oblivious to what was about to happen. The crowd had gathered below the podium, with military personnel, important figures, and journalists all packed tightly together. Cameras were already set up, ready to capture every moment of the speeches that were about to take place.

The Russian president walked up the steps and made his way to the podium.

But where was President Pash? He wasn't in my line of sight. If I couldn't see him, then neither could A-Rad.

I had a clear shot at the Russian president but couldn't risk taking it at this point. Not until we had both of them in our crosshairs.

"Where the heck is Pash?" I muttered under my breath, shifting my position to get a better view. I swept the scope from left to right, scanning the entire area, but the American president was nowhere to be seen.

A-Rad's eyes were glued to his own scope, his brow furrowed in frustration. "This is a nightmare," he grumbled. "I can see the Russian president clear as day, but Pash is nowhere near him."

The Russian president stood tall, soaking in the attention. My gaze shifted to the right where I finally spotted Pash, sitting in one of the chairs, flanked by his security detail.

"He's over there," I whispered. "Two o'clock behind the podium."

"I don't see him," A-Rad replied.

In truth, I couldn't see him either. But every so often, I caught glimpses of his tie as the members of his security team moved back and forth in front of him.

"I don't have a clear shot," A-Rad said with urgency in his voice.

The Russian president began speaking, his voice booming over the loudspeakers. The crowd's attention was focused on him.

"They're not in the same spot!" A-Rad said with urgency. "We can't take them both out at once."

I bit back my frustration, my mind racing. It felt like they knew our plans and purposely positioned themselves to make it impossible for us to take them both out without getting caught.

"What do we do?" I asked, my words tasting bitter in my mouth. Every passing second felt like a missed opportunity. We were rapidly running out of time, and my gut told me that hesitation would be our downfall.

A-Rad took a moment to think, weighing the options. I could see the struggle in his eyes. Kill one and risk losing the other or wait for a perfect chance that may never come.

"If we take out one now, the other will go into full lockdown," he finally said, still keeping his gaze fixed on the scope. "We'll lose any chance of getting them both."

"Let's wait and see," I suggested. "Maybe the Russian president will introduce Pash, and they'll shake hands at the podium."

But my hopes were shattered when the Russian president finished his speech and turned to walk back towards Pash, who emerged from behind the security detail and made his way to the podium.

The Russian president was no longer in my line of sight. I had missed my opportunity to kill him and I didn't know if I'd get another.

"We can't count on them being together at the same time," I blurted out, feeling hopeless. "We have to do something now. Waiting is not an option."

A-Rad let out a deep breath, his expression betraying his decision. "I'll take out Pash," he declared. "It's our only chance to stop the nuclear launch."

Are you sure about this?

I wanted to ask, but already knew the answer. A-Rad was determined and I understood why. The American president was the key player in this dangerous game. If we could eliminate him, it would disrupt their plans.

"I'm positive that's what we should do," A-Rad replied firmly as if he was reading my mind.

"Me too," I whispered under my breath. "If Pash is gone, the Russians won't follow through with the attack. The Vice President will take over and if the codes don't match, they'll initiate emergency protocols to fix it."

I shifted slightly, keeping my aim on the Russian president just in case. But everything inside me told me this was our only opportunity. Circumstances had changed and we had to adapt.

I could take out some of the guards in front of the Russian president and then possibly kill him, but there were innocent people among them. They were just doing their jobs and I didn't want to harm them unnecessarily.

But if it meant stopping a nuclear war, I would do it without hesitation.

We had a clear shot at Pash and that's all we needed.

The crowd erupted in applause as Pash stepped to the podium. Cameras flashed and I watched as he began his speech.

My heart raced as the enormity of our decision weighed on me. We were about to assassinate the President of the United States of America—something I never thought possible.

Pash adjusted the microphone with a calm demeanor, almost smugly unaware of the danger looming around him. The cameras captured his every move as he straightened his tie. A-Rad adjusted his aim, his finger hovering over the trigger.

"Make it count," I whispered, knowing it was our only hope. The shot had to be true. We'd probably only get one chance at it.

"You take a shot as well," A-Rad said. "That will double our chances."

I didn't hesitate and got Pash in my sights.

"On my count. Three, two, one, fire."

We pulled the triggers at the exact same time and the sound of the gunshots reverberated off the buildings. Through my scope, I watched as both bullets hit Pash in the chest, causing him to jerk violently before collapsing to the ground in a silent scream.

Pandemonium erupted in the once peaceful scene. Guards bellowed, their weapons drawn and ready as they scrambled to protect the fallen president. The panicked crowd screamed and scattered in every direction, creating a chaotic frenzy.

With my heart pounding in my ears, I took one last desperate look through my scope, hoping for a clear shot at the Russian president amidst the chaos. But he was now being smothered by his own guards, making any chance of a clean hit impossible.

"Go, go, go!" I shouted, instinctively springing to my feet. We had mere seconds before our location would be compromised.

We leapt off the roof, sliding down the side of the building and landing hard in the snow below. We sprinted toward our plane, but it was already swarming with enemy soldiers.

"Blocked," A-Rad hissed, skidding to a halt. Frustration etched deep lines on his face as our carefully crafted plan crumbled before us.

"Run!" I yelled, grabbing his arm and pulling him towards cover behind the nearest building. Bullets whizzed past us, grazing dangerously close as we darted between vehicles for protection.

Finally, we found temporary refuge inside an abandoned warehouse. Gasping for breath, we slammed the door shut behind us and tried to regain our composure. But we knew it wouldn't last long.

"This way," A-Rad urged, leading us through a maze of corridors and out a side exit. We emerged into a desolate alleyway, pausing momentarily to catch our breath before taking off again.

"I think we lost them," I panted optimistically as I scanned our surroundings. But just as I allowed myself a glimmer of hope, headlights blazed to life and a convoy of military vehicles barreled around the corner towards us.

"Move!" A-Rad shouted, and we were off again, racing towards a row of abandoned buildings for cover. We burst inside an old warehouse, weaving through dusty corridors and rusty machinery in an attempt to shake off our pursuers.

The sound of boots and shouts grew louder behind us as they followed us inside. They were gaining on us, closing in with every step.

A-Rad's panicked muttering filled the air as we searched desperately for an escape route. I scanned our surroundings, reminding myself to control the adrenaline pumping through my veins.

"Over there!" I shouted, pointing to a ladder leading up to a narrow metal catwalk. We scrambled up, fear and determination fueling our movements. When in a gunfight, always seek the high ground.

Reaching the top, we looked down at the soldiers swarming into the warehouse below. They were getting closer by the second and it wouldn't be long before they spotted us.

"We need a way out," I whispered urgently, frantically searching for a solution. "They'll search every inch of this place."

A-Rad's jaw was clenched as he nodded in agreement. But deep down, I could see the doubt in his eyes. We were trapped, and we both knew it.

From our elevated position, we watched helplessly as the soldiers spread out, their weapons ready to kill, and their voices echoing off the walls.

A-Rad's gaze met mine, his dark eyes filled with determination. "We're getting out of here," he declared with conviction, though I could sense his uncertainty.

I tightened my grip on my weapon, steeling myself for what was to come. "We have to," I replied tersely.

As the soldiers closed in on us like vultures, I knew that our survival depended on us finding a miracle. We were backed into a corner, but we wouldn't go down without trying everything we could think of.

Our resolve would never waver, even if it meant facing death head on. We had come too far and fought too hard to let them defeat us.

Our mission wasn't over yet. We were getting out of Russia alive, no matter what it took.

31

The thunderous sound of heavy boots echoed against the cold, uninsulated warehouse walls, reverberating like a haunting drumbeat shaking the very foundation of our precarious hiding spot. We were trapped, cornered with nowhere left to run. A-Rad and I huddled behind an old stack of rickety shipping crates, the dim light casting long shadows across our faces.

My chest tightened with each breath, and the realization hit me hard—we weren't getting out of this.

"They've got us surrounded," A-Rad whispered, his voice raw with exhaustion.

He peered through a crack in the crates, his eyes scanned the sea of soldiers cautiously moving around the warehouse below. They were organized, disciplined, and closing in like a tightening noose.

A-Rad poked his gun through one of the crates and fired several rounds causing the soldiers to scatter. It gave away our position but had the desired effect. They retreated out of the warehouse.

He was careful not to hit anyone. We had enough rounds to do a lot of damage, but that wasn't the goal. We didn't want a bloodbath. That's not what I wanted to be known for.

We targeted the two presidents and were able to take one of them out. Hopefully, that was enough to stop the nuclear disaster.

We had to be satisfied with that outcome.

Since A-Rad had already sent Alex and Jamie the proof of Pash's involvement in the scheme, our motives would be clear to the world, and we'd be looked at as having done a good thing. Killing a bunch of Russian soldiers would tarnish that image.

I clutched my gun tighter, my palms slick with sweat. "We can't let them take us," I said, my voice trembling slightly. "We know what the Russians will do to us. If they catch us, it won't just be the end—it'll be torture, interrogation ... they'll use us, break us."

A-Rad and I locked eyes, and in that split second, I saw the same thoughts racing through his mind. We had been through battles that would break lesser people and survived but somehow this felt different.

This felt final.

He nodded in agreement, and I could see the resolve hardening in his gaze. "We've given too much. Sacrificed everything to keep the world safe. We can't give them what they want."

I voiced a low moan of resignation, feeling every mission, every decision, and every loss bearing down on us. This wasn't how I imagined our last stand would be. I always thought we'd have a fighting chance, that we'd be able to claw our way out of any situation.

But here we were, trapped like a couple of desperate animals with no way out.

I turned to A-Rad, tears stinging my eyes. "I'm not ready for this," I whispered, my voice breaking. "There's so much I still want to do ... with you."

A-Rad reached out and gently held my face in his hands, wiping away a stray tear with his fingers. "I know," he spoke softly, his own eyes shimmering with unshed tears. "But if this is how it ends with us ... if this is our fate, then I'm glad it's with you."

I leaned into his touch, seeking solace in the warmth of his skin amidst the chaos surrounding us. "I love you," I confessed through choked sobs. "From the moment I met you, I've loved you. I just wish we had more time."

A-Rad's expression softened, and he pulled me closer, resting his forehead against mine. "I love you too, Kaley. More than anything else."

He paused and smiled wistfully.

"We shared some amazing moments together, didn't we? We did things that no one else could do."

His voice grew somber as he continued, "We saved people. We made a difference."

As we held each other in that moment, my heart ached for more. "Yes, we did," I whispered back, struggling to hold back tears. "And no matter what happens now, they can never take that away from us."

He looked around anxiously, as if he was looking for a way out. Jamie had instilled that in us. Fight to the end. When things look hopeless, find hope somewhere. Anywhere.

A-Rad's eyes searched mine for that hope, for answers, but all I could offer was a grim reality.

"What do we do now?" he asked, desperation creeping into his voice.

An unthinkable thought crossed my mind, sending chills down my spine. "Remember the movie Masada?" I asked, my heart dancing all over my chest with irregular beats from the prolonged and intense surge of adrenaline.

His nod was enough to confirm that he too remembered the tragic history of the mountain in Israel. I took a deep breath, trying to steady myself as I spoke. "We visited that mountain before ... do you remember?"

The story was heartbreaking. A group of Jewish rebels were trapped on top of that plateau during the Jewish Roman war. Rather than surrender, they committed mass suicide.

"I do," A-Rad replied, his voice heavy with sorrow. "But forget about it. I couldn't ... I couldn't shoot you."

My mind raced with possibilities and alternatives, but A-Rad's words brought me back to the harsh reality of our situation.

"I could shoot you," I said with a forced smile, so he'd know I was kidding.

A-Rad pulled away slightly, his expression a mix of determination and sadness. "I was thinking about a different movie," he said softly. "That one we watched on the yacht. The two bandits being chased by authorities ... they died together in the end."

"Bonnie and Clyde?" I asked. Our situation felt all too similar—a legendary couple facing down an inevitable end.

"No, the other one," A-Rad said, his lips curling into a faint, bittersweet smile. "The one where the two main characters are trapped in a building. Sort of like this. Instead of giving up, they decide to run out together, holding hands. Go out in a blaze of glory."

I furrowed my brow in confusion until the memory clicked into place. "Butch Cassidy and the Sundance Kid," I said.

A bittersweet smile tugged at A-Rad's lips as he nodded. "They knew they couldn't win, but they didn't care. They just ran out together."

My heart constricted at his words, knowing exactly what he meant. "That's how I want to go out too," I admitted. "Not scared or hiding or taking the coward's way out. Not killing ourselves. But facing whatever comes next . . . together."

"Together for the entire world to see. I assume there are cameras out there by now."

I looked at him, feeling a surge of emotions that I couldn't put into words. There was fear, yes, but also a fierce love that burned brighter than anything else. If we were going to die, then we'd die on our terms, as the warriors we were—side by side, unbroken.

A-Rad squeezed my hand, and I saw the glimmer of a tear roll down his cheek. He wiped it away quickly, his resolve unwavering.

"We don't die as prisoners. We go out as martyrs. Alex and Jamie have all the facts. They'll tell our story. People will know why we did this."

I nodded, while trying to swallow the lump in my throat.

"They'll know we had no choice. That we did what we had to do to save the world. Maybe . . . maybe they'll even see us as heroes."

A-Rad smiled, that old familiar grin showing through on his new face. His smile had always been a source of comfort to me.

"I hope so. And if not, well, we'll know the truth. That's enough."

He pulled out his phone.

"Good idea," I said. "You need to destroy that."

"First I want to send something to Alex and Jamie."

I peered down as he typed, *Love you both, A. More than you'll ever know.*

"Add me too," I said.

Me too, K.

When the message was sent, A-Rad shattered the phone into pieces. He fired a number of shots into it, completely destroying it. So, no one would be able to trace us back to Alex and Jamie.

"Are you ready?" I asked.

"Ready as I'll ever be."

We rose together, backs straight and heads held high. Our hands were intertwined, a lifeline connected us as we faced the fate that awaited outside. With each beat of our hearts, I could feel the strength of our bond grow even stronger.

The sound of impending danger from the activity outside echoed through the building, but it didn't faze us. We had made our decision, and nothing would stand in our way.

I looked at A-Rad one last time, committing every detail of his face to memory—the sharp lines of his jaw, the intensity in his eyes, and the way his smile always had a hint of mischief.

This was the man I loved, the man I would run into death with. To our future on the other side, where I knew we'd still be together in heaven.

"You good?" A-Rad asked, his voice calm and steady, as if this was just another mission.

I nodded, gripping his hand tightly. "Always."

Together, we took a deep breath, steeling ourselves for what was about to happen. We shared a final, desperate kiss, full of everything we couldn't say. When we pulled back, there were no more words left. Just action.

We raised our guns, gripping them firmly in our free hands. We took a look out of one of the dusty windows. The sight was daunting. We were completely surrounded by a small army. I could hear them barking orders, their weapons clattering as they prepared to storm in.

We were doing the right thing going now.

"This is it," A-Rad said, his eyes locked onto mine. "Let's give them one heck of a show back home."

With my heart pounding and adrenaline coursing through my veins, we burst through the door and ran. We sprinted out of the warehouse, firing our guns into the air with one hand and our other hands clasped together.

I could feel A-Rad's grip on me, strong and unwavering, as we were in the open now, facing the soldiers head-on.

Bullets flew through the air, whizzing past us in a deadly hailstorm. The world around us blurred into a frenzy of noise and light, but I looked straight ahead. I willed myself to keep running, side by side with the man I loved, refusing to let go.

In that split second, everything seemed to slow down. All I could feel was the wind hitting my face and the warmth of A-Rad's hand in mine. We were untouchable, unstoppable, even in the face of certain death.

This was our final stand, and we were making it count.

The soldiers opened fire, and I felt a sharp pain rip through my side. But I didn't stop. I wouldn't stop. We kept moving, defiant. A-Rad's hand tightened around mine, a silent promise that he was with me, no matter what.

In those last moments, I wasn't afraid. I wasn't sad. I was at peace, knowing that we had done everything we could, that we had fought until our very last breath.

We went out together, just as we had promised, holding on to each other until the very end.

Maybe they'd remember us as heroes. Maybe they wouldn't. But as the darkness closed in, all that mattered was that we had stayed true to ourselves, to each other, and to the mission that had defined our lives.

And that, I knew, was enough.

32

Arlington, VA

Jamie's hands trembled as she hung up the phone. Brad's words rang in her ears, drowning out everything else in the room. She felt frozen, unable to fully process what she had just heard. And helpless since she didn't know what to do next.

"Kaley and A-Rad shot the president," Brad had said with disgust and disbelief. "It happened in Russia. The Russian forces have them cornered in a warehouse. It's over, Jamie. There's no way out."

Or something to that effect. Everything had suddenly become a blur.

She squeezed her eyes shut and sobbed, fighting back the wave of nausea that threatened to overwhelm her. Kaley and A-Rad were like family. They'd been with her through more life-and-death situations than she could count. Now they were trapped like animals, thousands of miles away, and there was nothing she could do to save them.

None of it made sense. Why were they in Russia? The last time she spoke to them, they were taking a well-deserved break from their dangerous missions.

But an even bigger question gnawed at her gut: Why would they kill the President of the United States?

Brad thought it was an act of revenge. The president had vowed to track them down during the campaign. But A-Rad and Kaley weren't cold-blooded killers. They didn't kill someone without a good reason. They only targeted tyrants and threats, and certainly not American leaders.

There had to be more to the story.

An alarm blared from the security system, signaling someone entering through the gate. It had to be Alex. Dread washed over Jamie as she thought about how she would break the news to him. He'd be devastated.

A-Rad was like a brother to Alex.

Telling Colonel and Bond would also be heart-wrenching. The members of AJAX shared a bond that few could understand, and somehow had managed to avoid tragedies like this.

The front door slammed shut, jolting Jamie from her thoughts. Alex burst into the house, his face flushed with urgency.

"Jamie!" he called out, his voice tinged with fear and excitement. "I got something, a message. It's from A-Rad."

Jamie bolted to her feet and ran to him, her heart hammering. "What? A-Rad? When?"

"About an hour ago," Alex said, holding up his phone. "I just got it."

"What does it say?"

He handed her the phone. The screen was still lit, the message displayed in stark, ominous capital letters:

NUCLEAR WAR IMMINENT! PRESIDENT IS COMPROMISED! NUCLEAR CODES HAVE BEEN SWITCHED! ACT NOW!

Jamie stared at the message, her mind struggling to comprehend it.

Nuclear war? Imminent? Compromised?

She looked into Alex's eyes, searching for answers, but all she found was the same fear and confusion.

"What does this mean?" Jamie asked, her voice breaking. "Switched codes? Could A-Rad mean nucle—"

The words were so unbelievable, she couldn't force them out of her mouth.

Alex shook his head, rubbing his eyes roughly with his hands.

"I don't know, Jamie. But it sounds like ... something bad. Like the president is working with someone. And Kaley and A-Rad found out about it. But what did they find out?"

Jamie's breath caught in her throat. The assassination, the reckless decision to kill the president—it wasn't impulsive. It was something they felt they had to do.

But why?

She pointed to the television screen and Alex's eyes followed her finger.

"Have you heard?" she asked.

"Heard what?"

"The president is dead."

"Dead? What president?"

"Ours. Pash. A-Rad and Kaley killed him."

Alex's mouth flew open in shock. "They killed the president?"

"This has to be related to his message!" Jamie exclaimed, the pieces clicking into place in her mind. "They knew something. They were trying to stop him. Something to do with the nuclear codes. What does it mean that the president is compromised?"

Alex paced back and forth, clearly deep in thought as his forehead furrowed so tightly his head was going to hurt.

"We have to call Brad," he said. "He needs to know. If there's any truth to this—"

"No." Jamie's voice was firm, cutting him off. "We can't. We can't call him on our phones. If this is as bad as it sounds, they'll be tracking every call, every connection. We could get implicated, too."

Alex paused and looked at her, then nodded slowly in agreement. "You're right. If they find out about our involvement, it's over for us too. Brad must know that we've been using A-Rad and Kaley to carry out these missions."

Jamie nodded in understanding. "He hasn't intervened because of the positive impact they're making. They're changing the world in ways nobody thought possible."

"They're doing what governments can't do. That's the beauty of it. They can't be tied back to a government. But killing *our* president. That's huge. They can't do that. Brad can't cover this up. There'll be congressional investigations. We're going to have to distance ourselves from the whole mess. I have to make sure we have covered our tracks."

He walked over to his laptop sitting on the desk.

"Let's not get ahead of ourselves," Jamie said, following him. "Let's think this through."

"All our communications with them are secure. But it won't be hard for them to make the connection back to us. They've been using our yacht and planes. We've been funding them. We'll have to say that they went rogue."

"I'm not prepared to say that yet. A-Rad sent you that message for a reason," Jamie said. "He would never risk compromising us unless he had no other choice. Nuclear war is imminent. That's what he said. That means we have to do something about it. We can't sit on that information."

"You're right. Brad needs to know, even if our involvement gets exposed somehow. We had nothing to do with killing the president. We only told A-Rad and Kaley to kill our enemies."

"If there is even a minute chance of a nuclear war breaking out, someone has to stop it," she said.

Alex started to log off his computer. Jamie grabbed his arm, her grip tight. "Check your email," she said suddenly. "A-Rad may have sent more info through the secured server. Surely he did."

Alex began typing on the keyboard and navigated to the secure website he set up on the dark web. And there it was—a message plain as day. The subject line was a single word: URGENT.

"You were right. It's here," Alex said. He clicked on the email, and the screen filled with a long list of attachments, documents, and paragraphs of hastily written text.

Jamie leaned in close, her eyes scanning the words as fast as she could read them.

There were records—detailed files from Iran that she had never seen before. Reports on Andrew Pash's background, his connections to shadowy figures in the Middle East, high ranking Iranian government officials, and transcripts of conversations between the president and foreign operatives.

It was all there—the plan to switch the nuclear codes, the deal Pash had made to sell out America in exchange for power.

Jamie's stomach churned as she read. "This can't be real," she said, her voice faint. "The president was going to let them bomb us. This was all . . . all part of some sick plan to usher in a new world government."

Alex's face was pale, his eyes glued to the computer screen. "This is unbelievable," he said. "The plan, the money trails, the people involved. They were going to use Russia's nuclear arsenal, and America wouldn't even be able to respond. Pash would step in after the devastation and lead a new world order, like some people in this country have always wanted."

Jamie's mind reeled. "We have to call Brad," she said, her voice urgent. "We have no choice now. He has to see this. He has to know why Kaley and A-Rad did what they did. If he doesn't act now, it might be too late. We'll be defenseless if Russia launches those nukes. Which might happen. Especially now that the president is dead. As far as we know, the vice president might be in on it. Who knows how deep this goes?"

Alex hesitated, but she could see in his eyes that he knew she was right. With a quick nod, he grabbed his phone and dialed Brad's number. The line rang once, then twice, before Brad's voice came through, sharp and agitated.

"Do you know anything about what Kaley and A-Rad did in Russia, Alex?" Brad snapped.

Alex took a deep breath, choosing his words carefully. "Brad, you have to listen to me. I just got a message from A-Rad. He sent me everything—the truth about the president, the nuclear codes, everything they uncovered. You have to see it."

"What are you talking about?"

Alex tried to explain everything to him. Jamie filled in some of the blanks that Alex didn't include.

There was a long pause on the other end of the line, and when Brad spoke again, his voice was filled with disbelief. "Are you seriously telling me that the president was a traitor? Do you realize how insane that sounds?"

"I know it sounds crazy, but you've trusted us before. You have to trust us now," Alex insisted, his voice pleading. "We don't have time to debate this. If you don't act, we could be looking at nuclear war."

"The vice president has already been sworn in," Brad said, with urgency behind his voice. "He's in charge now."

"Check his nuclear codes. They could be compromised as well," Alex said.

"I'll get back to you."

Jamie turned her focus to the computer and read back through the email, feeling a deep, gut-wrenching certainty that this was real. Kaley and A-Rad had risked everything for this. She could only hope that Brad would believe them and could find the proof on his end to justify their actions.

Alex's face was tight with tension. "He said he'll look into it, but I'm not sure if he believes us. And even if he does, I don't know if he can do anything in time."

Jamie walked back across the room and collapsed onto the couch. She turned her attention to the television, hoping for any updates or clues. The news channels were already buzzing about the assassination of the president, speculating on motives and describing the chaos in the streets.

The screen cut to a live feed from Russia and Jamie's heart stopped even though she had seen the same scene earlier. The warehouse where Kaley and A-Rad were hiding was completely surrounded by armed soldiers. Jamie could see tanks, snipers on rooftops, and barricades blocking all escape routes.

"Kaley and A-Rad are in that warehouse," Jamie whispered, her voice trembling. "They're trapped."

Alex sat beside her, wrapping his arm around her shoulders. Together, they watched wondering what was about to unfold. Jamie held onto Alex tightly, her nails digging into his arm as they stared at the screen, praying for a miracle.

And then they saw them.

Kaley and A-Rad burst out of the warehouse, holding hands and brandishing weapons in defiance. It was like watching a scene from an action movie, surreal and heartbreaking at the same time.

Jamie gasped.

"What are they doing?"

"They're choosing to go out on their own terms, refusing to be taken alive," Alex said soberly.

Tears filled Jamie's eyes as she watched them sprint forward, bullets whizzing past them. She could almost feel the impact as Kaley stumbled, her body convulsing as she was struck. But A-Rad didn't let go of her hand. They kept moving forward, standing their ground until the very end.

The camera zoomed in, capturing every excruciating moment. Kaley fell first, and then A-Rad went down right beside her, their hands still grasped together. The soldiers quickly closed in, surrounding their lifeless bodies with guns still drawn.

Jamie couldn't look away, even as tears streamed down her face. She felt Alex pull her closer, his own tears falling freely now.

She still couldn't believe it. They had just lost two of the bravest people she had ever met.

They sat there in suffocating silence. A heavy shroud of grief filled the room like clouds blocking the sun. Alex's phone blared out an alert piercing the sadness. It was still tightly clenched in his other hand.

"It's from A-Rad," Alex said.

They both stared at the screen. The tears stopped momentarily.

Love you both, A. More than you'll ever know.

Me too, K.

As quickly as they stopped, the tears began flowing again. Unrestricted this time.

Jamie looked at the television again, the images fuzzy from her tears. The taste of salt lingered on her lips as she tried to keep them from turning into sobs again.

A-Rad and Kaley were lying on the ground, their hands still clasped together in death, a final act of defiance and solidarity. The image would be seared into Jamie's memory forever.

"We can't let their sacrifice be in vain," Jamie said, her voice steady even though every part of her being had been shaken to its core.

"This is why we do what we do," Alex said. "We all knew this day would eventually come."

"I thought I was ready for it," Jamie said. "But I'm not."

"Neither am I."

The only consolation for Jamie was knowing that A-Rad and Kaley had made the ultimate choice—to stand against the darkness, no matter the cost. That was the legacy they would leave behind.

I will make sure of it.

33

Jamie stood in the vast lobby of CIA headquarters, where she faced the Wall of Stars—a graveyard of the unseen, a quiet tribute to the fallen. She had been there before not that long ago, but today was different.

Today, they were there for Kaley and A-Rad.

Her chest tightened with a mix of grief and pride she couldn't untangle. Two months had passed since that day in Russia, but the memories felt fresh—Kaley and A-Rad sprinting from the warehouse, defiant, choosing to die on their own terms.

Hand in hand. A bond of love that most couples would never achieve.

The lobby was filled with agents, analysts, and officials gathered to honor two of the Agency's best that ever lived. At the front stood Brad, his usual stoic demeanor softened by the solemnity of the occasion.

Jamie glanced at Alex beside her. He looked exhausted, his eyes red from nights without sleep. He had worked with Brad nonstop to try and avenge their deaths and bring the parties responsible to justice.

She squeezed his hand, drawing comfort from his presence.

Brad began to speak, and the room fell silent. He glanced at the large number of engraved stars on the wall, then at the faces around him, his expression grim. A small black curtain covered what Jamie knew were two new stars.

"We gather today to honor two extraordinary individuals," Brad began, his voice steady but strained. "Kaley and A-Rad were more than operatives— they were legends. They gave everything to protect their country, and their sacrifice will never be forgotten."

Brad's words cut deep, bringing back memories of missions, victories, and losses. Kaley and A-Rad had saved the world in ways few would ever know.

"They redefined what it means to be a covert operative," Brad continued, recounting their achievements. "They played a pivotal role in the reconciliation of North and South Korea, eliminated threats to global stability, and exposed Iran's secret nuclear ambitions. But their final act, uncovering a plot that would have led to nuclear war, saved millions of lives. They stopped a traitor in our highest office, even at the cost of their own lives."

Jamie blinked back tears. Brad's voice wavered, but he pressed on.

"Because of their actions, we exposed the compromised nuclear codes, arrested many of the secret Iranian spies, and prevented a catastrophe. Because of them, America didn't fall into chaos. They stopped a chain reaction that would have ended in nuclear devastation."

Jamie knew Brad regretted that they were never able to arrest the chief of staff, the president's wife, or his parents. Pash's parents fled to Iran and the chief of staff and the president's wife were being harbored in Russia, sparking a new cold war.

Alex, Colonel, and Bond wanted to go to Russia and take them out. Someday they might if the opportunity presented itself.

Brad continued. "We owe our very existence to Kaley and A-Rad's bravery. Most of us would not even be alive today if not for them."

Jamie felt a shiver run through her. The truth about what could have happened was a terrifying thought, and she was grateful that everyone in the Agency knew the full story even if the world didn't know all of it.

Brad's voice softened. "Kaley and A-Rad were more than just colleagues. To many of us, they were friends, confidants, and family. Their courage will inspire us for generations. Today, we add their stars to this wall, a testament to their heroism. Though their names remain classified, their legacy will live on in every mission, every operation, and every life they saved."

Brad stepped back, and Jamie knew it was her turn. She didn't want to speak, but she couldn't leave without honoring her friends.

She approached the podium, her gaze fixed on that black curtain, the two stars that would soon be unveiled.

"I met Kaley and A-Rad several years ago, and from the moment I met them, I knew they were different," Jamie said, her voice shaky but resolved. "They were fearless but not reckless, committed but never blindly. They were the kind of people you wanted on your side because they truly believed in what they were fighting for and would give everything to protect you."

Jamie paused, struggling to find the right words since she wasn't reading from notes. "To me, they were family. We laughed, fought, and faced things few could ever understand. Losing them feels like losing a part of myself."

She glanced down, collecting herself. She had caught a glimpse of Alex dabbling at his eye and almost lost it.

"Kaley always believed that every mission was more than just an operation—it was a chance to change the world. And A-Rad, no matter how dire things got, would remind us that there was still hope, still something worth fighting for. He would literally run through a wall for those he loved."

She paused trying to think of what to say next. The words seemed so shallow compared to what they had done and had meant to her. They deserved so much more.

Truthfully, no combination of words would be enough.

"I think about them every day. Their determination, loyalty, and unwavering courage. They died as warriors, fully aware of what was at stake. Their missions and tactics should be taught to every new trainee in the CIA, not just for their skills, but for their unmatched bravery and love of country."

She could almost hear Kaley's laugh echoing in her ears, see A-Rad's half smile and how he was so overprotective of her. She missed the banter between all of them. Things would never be the same at AJAX.

Her voice cracked, but she continued. "Jesus said there's no greater love than to lay down your life for your friends. Kaley and A-Rad did that, not just for us, but for everyone. The world will never know their names, but we will. And I'll never forget them. Not as long as I live."

Jamie stepped back, her heart heavy but filled with pride. Brad returned to the front, gesturing toward the black velvet curtain.

"With these stars, we honor Kaley and A-Rad," Brad said, his voice thick with pride. "Their names won't be recorded in public history, but they will be remembered here, among those who knew what they did."

Brad pulled the curtain aside, revealing two new stars etched into the marble. Jamie felt a bittersweet pride as the stars caught the light and everyone burst into applause.

In front of the wall was the Book of Honor, open to blank pages where Kaley and A-Rad's names should have been. Because of the sensitive nature of their missions, the identities next to the stars would remain secret, known only to those who had worked alongside them.

Jamie ran her fingers along the smooth, empty pages, feeling sadness for what was left missing. Kaley and A-Rad had given everything, even their names, to protect others.

As the ceremony ended, Jamie stood with Alex, gazing at the stars that now marked her friends' legacy. "They'll never know," she whispered. "The world will never know what they did."

Alex squeezed her hand. "We know."

They turned to leave; the loss bearable because of the honor Brad was willing to bestow upon them. Technically, A-Rad and Kaley weren't working for the CIA when they died. As CIA director, Brad made an exception.

Word was that the current president intended to bestow upon them the Presidential Medal of Freedom, America's highest civilian honor.

Jamie took one more look back at the wall as they were leaving. The stars gleamed under the lights, tiny yet profound, etched into the wall as a silent declaration that their sacrifices mattered.

Jamie knew that Kaley and A-Rad would eventually be forgotten. A new generation of heroes would emerge, and more stars would be added to the wall.

But at least their stars would shine on that wall as long as it stood—a silent tribute to the extraordinary lives they had lived and the incredible difference they made.

The End

Thank you for purchasing this novel from best-selling author, Terry Toler. As an additional thank you, Terry wants to give you a free gift.

Sign up for:

Updates
New Releases
Announcements

At terrytoler.com

We'll send you an eBook, *The Book Club*, a Cliff Hangers novella, free of charge.

READ MORE BOOKS FROM TERRY TOLER

Jamie Austen Thrillers

Read all the Jamie Austen Thrillers. They must be good.
They've been number one on Amazon in ten different countries.
Click on the link below.

THE JAMIE AUSTEN THRILLERS (12 book series)
Kindle Edition (amazon.com)

https://amzn.to/3vmPUy7

Cliff Hangers Mystery Series

Who wants to read a good mystery? We've got you covered! Read the Cliff Hangers where homicide detective, Cliff Ford, solves crimes in Chicago, with help from his wife Julia. These books have everything Terry Toler is known for. Page turning suspense, a hint of romance, and an ending you won't see coming.

The Cliff Hangers Mystery Series (4 book series)
Kindle Edition (amazon.com)

https://amzn.to/36WX3go

About Terry

Terry Toler is an Amazon international # 1 best-selling and award-winning author. He writes clean fiction with a message and life-changing nonfiction. He's a public speaker, entrepreneur, and has authored more than forty books.

Sign up for his newsletter where you'll get free stuff, exclusive content, and news of releases and promotions. He can be followed at terrytoler.com.

If you like his books, please take a few minutes to leave a review on Amazon. We really appreciate it. It helps draw more readers to his books. Thanks!

www.ingramcontent.com/pod-product-compliance
Lightning Source LLC
Chambersburg PA
CBHW050401260626
47156CB00003B/825